# Blindside Love

## Empire State Hockey Book Three

Lexi James

Copyright © 2024 by Lexi James

All rights reserved.

No part of this book may be reproduced in any form or by any electronic or mechanical means, including information storage and retrieval systems, without written permission from the author, except for the use of brief quotations in a book review.

This is a work of fiction. Names, characters, businesses, events and/or incidents are the products of the author's imagination or to be used in a fictional way. Any resemblance to actual persons, living or dead, or actual events is purely coincidental.

**Cover Design: Candice Butchino, @sugarandspicybooks**

**Editor: Mattingly Churakos**

**Proofreader: Caroline Palmier**

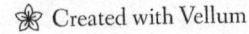

❦ Created with Vellum

*For all the women who do it on their own, and the men who show them they don't have to.*

*May all your days be bright and your orgasms magical.*

# Chapter 1

## *Trevor*

"How in the actual fuck am I even awake right now," I yell to no one as I slam my Jeep into park, my music continuing to blare through my headphones as I lean my head back on the seat. I'd give just about anything right now to be able to teleport to my bed. I feel like I'm about two seconds away from dropping into the fetal position and begging for my mommy. But, unfortunately, I'm a thirty-four-year-old grown-ass adult who's supposed to be able to handle life on his own.

I'm not sure when playing hockey started to be this tiring, but this is the tiredness you feel deep in your bones, the type that even a few good nights of sleep wouldn't touch. I definitely don't bounce back from these long road trips like I used to and I'm starting to really feel it. As I've gotten older, I've learned I thrive on routine, which includes being in my own house and my own bed, at a reasonable time to get a good night of sleep. It doesn't help that these hotels we stay in for away games have paper-thin walls, so I'm usually up late having to hear the music my teammates play in their rooms as they hook up with puck bunnies until the early hours of the morning.

Wow, I sound like the grumpy old dude who's become allergic to fun. I was supposed to be out on a date tonight, which I'm sure I would've been an absolute joy, but I canceled at the last minute because I can barely keep my eyes open, let alone carry on a meaningless conversation.

But in my defense, I'm not even sure tonight could be classified as a date—more like an attempt at figuring out a dating app. When everything went to shit with Claire, I caved and finally downloaded one of the apps Sawyer is constantly bugging me to get. I guess I figured that if the old-fashioned way of meeting women wasn't working, I might as well try this method, even if most of the people on this app just want a quick fuck, and tonight's girl was no different.

It didn't help that last night with the guys was depressing. Even thinking that makes me feel like I'm a complete asshole, but it was just hard for me to hear about everyone's happiness. Well, mainly Rex and Max's. Hearing both of them dote on about their women was adorable but made me more fucking jealous than I realized I was capable of.

Those two have everything I've ever dreamed of, and I'm so happy they found their match. But I get so frustrated and tired of waiting that it's so goddamn fucking hard seeing everyone so happy. I can't even remember the last time I was naked with a woman, let alone actually liked someone.

It's like the older I get, the pickier I am about who I

# Blindside Love Playlist

1. The Offering - Sleep Token
2. Say You Won't Let Go - James Arthur
3. Perfect - One Direction
4. Dial Tone - Catch Your Breath
5. Spotless - Zach Bryan
6. Fine Apple - Nic D
7. THE DEATH OF PEACE OF MIND - Bad Omens
8. Glass Houses - Bad Omens
9. King Of My Heart - Taylor Swift
10. Love Me Like You Do - Ellie Goulding
11. Chokehold - Sleep Token

spend my time with, and unfortunately for me, most of the women that I'm around are puck bunnies who are either chasing clout or my money, and that's an immediate turn-off for me. I want to meet someone who doesn't know anything about hockey and isn't attracted to my last name or my career, which is hard to find when we play eight months out of the year; it kind of cuts down on my dating pool.

So now, I'm trying this dating app nonsense, even though I hate it.

Don't get me wrong, the swiping is interesting, although a little unnerving at times. It's hard to believe some people are *so* comfortable with what they are willing to share with the world.

*Interested in being filled… completely?*

*Supernatural interests? Yes, please. Monster dildo? Unicorn horn? Double yes.*

I get being comfortable with yourself and your sexuality, but come on now, save something for the first date. It feels like a compilation of sex ads, which I guess it is.

Fuck me, I'm way too old for this shit.

And this is why I bailed on my date tonight. She wasn't upset in the slightest, so I'd be surprised if I was her only option for tonight.

I ended up staying a little later at dinner with my parents tonight anyway. My mom hooked me up with meals for the week like she always does. She tries to play it off like she just made too much food, but the woman has done it for years and she always makes my favorite. She knows I can't cook for shit, so she probably just wants to make sure I survive.

Our dinners are easily my favorite part of the week, but today, I was exhausted and couldn't shake it. I've been off lately; I can own it. I mean, hell, everyone around me has noticed, even Cade called me out for it during practice last week when I couldn't get the puck in the net to save my life. Then tonight, my parents both said I was oddly quiet. I could see it in their eyes that they were worried about me, but they couldn't figure out how to help.

I don't feel like anyone can right now because, hell, I don't even know how to help myself.

I've lost my spark, my drive. The excitement I used to feel every day is gone. Dare I say it, my "zest for life" is almost non-existent. I feel like I've been going through the motions and not doing anything that excites me anymore, and I hate it.

Every week is the same. I see my friends and family once a week, and I play hockey, and honestly... I'm bored. I know I need to make a change, do something different, something exciting. And I've been wondering if this might be my last year in the NHL. I'm thirty-four years old and I still lead the league in goals, so I'm sure I could easily get one more good contract out of 'em, but I'm tired.

The only thing holding me back from making the call to retire after this season is my father. I spent tonight listening to him go on about how excited he is for the next season and how he can't wait to see what they offer me for a contract extension. I felt like I would break his heart if I told him I'd been considering retirement.

He's coached me a couple of times throughout the

years, including in college when he got to coach both Rex and I at Brooklyn University. It was fucking exciting—Rex as left winger, me as right, and my dad as the coach. It was always an absolute blast and something we could bond over. But at thirty-four, I feel like it's time to face the facts. My time on the ice is starting to come to an end, at least professionally.

The worst part about all of this is that without hockey, I have no idea who I am anymore. Which terrifies me more than *anything*. I'm always the happy one, the positive one, but right now, I'm the lost one.

*Fuck me.*

Grabbing my stuff, I head toward the parking garage elevator, and press the call button with more force than I intended. As it opens, I step in, hit the number fourteen before leaning back to rest my head against the wall. Just as I go to close my eyes, trying to steal just a tiny moment of peace, all hell breaks loose in front of me. At the center of the mess is the hottest little thing I've ever seen, rocking pink hair.

It feels like everything happens in slow motion, yet it's somehow fast at the same time. I can't think, can't react; it's like all I can do is stand frozen in place as I watch everything unfold.

One moment, I see this absolute stunner of a girl, wearing these cute little jean overalls with pink hair at her shoulders. The next, I see her mouth open in a scream as she trips and drops the box she's carrying, the contents flying everywhere.

I look down at her for what feels like minutes but is probably only seconds, as neither of us has moved or even taken a breath. Before I can say anything, something in the elevator catches my eye.

It's a dildo.

There's a fucking dildo in the elevator with me.

And it's not just a regular dildo. No, this is an angry-looking thing, a bright-as-fuck hot pink dildo, which apparently vibrates as it's now rattling against the elevator floor. The doors start to close, leaving us trapped in this fucked up moment where neither of us can move; we just stare in shock at the dildo, like we're waiting for it to stand up and walk away or do a little dance. The moment before the doors finally close, she looks up at me, her cheeks now a rosy pink and her eyes filled with a mixture of shock and embarrassment, and goddamn, it only makes her that much cuter.

There's something about this girl, something I like. Maybe like is too strong of a word for someone you haven't technically even met. I guess there's just something that intrigues me about her. She has these gorgeous, bright blue eyes that I felt like I could drown in. It's almost like she can see into my soul. Through her vulnerability and my shock, she somehow is able to see who I truly am, and it's unnerving as fuck, especially since I'm acting like a goddamn lost puppy just staring at her like she's my home.

I feel like a damn teenager, but she's easily the hottest woman I've ever seen in my life. Her deep blue doe eyes were silently urging me to help her up, but all I could do was stare until the doors shut between us. In that split second before the elevator shut, I could see so many emotions cross her face, from embarrassment to anger, but there's this overwhelming sadness I could tell she was trying to keep hidden deep down that matched my own. It was defeat.

She had it written all over her face, and now I feel like the world's biggest jerk for not helping her. I know I should go down there and check on her, but I'm too fucking embarrassed to face her, especially given that I still have her hot pink dildo now riding up in the elevator with me. Without a second thought, I grab it from the floor as I step off the elevator, not sure what the fuck I'm supposed to do with it, but I know damn well she probably doesn't want it riding around the apartment building where old Mrs. Brinley might just have a heart attack if she sees it.

By the time I make it into my place, I head straight to my bedroom and into the bathroom. I throw the damn vibrator into the sink before undressing and jumping in the shower, turning it on as hot as it will go. I know damn well I should be taking an ice-cold shower with how turned on I am right now, but I'm only human.

I still shouldn't be thinking about her. I shouldn't be thinking about the way she looked, down on her knees, her big eyes staring up at me, just waiting for me to move, to do something—although I'm sure she hoped it would be to help her and not face fuck her like I'm imagining doing right now.

If I wasn't rock hard before, I am now.

Placing my hands on the tile, I lean my forehead against the shower wall, letting the water run down my muscles. I'm trying to relax in the heat, yet she's the only thing I can think about right now.

What is it about her?

Is it her overalls that somehow highlighted her curves perfectly while being adorably modest at the same time? Or her blonde hair that's been dyed to look like bubblegum? It's just long enough to wrap around my fist, holding her in place as I slide my cock between her plump fuckable lips.

Fuck.

I really, *really,* need to get laid.

Without another thought, my right-hand drifts down from holding myself up on the tile, sliding down to grip my throbbing cock that's practically begging to be touched, even if it is only by me. I squeeze tightly, trying to alleviate some of the ache that's been building since the moment I saw her. An innocent moment that lasted practically no time at all, yet somehow, has made quite the fucking impression on me.

It's not long until just gripping my cock is no longer enough; my hand starts to pump, my hips acting on their own as I begin thrusting. Slowly fucking my hand to the dirty, depraved thoughts I'm having, starting with her on her knees, beneath me as my hand grips the hair at the back of her neck. Her mouth opening eagerly as I slide my cock between those pretty plump lips that look like they'd be even prettier wrapped around my cock.

I bet she'd take me so well. Be a good little slut just for me, letting me take her as I please and loving every fucking thing I give her.

*Fuckkkk.*

Just the thought has me thrusting my hips wildly.

Faster and faster as I chase my release, imagining just how fucking hot we could be.

I bet she'd be disgusted by the things I want to do to her. Disgusted by me imagining how I'd grip her hair as I fucked her mouth. How I'd slide my cock further and further down her throat until eventually pouring my cum down her throat, keeping her mouth closed until she swallowed every last drop. Rewarding her, I imagine forcing her jaw open, and spitting into her mouth, before dropping to my knees and letting her know just how much I love what a dirty fucking girl she is by tongue fucking her until she comes all over my face.

*Goddammit.*

I groan as I finish, my cum splashing the shower wall. Holding myself up against the shower as I nearly pass out, I come so hard. I slam the shower water off and grab my towel, now somehow more irritated than before. I know damn well there's no way a girl like her would ever be interested in the things I want.

As I get in bed, I realize Sawyer might've been onto something with that dating app. At least with the app, I can set the boundaries beforehand and find out if we'd be a good fit before jumping into bed. That way, I could find out what she likes.

Maybe, just maybe, I can find someone who enjoys what I like. The ability to bring a woman to the edge of pain, a moment where she can see just how strong and capable her body is, right as I turn that pain into unimaginable pleasure, making her crave more.

I like it all. Spanking, biting, whipping. I especially love seeing my mark on their bodies, knowing they trusted me enough to know that I would treat them with respect—no matter how disrespectful I may be, as I give them everything they can handle.

Even though I know she would be horrified by me, I can't stop thinking about the girl I saw for only 3.7 seconds.

I know nothing about this woman except for the fact that she owns a bright pink vibrator, but now I want to know more.

I *really* need to get fucking laid.

## Chapter 2

## *Ellie*

"Wait, what? Say that again. Set the scene; I want the full experience," Natalie says as she laughs into her margarita. Her ass is perched on my island as I attempt to unpack before Addy comes home tomorrow. She's a brat for laughing at my expense, but she wouldn't be my best friend if she didn't poke fun at me.

"I dropped the box, Natalie! Like, I full-on tripped right in front of this hot guy, and the box went flying. My god, it was so embarrassing. Scratch that, it was mortifying. Like, for fucks sake, who else but me would be clumsy enough to trip over their own damn feet. Not to mention, I was carrying a box that should've been labeled top secret or fragile, so I knew not to drop it in front of the hot guy!" I shriek, slamming the plates down much harder than I meant to. "Also! Has my dumbass ever heard of tape? I should have just taped the actual shit out of the box," I grumble, both laughter and embarrassment filling my words.

Natalie silently cackles as she wipes tears from her cheeks.

I suddenly have the urge to push her off the counter.

"Natalie, I don't think you understand. Not only did I drop the box full of my toys, but the big one—yeah, you know *the one*. The pink one you sent me the link to demanding I buy *immediately*. Yeah, not only did she fall out, she rolled her happy ass right onto the elevator with him like we were in a movie. It was awful."

"But you said the guy was hot?"

"He was so fucking hot; it should be illegal. He looked like he was some mythical creature or a Greek god or something—I don't know, but he belonged in a damn museum. I swear I've felt like I've seen him somewhere, but then again he has a face that's hard to forget, so I feel like I would remember if I'd met him before." I slide to sit up on the counter across from Natalie as I think about Mr. Tall, Dark, and Fuckable.

"You could tell he was built tough, he was tan with dirty blonde hair that was long on top, just begging to be tugged on. And Natalie, he had so much scruff. He was all man. Jesus, it was fucking hot. He had these broody eyes that just stared at me. I was caught between wanting to shrink away and disappear or go up and touch him just to see if he was real or not. But of course, when those damn doors were closing, and I was left sitting on my ass, the jerk never moved, didn't even say anything—he just stared. I felt like I was inconveniencing him, like the hot God couldn't be bothered to waste his time helping out a mere mortal as she has a damn sex toy catastrophe in the goddamn parking garage! I don't know, it made him lose

*Blindside Love*

hotness points because it just proved that all men are assholes."

By the time I'm done, Natalie is full-on crying—tears streaming down her cheeks as she laughs hysterically.

"So, what'd you do? How'd you get her back?"

"I didn't! As soon as those doors shut, I immediately picked up everything, threw it back into the half broken box, and then hoofed it up the damn stairs because I was way too nervous that I'd run into him again if I went onto the elevator. Instead, I walked up fourteen flights of stairs in what felt like some shitty version of a walk of shame."

"What if it's still there? What if he left your toy in the elevator, thinking you'd go back for it? Now it's just riding alone in the elevator all cold and scared," Natalie says with a wink.

"Christ on a cracker, Natalie, don't tease me right now. This is bad enough. She's gone for good," I whine.

"Just order a new one, you big drama queen."

"Oh, I did, but it won't be here for a couple of days."

I ordered a new toy the second I got back up here. It's seriously the best toy ever, and it works its magic every single time, unlike my soon-to-be ex-husband, who couldn't give me an orgasm if his life depended on it. I guess it finally came in handy that I was raised to put on an act and be pleased with everything, because I had to do it every time with Tom to protect his fragile ego.

Now, I refuse to fake anything. I've realized it's pointless—no one learns, so it remains the same, and this goes for things in *and* out of the bedroom. I will no longer fake emotions, friendships, or orgasms.

"That's the worst. Online shipping and their ridiculously fast deliveries have ruined us. Now if we have to wait more than twenty-four hours, we get twitchy," Natalie says dramatically before her expression turns downright mischievous. "You know... you could always go look for him."

"And say what? Hi, it's me, the girl that fell on her ass while you rode up in the elevator with my bright pink dildo. I was just wondering if I could get that back?"

"I mean... you could say that if you want to be a total weirdo. But could I suggest you try to be normal and just ask if you could take his dick for a ride?" Natalie says with a shrug as she switches the music on my phone from a random country station I selected to our usual Taylor Swift playlist.

The perfect playlist for my mood.

Feisty, fearless, and *fucking* single.

I hope Tom and Lena are happy and that they have a long life full of mediocre sex, which with his small dick and vanilla tendencies, that's about all she's going to get. He's an absolute bore in the bedroom, a pillow prince who only cares about his release. I hope she doesn't expect him to talk dirty during sex because the man is silent unless you count the awkward groaning sounds that always reminded me of a hyena mixed with a feral cat. It was like some fucked up love child that could only screech and howl.

"Yeah, Natalie, that's exactly what normal people do. It's definitely normal to just walk up to a random stranger and ask if they happen to have your sex toy, and if not, if you could use their cock instead," I deadpan, as I grab another box of dishes and start placing them on the shelves, passing a box of silverware to Natalie.

She doesn't even say anything; just grabs it and starts setting up the drawer. This is what I love about our friendship; she always knows exactly what I need. We've been friends for so long that I don't even know if that term is strong enough for the two of us. She's practically my sister. We've been there through a lot together, and she stuck by me through my shitty marriage—even though she has always hated Tom.

*I should've just listened to her six years ago when she said he was a twat.*

"I mean, who knows, the guy could be nice. I'm not saying you have to date the guy. Hell, you don't even have to sleep with him, although, based on your description, that sounds like it would be a mistake not to. I'm just hoping you can see that not every man in this world is a complete and total douche nozzle like Tom. There are actually good guys out there, even ones who are absolute givers in the bedroom." Natalie smiles the entire time she's talking, like she's trying to sell me on it. "I just want you to see that. I want you to meet someone who shows you how you deserve to be treated. You and Addy both deserve a real man in your life, and sadly, I doubt that's ever going to be her sperm donor."

"Dramatic, much? First off, it's not that I'm against men; I'm just not in a position to date right now, especially while in the middle of a divorce."

Tom is fighting me, trying to force me to take the blame for our marriage falling apart since he's being considered for partner at his father's firm this year.

Apparently, my citing 'infidelity' as the reason for our divorce won't make him look too good to daddy.

"Besides, Natalie, it's not like I'm ever going to see the guy again. This building has hundreds of apartments, so the likelihood of ever even seeing him again is slim."

"Improbable, yet not impossible." She shrugs.

"Even if I did see him, it's not like I could actually do anything about the attraction. I don't exactly have a lot of time for fun, especially not for the fuck-boy type, and with how hot he was, there's no way he's not a complete and total man whore. I have Addy to think about, and I can't do that to her. I don't want to bring something like that into our lives. It'd just be someone she met that would end up leaving again."

"Whatever," Natalie grumbles as she crushes the box she just unpacked before throwing it into the ever-growing pile of recycling. It's going to suck lugging all of this out, but it's not like I really have a choice anymore. It's just me now, and I don't exactly have a long list of people that I can call for a favor since I'm the one who filed for divorce. I guess that's the downside of being married to a lawyer— they can be rather convincing and downright manipulative. And unfortunately for me, people often take sides based on how others will judge them, regardless of the facts.

My mother happens to be one of those people. It definitely didn't help that her best friend is Tom's mother.

"Can I unpack this box of art supplies in that last bedroom?" Natalie asks quietly.

"No, there's no point. I haven't sat down to paint in months."

"What? Why? I thought you loved it."

"I do, but every time I would start something new, Tom would make some underhanded comment about how I should be spending time with my daughter instead of my silly 'hobby,' as he put it. He always liked to point out that my art was basic at best, that there was nothing special about it. I guess after a while, I just lost the desire to do it."

If I'm being honest, it felt like all the joy had been stripped from it. The peace I used to feel when I painted was gone, along with all the color in my mind. Like it was sucked dry from my life, leaving only shades of black and gray. I've been living in a monochrome world. Even now, it feels like that most days unless Addison is here with me.

"Well, Tom's a piece of shit, but I've been saying that for years. It's so much worse now, though. The fact that he tore you down and ignored your incredible talent just shows how insecure he is about himself. Still, it doesn't give him the right to be a complete douche-canoe," Natalie says, her eyes filled with rage as she bites her lower lip in frustration. She looks like this anytime he's brought up. She's very passionate about protecting me. "Have you shown Betty any of your pieces yet? I know you told me she'd been asking."

Betty is this sweet lady who owns the art studio I've volunteered at for the last five years. Her art shows are always packed and a huge hit, probably because she lines up some of the best of the best to host shows. I feel lucky just to be able to volunteer with her. She offered me a job a couple of years back, but Tom didn't like the idea of his wife working—he said it made him look bad. I didn't have the time or energy to tell him that we no longer lived in the Stone Age and women actually have rights and their own lives.

"No, I'm too nervous. She actually asked me again last week, but I just can't. I always come up with excuses that I know she can see right through. I'm just stalling. Tom hated them, said they were boring, and were done by someone just messing around. Addison has seen them, and she loves them, obviously, but that's because her mommy painted them, and she thinks I hung the moon. But, Betty? Hell, that's asking a professional what they think of my amateur art. It's too fucking terrifying, Nat," I ramble, still stalling even just talking about it.

"You should. I know she'd absolutely love them," Natalie says, her voice quiet, sincerity filling each word. "You're way more talented than you give yourself credit for. But I guess now we know who's to blame for that."

"Maybe," I say quietly, ignoring her little jab at Tom.

My mind is already elsewhere, thinking about my art. Maybe I should show her.

*Maybe* I'm good enough.

# Chapter 3

## *Ellie*

*Knock, knock, knock.*
   *What the fuck is that noise? It's not even eight in the morning.*

The knocking returns, proving it's not just from my hangover. Someone is actually here, knocking on my door when I should still be sleeping off the tequila.

"Who the fuck is knocking? Were you expecting someone?" Natalie grumbles from beside me.

"No. I don't even know anyone who lives here. Besides, you need to be buzzed in to come inside. There's no way it could be Tom. He's not desperate enough to try and sneak in, right?"

Tom's upset because I won't let him know exactly which apartment I'm in and because I declined his request for access to the building. I told him it was none of his business where I sleep, and that he knows which building his daughter is in and can contact the front desk if he can't get through to my cell phone. I thought that seemed more than sufficient.

Although I thought his head was going to explode when he realized he wasn't getting his way.

"Go look," she says, nudging me to walk along with her as another more forceful knock taps on my door. "Why do I smell like tequila?"

"Because I'm pretty sure we finished that bottle of Patron we opened while belting out Taylor Swift like we were seeing her in concert.

Peering into the peephole, I nearly shit myself when I see who's standing on the other side of my door.

"It's him," I whisper-shriek, unable to believe my shitty luck. How did he find me? The man who is currently knocking on my door just so happens to be the hot God who saw me make a fool of myself in the elevator. But it's not like we even talked last night, so why would he be stopping by now?

"Who?"

"Elevator guy!"

"Open the door. Maybe he brought your toy back. Either way, I want to see this sexy piece of man meat you need to get a slice of."

"No!"

*Knock, knock.*

"Look, he's being rather persistent. Maybe it's important, or like I said, maybe he brought your toy home... or his dick."

I'm intrigued, but only because she's right; he is being rather persistent. Only Natalie doesn't give me a choice as she steps to the side hidden by the door and opens it.

Leaving me front and center, by myself, facing this damn Adonis.

"Hi," I say, unable to come up with anything somewhat intelligent to say as I stare at him.

He's currently engrossed in his phone, one hand already raised to knock again. The moment he looks up at me, his entire disposition changes. He recognizes me if his little smirk means anything. Just fucking fantastic.

"Uh, hi, I was looking for the guy who lives here," he says, tucking both hands into his joggers as he looks behind me like he's looking for someone.

"Can I help you?" I ask, my voice clipped. I can't help it that I'm annoyed, especially with Natalie peeking through the crack of the door, watching this entire situation she's forced me into.

"I don't know," he says plainly, still staring at me.

Weird. This whole conversation is weird, but for some reason, I'm not slamming the door in his face even though he's standing there like he's expecting something from me. *He* knocked on *my* door, yet it feels like the conversation is up to me, and if I'm being honest, I just want to shut the door and hide as thoughts of last night invade my mind.

Looking down, I see Natalie smirking as she mouths, "Ask him about big pink."

I flip her off.

Nope. No thanks. This is already awkward enough.

"I, uh... I guess I came over here to introduce myself. I live next door. I thought someone else lived here, so I didn't expect you to open the door," he rambles, running a hand down his face as he looks anywhere but at me. It's irritating, but I can tell he's nervous.

"Sorry to disappoint you with another inconvenience," I snap, surprised when he looks offended and confused by my response.

"Huh? What? No. I didn't mean it that way, I promise. Fuck, I'm sorry. I probably sounded like such an asshole. I looked up who lived here, and I thought it said Mr. Thompson," he says as he runs his hand through his hair. "Look, can we start over?" he asks as he reaches his hand out to me. "I'm Trevor. I—uh, I guess I wasn't expecting to run into you again, so I'm sorry I've made an ass out of myself... again. I'm really sorry about last night. I—"

"Nope, not talking about that. If we're starting over, can we please not go there? I'm embarrassed enough as it is without having to relive it." Reaching out I place my hand in his, surprised by his firm handshake and warm smile. "I'm Ellie. It's nice to meet you but—" I start to say when Natalie rudely cuts me off as she pops up behind me with a shit-eating grin that can only mean trouble plastered on her face.

"You're the hot guy from last night? I think you might have something of Ellie's," Natalie says without introducing herself, surprising both Trevor and me in the process. As I register her words, I want to punch her in the twat.

"Some... thing of Ellie's?" Trevor asks, and I feel my face heat from embarrassment as I watch him connect the dots. This bitch is throwing me under the bus when all I want is to never discuss it again.

"Please, for fucks sake, just ignore her," I interrupt his thoughts. "She went around the teapot ride one too many times at Disneyland and has never quite been the same."

Turning to Natalie, I glare as she just winks, loving this entire situation. "Natalie, go to my room; you're in time out."

"Aw, but maaaahhhhhm. It was just starting to get interesting," she whines like my five-year-old as she drags herself towards my room, one arm waving above her head.

It isn't until she's at my door that she turns around with one last comment, which is always the worst. "Yo, hot guy. If you don't have her toy anymore, you could always just loan her your cock. Ellie could use a good railing and an orgasm... or five, and you look like you might just know your way around a woman's body. At least more than Tom."

I could die.

Right here, right now.

I've never prayed for spontaneous combustion to happen to me until this very moment. I'm praying to every god in existence to take pity on me and just sacrifice my life. Looking up at him, I hope that by some miracle he didn't hear her or that he could just be mature enough to just pretend it didn't happen. Unfortunately for me, everyone wants to watch me squirm today because he just stares, a downright devilish grin on his face as he watches me.

Goddamn, this look alone feels charged. Electric tingles move throughout my body in places I forgot I could feel. That's when I realized we never dropped our hands.

He looks at me, one hand on his face as he rubs his bottom lip with his thumb, his forearms flexing with the movement, and holy shit, his arm is covered in tattoos. His other hand, the one still gripping my own, starts to rub tiny circles on top of my hand.

*Fuck,* why is that so hot? He looks down at my feet, which are currently tucked into pink fluffy bunny slippers; he smiles at that and continues his perusal. When his gaze moves up, finally reaching my bare legs, I see his obvious arousal beginning to tent in his joggers, but he makes no move to hide it. The thought that I'm turning on a man who is *so ridiculously hot* is the biggest confidence boost. And I definitely need it right about now.

But that's all this is. I need nothing more from this man other than these delicious looks he gives me that make me feel like he's thinking about devouring me. It's slightly awkward because he's so intense and just stares at me like he's waiting for something. But his intensity feels safe. Something about him feels safe, and the fact that I don't even know him makes that even more terrifying.

Should I ask him? About my toy? About his... cock?

"You need orgasms?" Trevor asks, a cocky smile on his face as he continues to peruse my body, making me feel even more confident in this moment.

By the time his gaze makes his way back up to my face, his eyes are no longer playful and bright. They've darkened and are filled with a hunger, which I can only imagine mirrors my own. It's at this moment I realize that I'm well and truly fucked when it comes to this man. There's something about him that just calls to me.

Which is exactly why I need to stay away. Back up and stay far away.

Far, far away from this man and his come fuck me eyes.

I just hate how much I love the way he looks at me with approval written all over his face, as well as in his pants. I feel desired, and I like it. Even though I was married, this was never something I truly felt.

Arousal starts to build inside me, setting my core on fire as he continues to check me out.

"I'm definitely not opposed to letting you use me," he says playfully. "I could definitely help with a handful of those orgasms you're looking for," Trevor says, adding a wink at the end.

"Down, boy. No one is using anyone, all body parts included. I'm sure you're great at what you do, but there will be none of that happening here—no rides. Jesus Christ, I can't even talk. Look, I suck at trust, especially with men. Hell, the only thing I trust to give me an orgasm is myself, my vibrator, and some good smut. Unlike men, they never let me down."

Why am I still talking? Why am I allowed to speak right now? He's smiling like he's enjoying this, but goddammit, I'm talking about orgasms and vibrators like it's what I had for lunch, and I can hear Natalie laughing from my room.

"I promise you, I won't—"

"Thanks again, but no thanks, Trevor. Now you have a good night," I cut him off as I step back, prepared to close the door, but he just stands there smirking.

"Well, Ellie, if you ever change your mind, I'm just next door. You could probably just knock on your wall if you need my assistance. Our walls are pretty thin if my listening to your renditions of the latest and greatest of T. Swift tells, screamed at the top of your lungs at two a.m. tells me anything."

*Motherfucker, swallow me whole.*

I feel my face redden as he smiles at me, and I shut the door in his face.

*This is my new neighbor?*

*Fuck. My. Life.*

## Chapter 4

## *Trevor*

"Hey, Trev, where are you?" Rex shouts, slamming the front door behind him.

"On my way out," I shout back as I head out of my bedroom. "You brought beer, right?"

It may only be eleven in the morning, but it's a Giants game. Football Sunday with no hockey to play means no rules. I like football, and I like beer. Win-win.

We used to watch these games religiously when we played for the same team. It was always our thing whenever we had the day off. But now that he's coaching a different team, our schedules don't always line up, but when they do, we try to never miss a Sunday. Today just so happens to be the last game of the season.

I smile when I see Rex in the kitchen, beer in hand. He's probably the only person I'm fine with just walking into my place without knocking. But we never knock. The only time I do now is if I go over unannounced, but I'm pretty good about letting both Rex and Sawyer know when I'm coming over, just so I don't walk in on something they don't want me to see.

"Do I ever let you down, Trev?" Rex says with a laugh as I walk into the kitchen, his laughter immediately dying when he sees me. "What the fuck happened to you? Someone kick your dog? Did you fuck up and sleep with a puck bunny again?"

"Fuck off. I'm too fucking tired and way too goddamn confused to think of a witty comeback right now. Beer first, talky-talk after."

"Fine. Here, whiny baby," Rex grumbles as he grabs us each a beer and puts the rest in the fridge.

"Thanks. What're Sawyer and Rory doing today?"

"They're going with Cassie to get pedicures and then to brunch. Rory was definitely more excited than I expected, so I'm sure they're planning on eating a bunch of garbage," Rex says with an eye roll, but he'd give those girls anything they dreamed up.

"Sounds like fun," I say with a sigh, leaning forward until my head rests in my hands.

"What's going on?" he asks, his tone no longer grumpy. It's what I call his 'dad voice.' He's always had it, but it definitely got more intense when he became a dad. It's all concerned and protective with just the right amount of judgment that keeps you in your place.

"I don't even know where to begin. Everything has just been a fucking mess lately. Honestly—for months now. Between hockey and Claire, I've felt lost and confused. Through my lack of dating, and the fact that I don't know if I want to play hockey next year or not, I'm just a mess. Then, to top it all off, I met this girl yesterday, well, kind of met her. She had a bright pink vibrator in the elevator, and because of her, I got three hours of sleep. And before you say anything, no, it was not for fun. It was because my neighbor and her friend stayed up belting Taylor Swift until three in the morning, yet somehow, my body still woke me up at five this morning. And the kicker is that Dildo Girl is also my new neighbor. So not only is she infuriating for keeping me up, but she's also the first girl that's made my dick twitch since before Claire got in my head. Plus, today, I found out she's funny, and that just makes her even more attractive," I growl, out of breath by the end of my rant. "I can't explain it. I don't even know the woman, yet all I can think about is how badly I want to."

When I look up at Rex, he's speechless, probably for the first time in his life.

"Wait... a vibrator? What the fuck? Also, can we not call her Dildo Girl? It's weird as fuck."

"Out of everything I just said, we're starting with that?" I deadpan.

"Trevor, no offense, but I don't think you've let a woman touch your dick in three years, even when they've practically thrown themselves at you. If you hooked up with a woman in an elevator? *That* I want to know about. Hell, I'll throw you a damn party for it."

"It has not been three years. And no, I did not fool around in an elevator. I just ended up with her vibrator."

"Start over—from the beginning. This is not making any sense," Rex grumbles, taking a seat at the island.

"You've been spending too much time with Sawyer and your sister; you're starting to gossip like them."

"Shut up and don't stall. It's almost kick-off, and we still have to get food."

"Look, it was last night. I was just coming home from dinner, and when I got on the elevator, I turned right in time to see this woman fall. She ended up dropping everything she was carrying, and well, the box broke, and everything went flying. She just kind of stared at me while my dumbass was frozen—unable to move or think—which means I didn't even help her, and I have no excuse, except that there was just something about her, she has these gorgeous fucking eyes, and crazy pink hair, and I fucking love it."

"Oh boy," Rex chuckles, his thumb playing with his lip like he's thinking. Whenever he does that, I usually end up wanting to punch him.

"What?" I grumble.

"Nothing. Keep going."

"Okay, but no more talking until I'm finished. I want to get it over with. I'm hungry," I say. "When I finally looked up from the girl, I heard buzzing. Apparently, her vibrator not only fell out, but it turned on and rolled into the damn elevator with me. We both saw it and made eye contact right as the doors fucking closed, leaving me locked inside with this sex toy that I know damn well has been in that perfect woman's tight pussy. I'm jealous of a fucking toy, Rex."

"You definitely need to get laid," Rex laughs, obviously enjoying my discomfort.

"First Claire, now a new girl," Rex says.

"What do you mean 'first Claire'?"

My brain starts running a million miles an hour

trying to figure out what Claire has to do with this situation. Honestly? I haven't thought about her in a while.

"I think you find something you like about someone and run with it. At least sometimes. I don't mean that as rude as it sounds, either. I just mean, it's obvious that you crave a relationship. You always have. You're someone who enjoys being in a relationship, a partnership. So sometimes I think you like the idea of somebody more than reality. With Claire, I think she got drunk and told you that she liked the same kinks as you and your dick took over and ran with it, not believing anyone else would ever share the same interests. I also think you wasted years on her even when you were completely incompatible with her, solely out of fear of rejection. Not only that, but you two barely even interacted, so I'm not sure what you got out of that situation, if anything."

Well, he's definitely not holding back tonight. But unfortunately for me, he's not fucking wrong, and that pisses me off. I didn't try to date anyone because of Claire… but I also didn't really try to date Claire.

I guess since I knew she had the same interests as me and wouldn't think I was a freak, I knew she would accept me. Even if we weren't together, it helped me not feel so alone. I guess I didn't feel like I needed a relationship because I had a friend who understood me.

"Fuck, man. It's not even noon, and you're already throwing punches," I groan, taking a pull from my beer as I think about what he said.

"Sorry. Sawyer kept me up most of the night, so I'm fucking tired."

"Don't come at me with your sex talk, and expect me

to feel bad for you." I glare, earning me another laugh. "Look, when it comes to Claire, you're right. I was interested in her because of her interests. When she said she liked being spanked and tied up, along with her casual mention of how it made her wet when she was degraded, hell, I practically wanted to marry her right then."

Most women freak out, thinking you want to hurt them or make them feel cheap. But that couldn't be further from the truth. Yeah, I like to be in control. I always have, but especially in the bedroom. I don't do it for me, though, at least not in the way you'd think.

Yes, I get off on it, but it's not because I like hurting women but because of the trust and freedom that comes with it. When a woman trusts you enough to let you bind her and tie her up, she's trusting you with more than just her body. She's giving over all her control, trusting that you know what her body needs, what her body craves, better than she does.

It's a skill I've perfected over time, and it only works if she's truly into it. I've had women say they were into it because they'd heard something from a friend. But the second we started, they often would change their mind. I always respected them and stopped the second they said anything, but I'd be lying if I said it didn't start to get into my head, which is why I stopped trying.

I don't want one-night stands. I want that connection, the kind of connection with someone where you trust each other completely. You could tie them up, spank them, bring them just to the brink of pain, but it's so intermixed with intense pleasure that the orgasm it creates is unmatched.

At least in my experience—and hell, the women who have experienced it have never complained.

Well, one did... but we don't talk about her.

"I know. I had to convince you once not to go ring shopping for a girl you'd kissed once," Rex laughs.

"Shut up. I was drunk and thought I was in love."

"And now? Is this any different?"

"Honestly? It feels different. I can't explain it, and I know I sound like an idiot. I'm not saying I want to marry the girl. Hell, I'm not even saying I want anything to happen with her. I don't even know her, but I definitely *want to* get to know her. Especially after knocking on her door today and her friend trying to get me to lend Ellie my cock."

"Elaborate."

"There's not much to say. I went over this morning to yell at my neighbor for their late-night music, but it ended up being her. You could tell she was embarrassed, and I did my best to ignore the awkwardness, but her friend was not on the same page. She said that since Ellie lost her vibrator, I should, and I quote, "loan her my cock. Ellie could use a good railing and an orgasm or five." It was wild. But if she asked, I'd let her ride me like a Harley."

"Definitely can't blame you for that. Bonus points for easy access and close proximity," Rex says with a wink. "But in all seriousness, I think you need to actually go out on one of those dates you keep setting up and canceling. See what happens. Put it all out on the table, and the worst they could say is no. I just don't want you making this new girl your personality and letting something special pass you by."

"I get it. I do. Look, I'll think about it. That's about all I can promise."

Because that's not the worst they could do. They could call me a freak, tell me I'm disgusting, and get pissed off when I call them my dirty little whore, even though it's a term of endearment to me.

"So, now for the million-dollar question. Why the fuck do you still have her vibrator, and why the hell did you pick it up in the first place?"

I just laugh. Truthfully, I have no idea what the heck prompted me to pick it up and bring it home. As if she'd ever actually want it back. But fuck, I don't know. It felt weird leaving it.

"Fuck if I know. It was in the elevator. I felt like I couldn't exactly just leave it there."

"So, instead, you picked up the vibrator that you know was inside this woman's body, and just what? Pocketed it?"

"Yeah, I mean, I cleaned it, then took a shower."

"Bold, man. Really fucking bold."

We both laugh because, honestly, he's not wrong. It's fucking weird that I did it. I still don't exactly know why I did it but fuck it. If we had hooked up in the elevator, I wouldn't have thought twice about touching her. Why should that be any different? It's done and over with, and if I ever see her again, I guess I could actually return it.

"Let's go get food," Rex says, interrupting my thoughts.

"Lead the way."

By the time we make it back with our food, we have fifteen minutes until kick-off, and I'm ready to sit back with a beer and relax. Walking through the lobby, I can't help but smile when I see a little girl running over to her mom, the happiest smile on her face like she's the happiest little girl in the world. She practically leaps into her mom's arms with an excited squeal.

But then the mom stands up, and I'm shocked.

It's Ellie.

Ellie is a mom?

"Who's that?" Rex says from next to me, his eyes following mine to watch Ellie and the little girl embrace.

"That's her. That's Ellie, and who I can only assume is her daughter," I say, my eyes never leaving her.

The little girl holds onto Ellie's neck while she holds her, chatting away in her ear, and the brightness on Ellie's face is one of pure joy. Pure love.

*Stop going there, Trevor. Maybe fatherhood just isn't in the cards for you.*

The joy only lasts a moment as the man standing off to the side finally walks up, his scrunched-up sneer immediately pissing me off.

"Are you done with your little charade? Are you finally ready to come home, where you belong? Do you know what would happen if it got out that you were living here? You're lucky your father is letting you live here. I'm sure I could change his mind if I wanted to."

Ellie sets the little girl down, a forced smile on her face. Her eyes are dark with anger as she does her best to hold her composure.

It's impressive because I can tell from here just how pissed she is. I can feel it in the air, almost taste it.

"This is not a conversation we're going to have in front of our daughter."

"We need to have it, she'll be fine. Besides, this is more important. My father finally approached me about making me a partner at his firm. Unfortunately, I also have to convince the board I can live up to their ridiculous standards. My becoming partner is contingent on me having no red flags. *This* is a red flag, Eleanor."

I can't believe the audacity of this man. Everything he's said has been about him, not giving a single fuck about anything she's said. I can see her body language change as she just stares at him, her anger palpable. But in the blink of an eye, she's smiling as she looks back down at her little girl, who's still smiling as she holds her mom's leg. "Addy, can you do me a favor? Mr. Walker is right over there by the door and mentioned he had a butterscotch for you. Would you go say hi to him?"

"Okay, mommy. I'll be right back. Bye, Dad." She waves politely, with no emotion on her face as she walks away. No embrace. No hug or I love you—and even worse is the fact that her own father didn't even respond to her. I hate him.

"If this is a red flag, you should have thought about that before you stuck your dick in holes that didn't belong to your wife. So, no, I will not help you. I won't do anything for you. I didn't make this mess; you did. Not only that, but you *are* a walking, talking red flag with flashing lights and bright red glitter because glitter fucking sucks and ruins everything, just like you. So, the fact that they've even considered you for partner tells me you still have your father convinced you're a decent human being," Ellie says, her tone sharp, words cutting, but the volume just quiet enough that we had to walk closer to hear her properly.

He looks like he's about ready to explode at her words, but Ellie stands tall, a devious smirk on her face as he just glares at her. She remains unbothered.

"She's kind of scary," Rex grumbles under his breath.

"I know. I like it."

"Of course, you would." He shakes his head as we continue making our way towards the elevator, forcing us towards Ellie and a furious Tom. When we're close enough to hear everything perfectly, Tom decides to open his stupid mouth.

## Chapter 5

## *Ellie*

It doesn't matter that it's been less than a month since I left him; I already wish I could do it again for good measure. I wonder what the hell it is that I ever saw in him. He truly is a ginormous red flag and should come with a warning label.

Right now though, I've officially pissed him off, and I'd be a liar if I said I didn't love it. It brings me so much joy knowing I've pissed him off, especially because all I've done is tell him the truth.

"You better watch your mouth, Eleanor," he seethes through his teeth, but he doesn't scare me.

"Or what, Tom? What will you do? I have all the control here. I don't need you for *anything*, but you? You need me for *everything*. Your image. Your career. Your family. So, it's *you* who needs to watch their mouth," I snap, a little louder this time, shock written all over Tom's face.

Out of the corner of my eye, I recognize my new neighbor, Trevor, standing with another guy watching me. Trevor's jaw is clenched, his fists balled at his side as his other hand holds a bag.

"You think you have all the control, but you'll find no one to take your case unless I okay it. I have the power when it comes to our divorce, which is why I'm telling you there won't be one. I'm not sure who you think you are, but this is unacceptable. I expect you at the company dinner next month. Get your little"—he waves his hand over my outfit, looking disgusted at my scrubby overalls and pink hair—"rebellion out of your system while it lasts before I drag you back home. No one supports this. No one is going to help you. You're all alone; you're nothing—"

"I'm going to request you don't finish that sentence because honestly, I'm not really in the mood to explain why I knocked your ass through that window, but if you keep talking I'm going to have no choice," Trevor's rough voice says from beside me, with a smile that doesn't meet his eyes.

His bright green eyes are dark with anger, and I'm not surprised that Tom immediately takes a step back. I take a quick glance and see that Addy is sitting behind the front desk laughing with Mr. Walker and the front desk manager, Christy, so I know I've still got a few minutes to get this over with.

"Who the fuck is this, Eleanor?" Tom growls, his face almost turning purple.

"I'm Trevor," he says, and I watch confusion flash through Tom's eyes before turning back to anger.

"Why do you look familiar? Are you a lawyer, too?" Tom grumbles, his eyes narrowing between Trevor and I.

"No." Trevor chuckles before looking over at me and winking. I nearly died on the spot. "I'm far too interesting to be a lawyer."

It takes everything in me not to laugh at his cheap shot, but Tom just ignores it, probably because he notices someone behind Trevor. I've never met the guy, but goddamn, he's handsome. "Did you two need anything? I'm in the middle of a conversation with my wife."

"Yeah, I actually did. I was just coming over to see if Ellie was ready to come over to watch the game with us," Trevor says to Tom with a smile before turning to me, and at that moment, I'm certain he's doing all of this to piss off Tom, and honestly, I could kiss him for it. "And a piece of advice. If she was my wife, I'd treat her with much more respect than you just did. You don't deserve a woman like her."

The guy behind Trevor actually laughs, but I'm too afraid Tom might do something stupid like hit him to join in. To diffuse the situation, I figure it's best to take the out Trevor just gave me; even though I don't need his help, I had this figured out.

"Yeah, I'll come up now. This conversation with my soon-to-be ex-husband was over anyway," I say, winking at Trevor before turning back to Tom with a glare. Tom looks uncomfortable, like he's torn between being furious and running with his tail tucked between his legs. "Let me go grab Addy, and I'll meet you at the elevator."

Trevor's eyes light up as his smile widens; his friend behind him even smiles at my response before they both turn and head over to the elevator to wait. It's confusing because their smiles seem genuine, like they're truly nice guys. Every man I've ever known has wanted something from me, whether physically or socially, especially Tom.

Tom just needed me because of something we *both* fucked up, but I know he always secretly blamed me for it. It was one of those relationships where what the public saw was much different than what we experienced at home. Regardless of what anyone says, marrying a guy just because you got pregnant unexpectedly is *not* a good reason to get married. It doesn't matter what anyone says, you can't force anyone into acting like a parent. We got married because our moms are best friends, and together they decided they didn't want their reputation tainted by their children having a child out of wedlock.

*I still think this belief is barbaric and can't believe I let them convince me to marry the sleaze ball.*

Needless to say, we weren't a good match. I want someone who loves me, cares for me, and desperately needs me for my mind, my body, and my soul. I want a man who sets my body on fire with a single look, touch, or even just a word.

That was definitely not Tom. Tom wanted the closest warm hole that *didn't* belong to his wife, but he wanted me to pretend it wasn't happening. Now he's trying to make me take the fault for his mistakes, and I fucking refuse.

"It's time for you to go, Tom," I say, unable to keep the annoyance from my voice.

"Why? So you can go fuck those two guys?" he sneers, looking down at me like I'm beneath him.

"No, Tom, I don't fuck people when I should be spending time with my daughter, that's your M.O.," I say with a smile before turning to walk toward Addy. "Besides, the one on the left kept me up all night; I'll definitely be satisfied for a while."

With that, I turn and grab Addy to meet Trevor and his friend at the elevator. Tom waits just a moment before stomping out of my building like a toddler throwing a tantrum. Trevor isn't watching him, though. Instead, he's staring at me intently as I walk over hand in hand with my daughter.

I bet he's not gonna offer to let me ride his dick now.

"Hey," I say nervously as his eyes bounce back and forth between Addy and me. She's hugging my leg, but not out of nervousness this time. My girl's a snuggler and she missed her mama. I love it.

"Who's this?" Trevor asks as he leans down to Addy's level.

"I'm Addison, but you can call me Addy. All my friends do. Are you my mommy's friend? You could be my friend too. We just moved here!"

Addy is always so happy. It's adorable. I'm so thankful for how outgoing she is; it definitely made the idea of moving out of the only home she's ever known much easier. I know it'll be an adjustment, but still, at least I know she's not shy and is willing to meet new people.

"Hi, Addy. I'm Trevor. As long as it's okay with your mommy, I would love to be your friend," he says, looking up at me for approval, and I can't help but smile and nod. "How old are you?"

Addy beams up at Trevor, loving the attention. "I'm five, how old are you?"

First, he's angry at the way Tom was speaking to me, and now he's standing here meeting my daughter and being so damn sweet to her that it makes me wonder if Natalie was right. That there are good guys out in this world, and I've just been wasting my time on someone who wasn't worthy.

I can't risk it, though. It's not just my heart I have to think about.

Her daddy is already breaking hers. I can't let another man do the same.

"I'm much, much older than you," Trevor says with a smile. "This is my friend, Rex. In fact, he actually has a daughter your age," Trevor says.

"Really?! What's her name?" Addy asks excitedly.

Something about watching a dad light up at the mention of his daughter makes my heart swell. He's beaming with pride just at Trevor's mention of her, and I love that—even if it does hurt knowing my daughter doesn't have that.

"Her name is Rory. Maybe next time we're at Trevor's, you two can meet. I know she'd love that," Rex says, eyeing me cautiously the entire time, and it makes me respect him so much more that he's trying not to overstep. The fact that he actually cares about that means a lot, especially with him taking the time to talk to my daughter. I feel my eyes welling with tears. Her own father doesn't give her the time of day, but these two men are making her the center of attention.

Goddamn, I've been emotional lately.

"Mommy, mommy! Can we?!" Addy begs.

"I don't see why not." I smile down at her, looking up to see both of them smiling at us.

"Awesome, I'll get in touch next time they're over," Trevor says as he presses the elevator button.

It opens immediately, and we all step on. I do my best to stop myself from remembering that the last time Trevor was in this elevator, just twenty-four hours before, it was with my damn vibrator. The thought alone has my cheeks reddening, and I peek out of the corner of my eye and see Trevor watching me, a knowing smirk on his face as he shoots me a wink that sends all sorts of excitement to my core.

Addy wraps her arms around my leg and stares at me with a look only a sassy five-year-old could pull off. "Mommm," she grumbles. "How will Mr. Trevor let you know when my friend is there?"

"What do you mean?"

"Does he know how to call you? He does have your number, right?"

She's too smart for her own good.

"Actually, Ms. Addy, you make a very good point. I definitely think I *should* have your mother's number. You know, so I can let you both know when Rory is over, of course," Trevor says boldly.

"You're ridiculous," Rex says as the elevator opens, and we all walk off.

I feel my cheeks heat, but I can't deny that I love the idea of him having my phone number.

*Even if he never uses it.*

"You're not wrong, sweet girl. Here, give me your phone," I say as we walk towards our respective doors.

He hands me his phone without a second glance, leaving it open on the main screen for me to navigate my way to the contacts. Tom *never* let me anywhere near his phone unless I was reading something he had up for me. Hell, I don't think he ever let me hold his phone. He didn't trust me.

Or he didn't want me to realize I couldn't trust him.

Typing my number in quickly, I shoot myself a text so that I have his number, too.

For emergencies only, of course.

"Here you go," I say as I hand him his phone back.

"You know... you two could come to watch the game with us. If you'd like."

"Thanks, seriously. It's just that it's her, uh, it's her first day back with me, and I'm not really used to not having her all the time. I think I just want to hang out with my girl," I tell him with more honesty than I expected.

Trevor smiles as he looks back over to Addy and Rex, who are in a competitive game of rock paper scissors that Rex is obviously losing.

"I get it. Enjoy your day," Trevor says before heading over to Rex, looking back with a devilish smile. "You've got my number now. Use it whenever."

Busted. I thought I was slick, but obviously not slick enough.

"Come on, Addy. Let's go figure out lunch."

"Bye Ellie, it was nice to finally meet you," Rex says as they disappear into his apartment.

What's that supposed to mean? Why does he even know I exist?

## Chapter 6

*Trevor*

We've been on a streak of away games these past few days; it's been exhausting. We had two on the West Coast, and now we're in Nashville until tomorrow morning. We won tonight's game three to one. I wanted nothing more than to go directly back to our hotel and pass out on my bed, but Cade decided that wasn't happening and all but drug me out with them tonight.

At least when I'm out with Cade, I don't usually have to deal with the puck bunnies. We aren't the usual crowd who spend their entire night entertaining them. I'm not saying that we never dabbled in flirting with the bunnies —I, for one, took my fair share of them home in my earlier years in the NHL. But now, I don't want the one-night rodeo; I want more, and I definitely won't find that here.

Cade and I spent most of the night playing pool, while Harris snuck off early after deciding he wanted to stay in; I wish he'd told me so I could have gone with him. It's always surprising when Mr. Playboy doesn't come out, but I guess even he needs a break from the madness at times.

"Nice goals tonight, Adams. You played your ass off. I always like to see McQuinn get embarrassed out there every once in a while," Cade says, snapping me out of my thoughts as he slips onto the stool next to me. "That five-hole goal, though, that was so sick."

"Thanks," I say, tilting my beer towards him.

"Why don't you seem excited? I figured you'd be stoked. It's not every day you get a hat trick against last year's Stanley Cup winners, especially with McQuinn in the net. You should be celebrating."

Just then, our server comes over with another glass of bourbon for both of us. She's figured out that we aren't interested in flirting tonight, so she's quick to scurry off.

"Are you throwing a fit because the bunnies are ignoring you? I can always call a couple of them over. That brunette is pretty cute," Cade says with a grin, knowing damn well I don't give two shits about who they're paying attention to. Neither of us do. Cade hasn't dated anyone seriously in a very long time. That's not to say he doesn't have a couple of girls he can call when he wants a quick hook up, but that's about it. We both prefer a little familiarity when we're with a woman; we aren't good at one-night stands, there's no trust involved, and trust is important when you're pushing boundaries.

But that's not why I'm grumpy. I'm grumpy because I've been staring at my phone all week, waiting for Ellie to text me, and have been sorely disappointed. Why would she, though? We aren't exactly friends yet. She doesn't need anything from me. Hell, I doubt she's even thought about me since I saw her and her daughter.

Speaking of which, you'd think finding out about her daughter would be a red flag, maybe even a speed bump or a major turn-off. But instead, it just made her that much hotter, that much more of a confident, independent woman, and I love it. Ellie is feisty, if a little unsure, but I know deep down there's an absolute badass inside her.

"Yeah, no. They can continue directing their interest that way. That brunette has already come over twice. I'm just not feeling it."

"You usually aren't," Cade says with a shrug, his eyes on our teammates. His lips are curled up just slightly as he watches how ridiculous they are with the girls—especially the rookies; they eat that shit up.

Hell, we all have at some point.

"Yeah, that life just got old for me. Random one-night stands with women who only wanted me for my career and money. I'm just over it."

"I get it. I don't know... I guess I just figured after everything with Claire, you'd want to play the field a bit," Cade says with a shrug as he takes a sip of his drink.

He's not wrong. I had definitely planned to dip my toes back into the dating pool, but this last week, I just haven't been in the mood. Hell, I've opened the app up a couple of times, but no one sparks any interest. I want to feel defeated, but I know there's someone out there who will set my heart on fire and remind me what passion feels like again. Like the passion I used to feel for hockey that has been slowly slipping away the older I get.

"I mean, I'm not going to lie to you, that was my

plan." I smile, taking a sip of my drink as I consider how much I want to tell Cade. We're close, we always have been, but I don't even know what I'd tell him. *I met a girl twice, and nothing ever happened between us, but I can't seem to get her off my mind.* That sounds fucking crazy. "I've even gone on those dating apps—don't tell Sawyer—there's just no one that sparks any interest in me. On the app, at least," I mutter out the last part.

"What the fuck does 'on the app' mean? Is there a new girl, and I'm just now hearing about her?" Cade grunts out, annoyance saturating his voice.

"Well, there is this girl, she's actually my new neighbor," I sigh, my tattooed hands gripping the glass as I try to figure out the best way to explain this.

"And have you hooked up with this new neighbor?" Cade questions, his eyebrows furrowing as he waits. Very impatiently, I might add.

"God, I wish. No, that's the thing, nothing like that has happened. We just had this weird, awkward run-in, well, two of them, actually. But fuck, I don't know. There's just something about her. Something different. Then I found out she had a kid, and instead of wanting to run, it actually just made her more interesting because I could see this independence, this strength inside of her that was sexy as fuck. I don't know, man. She's cute as fuck with this goddamn pink hair and her little body that is usually rocking overalls. But the best part about the girl is her *feistiness*. She's feisty and confident and takes no shit. Not from me, not from her ex, no one."

Cade chuckles, shaking his head as he sets his beer down.

"You're a lover, T. And I mean that in the absolute best way. You always see the best in people. I love that about you, especially because you have so much love to give. Just be careful with it. Whoever they are, make sure they're worth your heart before you give it to them."

"Look, man, I'm not getting down on one knee anytime soon. I'm just intrigued, but that doesn't mean I want to give her my last name and fill her with babies," I grumble.

"Calm down, dude. Being interested in someone isn't a commitment, and wanting to get to know her isn't a crime. Chill out, have some fun, and get to know her a bit, that's the fun part. You don't have to have all the answers today—you never know what will happen tomorrow. Hell, we don't even know what's going to happen tonight," he says with a shrug, nonchalant like always.

Cade is right. We don't know. I've spent so much of my life trying to make it to my happy ending that I'm constantly on the go, never satisfied with anything. When it comes to relationships, it's almost like I don't want to date someone unless I know they're the one because I'm so ready to have my person. The girl I'm supposed to marry, the one who I'm supposed to start a family with. That's what I want, so spending time with anyone who seems less is hard. But that could also be stopping me from branching out, meeting new people, and, quite possibly, missing out on someone I could have a future with.

I hate when this motherfucker is right. The grin on his face makes me want to punch him.

"You're right," I tell him before grabbing my beer and taking a swig, doing everything I can to avoid eye contact.

"What was that, T? I couldn't hear you over the sound of the puck bunnies mating calls," Cade says, his lips turning up into a grin.

"Oh, fuck off. And wipe that smug ass grin off your face. It's not becoming on you."

"My grin is very becoming. Just ask your mom." He winks.

"You're such an asshole."

"Who? Me? No way. Your mom said it at dinner last month. Complimented my smile and everything. Said I had nice teeth."

I can't help but laugh.

"You're fucking ridiculous," I tell him.

"Yep, but I always keep things interesting."

"Damn straight," I say, tapping my beer against his.

"But now the question remains, what are you going to do about your hot neighbor?"

"Fuck, I don't know." I take my hat off and run my fingers through my hair as I think. "I mean, her daughter did get me her phone number, so there's that."

"She gave you her number?"

I smile, remembering the sneaky girl and how she was the best wing woman ever, even if it was entirely unintentional.

"Yeah, her daughter, Addison wants to have a playdate with Rory. We ran into them in the lobby when Rex was with me. She told her mom that I couldn't let them know when they were over if I didn't have her number.

*Blindside Love*

When she put it in my phone, I saw her text herself, meaning she has mine too."

"What's stopping you then? Just text her."

"That's the question, Cade. I don't know what's stopping me."

---

**REX**
When do you get home?

I am home. We got back this morning. What's up?

**REX**
Let's go out. Sawyer has been bugging me to get everyone together, but my schedule has been fucked lately. Mom said she'll watch Ro on Friday. Are you free?

We have a game. Meet up after?

**REX**
Sounds good.

Still on for dinner with everyone on Wednesday?

**REX**
I wouldn't miss all-you-can-eat wings for anything.

---

After our flight, I hitched a ride with Miles back to my place. The only downside is that I have to lug all my gear in through the lobby. I wave to Fred, one of the doormen who smiles back as he opens the door for me.

"Good morning, Mr. Adams. Glad to see you're back in one piece," Fred says with a nod. "Not that I had any doubts."

"Of course, and for the millionth time, call me Trevor."

"And for the millionth time, not a chance, Mr. Adams," Fred says with an attempt at a serious face, but he can't hide his smirk.

I just shake my head, smiling as I walk by, heading through the lobby. It's busy here, people walking around, the front desk staff talking on their phones, and some sort of oldies music playing through speakers, yet I can hear her.

I look around, trying to figure out where her voice is coming from and then I see her, standing over by the elevator with Addy clinging to her leg. Her facial expression is one I haven't quite seen before, her jaw clenched as she stares at someone I can't quite see yet, but as I get closer, I see that it's her ex.

I want to stop whatever is happening over there because I hate that this man is bothering Ellie. Even worse though, I hate that this man got to marry Ellie and have a baby with her, but that's not really something I want to dissect today. But by the look on Ellie's face, this conversation is far from over, but as I watch she keeps glancing down at Addy who's still hugging her.

But as I get closer, I catch Addy's eyes, smiling in her direction and she surprises me, letting go of her mom and running over, squeezing my legs in a bear hug. She catches me off guard, so I make a quick attempt to not take her out with my bag and gear, but she doesn't seem to mind.

"Hi Mr. Trevor," she says quietly, a voice I'm not used to hearing from her. Ellie looks over nervously as she watches us, but I just smile and wave her off, setting my things down in the chair next to us, and guiding Addy to the chair next to mine.

I'm not exactly in a rush to get upstairs, that just means back to the real world and I'm just not ready so I might as well hang out with one of the coolest five-year-old's I know.

Of course, next to my Rory girl, who is the OG mini-BFF.

"Hi, Ms. Addy." I smile, unzipping my bag and pulling out a mini paper bag. Guess now is probably the best time to give her a surprise gift and help her take her mind off the drama between her parents that looks like it might be simmering down. Handing it to her, her eyes widened in surprise, pure joy radiating from her face.

"What's this?" she asks quietly, her eyes bouncing from my face to the present, her excitement building.

"It's not much, but your mom told me that you like music, when I saw this I thought you might like it," I say, somehow nervous about what a five-year-old thinks about the present I got her.

She giggles, immediately tearing into it. If I thought she was excited about her present, it's nothing now that she's seen it. It's a simple snow globe I got in Nashville, but it plays music. The one I got for her and Rory are both Taylor Swift ones, and apparently, it's a winner.

"This is so pretty, Mr. Trevor! Thank you, thank you, thank you!" she squeals, winding it up to play another song, right as Ellie walks over. Her eyes still hold the anger I noticed when she was talking to Tom, but her fists aren't clenched like they were, and she actually smiles as she hugs Addy.

I'm glad that she's feeling better, I guess all it took was him leaving.

"Thanks for hanging out with my girl," Ellie says, a soft smile as she looks at me, mouthing the words thank you, again, her eyes are sad, and I hate it.

"Anytime, seriously," I say with a smile as I grab my bag and gear from the chair, Addy still playing the music as she shows her mom.

Ellie smiles over at me, her cheeks tinging pink before she looks back down at Addy and somehow a present for Addy made both her and her mom smile.

I call that a win.

———

THE WORST PART ABOUT HOCKEY SEASON IS BEING away from home for so long. It's always so exhausting trying to get back into a routine. There's laundry, groceries, mail, and all the other mundane tasks that we get to avoid while we're away.

Walking out of my laundry room, I put the basket back in my bathroom now that the last load is finally in.

You'd think with it only being me, I wouldn't have too much laundry, but I've practically been drowning in laundry today, and I still don't see an end in sight. I'd be thrilled to just sprawl out on my couch and watch a movie, but I'd most likely fall asleep immediately.

Instead, I make my way down to get the mail, checking another thing off my to-do list.

"Good evening, Mr. Adams," Mrs. Walker says as we pass in the hallway, her smile bright and cheerful like always. "You played one helluva game the other night. Kept me on the edge of my seat the entire time, watching you skate the puck through all those players like it was nothing. You're a damn fine skater, son. Mr. Walker would've loved to have watched you play."

---

HER HUSBAND WAS A HUGE HOCKEY BUFF AND LOVED the Cyclones nearly as much as he loved his dear wife. She's told me a million stories about him, but I always love to sit with her and listen to them. She's a dear friend. Plus, her oatmeal chocolate chip cookies are practically made with crack.

"Thank you so much, Mrs. Walker. I always love knowing I have you watching," I say with a smile.

"Oh, always. I see you're on your way out, stop by sometime soon and I'll whip up some treats, and we can have some tea."

"That sounds perfect. I'll let you know," I tell her before walking into the elevator.

When I get down to the mailroom, I'm surprised to see that I'm not the only one down here. Ellie's also here.

After talking with Cade, it's hard to not want to get to know the girl better. She's such a little kitten, but the kind of kitten with spiky claws. Now, I'm not saying that this is divine intervention or anything, but I did tell Cade that if I ran into her again, I would actually talk to her more. Maybe actually try to spend time with her.

"Fancy seeing you down here," I say with an overly cheerful smile as I walk over to my mailbox right next to her.

"How much of a surprise is it actually? I mean, we both live in this building and need to get our mail at some point," she mumbles, her face scrunched up as she grabs her mail.

"Well, I mean... yeah," I say, stuttering over my words. "I guess it would've been better if I'd just said hello, but for some reason, you kinda caught me off guard, kitten."

She looks at me quietly, worrying her bottom lip between her teeth as she stares at me, no doubt sizing me up.

"Kitten?" she asks, her eyebrows scrunched together, making her look even more adorable.

"Yeah, you're cute as fuck, but damn, you're feisty." I shrug. "I like it."

"Oh," she says, turning her head as she tries to hide the blush now taking over. Turning back, she bites her lip nervously. "Sorry. For snapping at you. That was really rude of me. I'm not really in the best mood right now—but that's still no excuse to be a bitch."

"Don't apologize for having feelings. We all have bad days. Everything okay?"

For the second time during this interaction, Ellie looks taken aback, like she's not used to people being nice and not judging her. Now I don't know if this has to do with the fact that we don't actually know each other or if everyone in this girl's life is just a complete and total piece of shit and doesn't ask her if she's okay.

Either way, I don't like it.

"Um, thanks... yeah, everything is fine, or I guess it will be. Just a lot to do between settling in and cleaning up, and then there was this asshole in the elevator that kept staring at me. I asked him to stop, and he started to yell at me. He was weird."

"That's Frankie. He's the nephew of one of the older tenants. Someone usually rides with him up to his place. He's harmless, just an entitled prick with a staring problem. If he bothers you again, let me know. I'll talk to his uncle or him if I need to."

"Thanks, Trevor. And, uh, thanks for coming over the other day when Tom, my ex, was there. He's kind of a douche," Ellie trails off as she chews on her bottom lip.

"You can take the word kind of out of that sentence. No offense, but the guy sucks. Where's Addy?"

"She's there. At her father's. Probably why I'm in such a shitty mood. Actually, do you have a minute to help me? If you don't mind, of course. I'm sure you've got somewhere more important you need to be, so, uh... never mind, just forget I said anything."

"Not a chance, kitten. What do you need help with?"

She still looks nervous, like she doesn't quite know how to ask for help.

No one should feel like a burden for needing help.

"Can you tell me where the recycling is? I've had to break down so many boxes that I practically have a mountain inside my apartment that I need to take out."

"Are you heading up there now? I'll show you."

"You don't mind? I don't want to bother you when I'm sure you have way more fun things that you could be doing."

"Nah, not at all. In fact, I'm starting to think I'm right where I'm supposed to be."

With a smile, I grab my things. "Now lead the way, kitten. We've got some boxes to move."

Her eyes stare up at me in utter and complete shock. It's a mixture of happiness and uncertainty, and I can't help but completely hate that she's feeling this way right now. I joked earlier about her being a kitten because she's feisty. She's also sensitive, and I can see that she's been wounded before.

This little kitten has been hurt, abandoned, and left to fend for herself—that much I can already tell. Maybe I can help her feel just a little less alone.

# Chapter 7

## *Ellie*

As soon as I woke up this morning, I had this intense urge to set up my art studio. I can't explain it, but it was like the second I was awake, the only thing I could think about was painting. After months of avoiding it, keeping everything in boxes, even back at our old house, I finally have the urge to paint again. I have no expectations for it, but I've missed the desire to create and design, and I can feel it building inside of me.

Natalie had put all the boxes in the last bedroom, but I refused to let her unpack them no matter how much she begged. I even held strong when she tried to be bossy. I refused to back down.

But now, I'm unpacking the last box before Natalie comes over to go out for a weekday brunch. Addy's back with her dad this week, and I don't have to be at the studio for work until tomorrow evening.

"Knock, knock, motherfucker!" Natalie sing-songs as she shuts the door behind her.

Why I thought I could finish unpacking this before she got here is beyond me. She's always early, which is why she has the only other key for this place. Well... that and just in case she needs to come watch Addy for me. She's all I have; it's not like I can call my parents, they'd just tell me to go back home, and my husband would be able to watch his daughter.

What they don't realize is that he just has a nanny that watches her. Addy told me last weekend that her dad was only there to tuck her in two of the nights that she was there. It broke my heart because she doesn't deserve an absent father.

"Where are you?" Natalie shouts from the hall.

"In the back room. Just finishing up something really quick."

I hear her come in, but am still surprised when she runs up behind me and wraps her arms around me, an excited squeal coming out of her tiny self.

"What's this for?"

"I'm just happy to see that you're finally setting up your studio." She giggles, giving one last squeeze before stepping back to look around. "It looks great. I see you got some new supplies, too?"

"Yeah, honestly, I woke up and just had this urge to paint. I went out first thing this morning to pick up some new supplies. I figured this way, if I do get more ideas for what to paint, I'll be able to start instead of coming up with another excuse."

Natalie smiles, pure happiness radiating off of her. It's why she's my best friend, my other half. Quite possibly, my soul mate. She's the only person I truly believe has always just wanted me to be happy.

She never cares about anything else, just that.

"Love that. What brought all this on?"

"What do you mean?" I ask.

"I mean that you went from being adamant you didn't want to paint to setting everything up and even buying new supplies. You're also smiling. Addy isn't here, and you're still smiling—that alone deserves some recognition."

I think about it. I have been happier, even with Addy being gone. I've been enjoying getting ready for the day, and doing my hair and makeup again, which I don't think I paid attention to for weeks leading up to leaving Tom.

Unless we had an event, I was in sweats and a messy bun. Now? I'm in sweats and a messy bun with some mascara on because comfort still matters, but I like to feel pretty. It's my mom uniform, and I'll never give it up.

But what's been different? My routines have been the same. I still work out and go to the studio. The only thing different is where I live.

It's Trevor.

He's the big difference. The main new thing in my life.

"You're blushing," Natalie says as she nudges me with her shoulder. "Go on, explain. You know I'll just bug the fuck out of you until you finally talk."

"There's nothing to tell. Nothing has happened, and it won't. You know I don't date."

"Yeah, yeah. I know all about how you won't put

yourself out there out of fear of getting your heart broken. But that doesn't mean you need to be a hermit."

"Natalie, I'm becoming a hermit, but I won't survive if I bring someone else into Addy's life just for them to leave us, to leave her."

"I know. I do. Trust me, I get it. If someone hurt her, I'd kick their ass myself. Is that what this is about?"

"I don't know. I guess my new neighbor has me all confused, and not just because he's hot, although that's a huge bonus. It's that he's genuinely a nice guy—or at least that's how it seems. He's always friendly, willing to help whenever, and he takes the time to make Addy feel special. I'm just confused."

Not confused enough to try to convince her that I don't want to see him naked, she's seen him; she'd know damn well it was a bald-faced lie. But I'm only human. When I ran into him last night on the way back to my place, he must've just gotten done with a workout. He had a baseball hat on backwards, his hair all scruffy, and he was wearing this black t-shirt that looked painted on. I'm pretty sure I might've drooled when I saw him, but it's the tattooed forearms fault, not mine. They're sexy, and you can't convince me otherwise.

I mean, watching him carry all my recycling out for me was hot enough, but add in his tattoos covering all of his muscles and his forearms covered in veins. Yeah, I was putty.

Who would have thought that the guy who has my hot pink vibrator would be the same guy I fantasize about riding until we're both screaming? Definitely not me, that's for damn sure. But nothing that I've predicted has actually panned out. In fact, Trevor has surprised me more times than I can count. Last night when I was stressed from a shitty day, he stepped up and it helped me realize not everyone sucks.

No, in this instance it's just my soon to be ex-husband who sucks donkey balls.

I'd spent most of yesterday arguing with him because he's still convinced that I'm going to take the fall for our divorce, so he's refusing to accept any of my terms.

He can have absolutely everything. Except Addy. I'm not saying I want to take her from him, I just want primary custody of her since I'm the *only* one who's taken care of her in the five years of her life. He can take the money, the homes, the cars; I literally don't care. I just want my daughter. The daughter he constantly reminds me he never wanted. The daughter who spends all of her time with me because her father can't be bothered to even acknowledge her existence unless our parents or the cameras are around.

So now, when all I've asked for is primary custody of her, he says no unless I take the fall for our marriage. Yet, in the same breath, he says he wants to bond with her, so I know damn well he's full of shit. The whole thing is a lie. He straight-up told me he had no interest in being a father. I obviously picked a real winner to knock me up and force me into marriage because our families would be devastated if our 'mistake' tarnished their image.

Yeah, Tom's a peach. A bruised, nasty peach that will probably make you sick if you eat it.

So instead of succumbing to a life of misery, I left his cheating ass with my now ex-best friend, Lena.

Trevor, on the other hand, is nothing like Tom, which I'm already confident in even though I've only known him a short time. He proved that when he helped me last night. Spending over an hour helping me take my recycling out, then building two side tables for me because I didn't have the tools. Yeah, Tom would've never.

"Earth to Ellie," Natalie says, her hands waving in front of my face.

"What?"

"You good? You definitely weren't listening to anything I said, were you?"

"Sorry, Nat," I mumble, shaking myself out of it. I don't want to sit here and think about Tom, and I definitely don't need to be comparing Trevor to him. "Guess all of this stuff with Tom is just messing with me. He's being a dick about the whole thing and trying to blackmail me, and I'm just getting frustrated. I don't even think he knows what he wants me to do except that he wants me to stop fighting him. Whether that's me going back home or taking the fall for our divorce. Either way, he's using custody of Addy against me in an attempt to force my hand."

"I seriously hate that guy. He makes me want to punch things."

"Me too, girl, me too."

"I want you to do me a favor. Can you do that?" Natalie asks hopefully.

"What is it?"

"You'll do it? You promise?"

"Pinky promise. Now what is it?"

"I want you to give this guy a shot. I don't mean to

date him. I just mean, get to know him. Be friendly, neighborly, hell, I don't know. Just see what happens. You're different when you talk about him, happier, and I like seeing you this way."

"But—"

"Nope. Pinky promise."

"Ugh."

*Knock, knock.*

I look at Natalie, confused at who could be knocking at my door. She just smirks, though, immediately running over to the door to see who it is. Stepping back from the door, she shakes her head as she laughs.

"Interesting. It's almost like he knew we were talking about him. Or he was thinking about you. Either way, lover boy is here."

"Fuck, Natalie, you're joking, right?" I ask, but she shakes her head no. "What do I do?"

"Well, step one is opening the door. Step two is to use your words."

"Oh, fuck off," I tell her as I open the door.

"Hi," I say meekly.

"Hey, kitten," Trevor says, his face bright, his tone cheerful; I can't help but return his smile.

"What's up?" I ask, noticing an envelope in his hand. "Is that mail for me?"

"Not mail, but it is why I'm here. So... I, uh... have two hockey tickets that I usually have family sitting in. I wanted to see if you wanted to come to the game tomorrow. Addy can come too if you'd like."

A hockey game? Why is he giving me tickets to a hockey game?

"A game? Who's playing?" I ask as Trevor starts to laugh.

"The New York Cyclones."

"Oh! Are you a season ticket holder?" I ask, knowing Tom used to love when we got to use his family's season tickets. They were always such great seats.

"Yeah, something like that. So, would you like the tickets?"

"Yes, she would," Natalie answers for me, jumping out from behind the door. "Hi, Trevor, it's nice to see you again."

"Likewise, Natalie." Trevor smiles before turning back to me and passing me the envelope. "Here, this is all you need. I'll text you the details and let you know where we'll be afterward if you guys want to come out with everyone."

"Thank you. It'll be a nice little escape before Addy comes home on Sunday."

"Of course. You ladies have a good rest of your day," Trevor says before walking away with a smirk.

Natalie looks me dead in the eye as I shut the door before turning back to her phone as she starts typing furiously. "What did you say his name was?" she asks, her eyes never leaving her phone.

"Trevor, why?"

"What's his last name?"

"I don't know."

"Never mind, I don't need it. Found him."

"Who?" I ask, but as she flips her phone around to show me the picture, and I'm floored. It's Trevor. But not like I'm used to seeing him.

*Blindside Love*

He's wearing a New York Cyclones jersey as he skates on the ice. He's a professional hockey player.

"Holy shit."

"Holy shit is right. Your next-door neighbor is a legend on the ice. He's played for the New York Cyclones for at least eleven years and still holds the record for most goals scored in a single season. No wonder he's such a hottie. I told you that you needed to ride that."

"Shut it, Natalie, I'm processing."

Why does this make everything feel more extreme? This guy is in the public eye—like my ex, albeit in very different ways—but he's interested in me. I'm no idiot, I know these athletes often have women all around throwing themselves at them. Yet, it's me he seems to be focusing his attention on. I mean, hell, he invited me to his game, and for some reason, that feels really important.

"Process faster, let's go eat and talk about hockey butts."

## Chapter 8

### *Trevor*

Wing Wednesday is always the highlight of my week.

Between hockey games, practices, and trying to have a social life, the guys and I are rarely able to make it here for wing night, but this week, it worked out perfectly.

Our favorite bar, Hudson's, does all-you-can-eat wings and beer until close on Wednesdays with easily fifty different sauces and rubs to choose from. It's absolutely incredible, even if they only serve shitty beers. Sawyer, Cassie, and Gwen have even joined us before.

Gwen surprised us all when she put down three full orders of wings, two of which were in the spiciest sauce they have.

It was impressive as fuck. I tried one wing and immediately chugged my beer because it was so spicy.

But tonight, I'm here, and my head is going a million miles an hour. Has been ever since Ellie accepted the tickets for tomorrow night's game. I'm so damn excited.

"Can I get you boys another round of wings?" our waitress, Sandy asks, her usual friendly smile in place. She's used to our shenanigans; we've been coming to her for years.

"Yes, please!" Miles says as he licks his thumb clean of BBQ sauce.

"Perfect, I'll bring out another random bunch, and before you even ask, I'll make sure there's extra ranch and none of that 'Bleu cheese' bullshit."

"That's why we love you, Ms. Sandy. You're our favorite," Harris says with a grin.

"Oh honey, that may work on the younger girls, but your smile just screams trouble to me, and not the kind of trouble Mr. Wilson would be too happy to find me in," she says as she swats Harris's shoulder.

He smiles even wider. "I'm wounded," he says with a laugh as he goes back to his wings.

We've already been here for an hour and done the usual bullshitting about hockey. Rex may be the coach of another team, but we've all played together long enough to know each other's ticks on the ice, so it's nice to just vent and let off steam together.

Tonight's big topic was how Harris has been fighting lately, much more than usual. He's been known to drop his gloves every now and then, but lately, it's been like every game he's getting thrown into the sin bin.

When Rex brought it up, he shrugged it off and said the guys deserved it. He's been weird ever since Mama Lockwood's gala, and none of us have been able to figure it out. I know he ran into his ex, Avery, that night, but he hasn't said much about it. He clams up every time she's brought up. It probably didn't help matters that she came in with a man who her father mentioned would be proposing soon.

But I'm not going to force him to talk. I know how hard it can be when you're trying to deal with shit on your own. Your own disappointments. He knows we are all here for him, and he'll talk when he's ready.

"So, how's everything going with the neighbor girl?" Cade asks, stopping my thoughts in their tracks. When I look up at him, he has a shit-eating grin as he bites into a piece of celery smothered in ranch. Whoever said celery is mostly water has obviously never met Cade. His celery is a spoon for his ranch.

"Is this the girl with the, um, rather unfortunate moving box mishap?" Miles questions.

*Fuck, I was not ready for this interrogation.*

"The one and only," Rex says with a grin as he leans back in his chair, drinking beer and trying to forget the burn of the extra spicy wings. "Although, I wouldn't say it was unfortunate based on the look on Trev's face right now."

"I don't know what you're talking about," I say, unable to stop myself from grinning, but I refuse to let Rex see it, so I bow my head. He'll push until he gets the information he wants, but I'm gonna make his pushy ass work for it.

All five of them have set their wings down and are watching me. Harris looks far too interested in this situation, but his interest is probably a mixture of curiosity and excitement at the idea of me back out in the dating world. He's been trying to get me back out there, but I've declined every single time. The rest of them just have this gleam in their eyes like they know something I don't—or that I'm not ready to admit.

*Which they probably do.*

"I heard you picked up some tickets for the game on Friday," Cade says, a smug look on his face as he breaks the silence.

My eyes snap to him, surprised that he knows. "Who told you that?"

"I went in the other day to pick up my tickets, and you must've just left because Mary thought we had shown up together. She told me all about your little visit," Cade says. So, he already knows and just wants me to be the one to say it. Even though it's really not a big deal, it's not like it's a date or anything.

All I did was invite Ellie and her friend to our game. It's not like they need to come hang out after, although I'd honestly love it if she did.

"Interesting. But I'm not sure what me picking up my tickets has anything to do with Ellie," I say, doing my best not to smile.

"Cut the shit, Trev," Cade's grumpy ass mumbles.

"Fine, yes, I picked up my tickets. I invited Ellie and her friend, Natalie to the game."

"Good job, Trev, you're making progress," Max says with a wink.

"What the fuck is that supposed to mean?"

"The first step is acceptance, my friend," Max adds.

"Oh, because you were so fucking quick to accept your feelings for Cassie?" Rex jokes back.

"That's different. She was my sister's best friend.

Speaking of sisters," Max jokes. "It's not like you accepted your feelings for Sawyer overnight, so don't act like you're Mr. Perfect."

"Well, no. But I had your fucking ass to deal with. It was complicated," Rex says with a shrug. "But your sister says I'm Mr. Perfect in bed, so I'll take that as a win."

"Oh, fuck off, Lockwood. I'm trying to eat," Max groans.

I don't have feelings for Ellie. How could I? I just met her a couple of weeks ago. But I'd be lying if I said that the times I've run into her haven't been the highlights of my week. It's so easy to talk to her, and she's funnier than I expected.

Sometimes we see each other in the gym, and fucking hell, her body. Watching her in her tiny little workout shorts and sports bra is pure fucking torture. The military could use that as an interrogation tactic because I was about to tell her all my secrets if it meant I could touch her, taste her, and feel her body on mine.

"So, are you still going to deny it, or are you going to fess up?" Max asks, a smug look on his face like he knows exactly what I'm thinking.

"I mean... no, yes, I don't fucking know, Daniels. My head is a hot mess when it comes to Ellie. I'm not exactly sure what to think."

Just then, our waiter comes over with a new round of beer and wings, halting our conversation long enough for me to look down at my phone. I have two texts—one from my mom telling me they were having fun with my sister, who convinced them to come visit her. The second message, however, is much more exciting. Ellie.

**ELLIE**

> Hi. What the fuck do I wear to a hockey game?

One thing I love about Ellie is that she doesn't pussyfoot around anything. She's curious about something? She'll ask. She wants to tell you something? She'll say it without a second thought. She's always kind, though. It's been nice falling into these easy conversations with her. It's like we've been doing it all our lives.

> Clothes? I mean I'm not opposed to you not wearing clothes, but it does get kind of cold inside.

**ELLIE**

> You're absolutely no help. :)

> Are you asking me to come help you get dressed? Because if so, *I'm on my way!* ;)

**ELLIE**

> For fucks sake. Good byyyyye, Trevor.

> Bye, kitten.

As I set my phone down, I feel everyone's eyes on me. Slowly looking up, I feel like a deer in headlights as they're all staring at me like they discovered the next wonder of the world.

Fuck. I feel my face slightly redden as I realize they know.

Even scarier? *I know*.

I like this girl way more than I should after just

meeting her. I mean, we've texted a bit here and there, and it's always so exciting for me, but I can't quite figure out why. There's just something about her that's so *real*. She makes me excited about life again because she's so full of it. She's like a damn unicorn. She's feisty as hell, passionate about so many things, and she's such a good mom, which makes her even hotter.

"Fuck my life."

I hear them clink glasses, but I just stare down at my phone. Shit, what am I going to do?

"So, what has you cheesing like a teenager in love?" Cade says, asking the question I'm sure all of them want to know. But honestly, why am I smiling so much over this little conversation?

"It's really nothing. Ellie texted me asking what she should wear to the game tomorrow," I tell them with a shrug. "I told her clothes or nothing, but I don't think that's really an option."

"Are you telling me you're not getting her your jersey?" Rex asks, his tone full of disbelief.

"Uh, I hadn't really thought about it."

"Don't be an idiot," Max says.

"Yeah, I'm single as a pringle, and even I know that if a girl's coming to the game for me, she'll be in my jersey," Miles chimes in. "I mean, unless you want her wearing my name on her back."

I hadn't even thought about that. What if she goes out and buys a jersey? What if she buys someone else's jersey? Hell, no. If she's wearing anyone's jersey, it's mine. My name on her back. My number for everyone to see.

God, what I'd give to see my jersey on her, *only* my jersey. Nothing else while I drive my cock into her until she's screaming my name.

"Fuck, you guys. I don't know how to do this. I haven't actually dated someone in years," I say, looking over to Rex. "Think Sawyer will help me out on this one if I give her my credit card?"

"Are you asking me if Sawyer will go *shopping* for you? For a girl you're interested in?" Rex chuckles. "Shit, text her right now, I'm sure she'll have everything for you by morning."

"On it," I grumble, pulling out my phone and sending the text.

> S.O.S.

Her response is immediate, the bubbles popping up almost as soon as I press send.

> SAWYER
> Everything okay? Rex isn't doing karaoke again, is he?

> Nope, he's definitely not that drunk. LOL. No, I need shopping help.

> SAWYER
> For you?

> No.

The dots start, then disappear, stop, then disappear. Until finally, my phone rings, and I see Rex start laughing.

## Blindside Love

"She loves this shit."

Answering the phone, I don't even get to say hello before Sawyer's yelling at me.

"Who is she?"

Her voice is filled with so much excitement. It's adorable.

"Her name is Ellie. She's coming to the game tomorrow with her friend. She, uh, asked me what she should wear to the game, and I said clothes. The guys said I was a dumbass for not having a jersey for her. Think you could help me out?"

"I'm already on it, Trev. Cassie and I were meeting up tonight anyway. We'll go shopping and get Ellie ready to support her man."

"I'm not her man."

"Not yet... not yet. Text me what you think her size is. You'll have it when you wake up. Tell Rex to wake me up when he gets home." She laughs as she hangs up.

"What'd she say?" Max asks.

"She's on it," I tell them, relieved for the first time since they brought everything up. "Oh, and Rex, she wants you to wake her up when you get home."

Rex smiles as Max fake gags. I laugh.

What's even funnier than these two, though?

The fact that for the first time in months, I'm looking forward to a hockey game—all because *she* will be there, even if she's only my friend.

# Chapter 9

## *Ellie*

> You'll never believe what he did.

**NATALIE**

Who? Twatwaffle or Twatmaster?

> Twatmaster.

> *SENDS PIC*

**NATALIE**

Are those jerseys? Are they for tonight?!

> Yes. One for each of us. Plus passes to go back with the players after and a sweatshirt and some other stuff. It's all super cute.

**NATALIE**

Interesting.

> What's interesting?

**NATALIE**

Your man is making sure you're wearing his jersey.

> **He got you the same one.**

NATALIE
> He just didn't want to make it obvious.

> **Fuck. Why do I love that? Are we still meeting there in an hour**

NATALIE
> Yep!

I went to the gym first thing this morning to get a quick workout in and try to kill some of my nerves. To say I'm a little stressed about going to Trevor's game tonight would be an understatement. I spent a solid hour running before lifting weights in hopes of exhausting my brain.

It didn't help.

Something about him inviting me to his game made me feel all giddy. It felt nice to look forward to something again, even if he only invited me to be friendly. I don't expect a man like him to be interested in someone like me. He probably dates supermodels and those Instagram fitness girls who always get the poses just right.

After Tom, I truly thought I would never enjoy a male presence again. Like, ever. I was going dick-free in 2023. But there's something about Trevor that's just so different. He's so kind, genuine, and so freakishly hot that it's hard not to stare sometimes. I had to stop myself from reaching out to touch his biceps the other morning when I ran into him at the gym. Just to see if they were real, of course. I blame his shirt, practically painted onto his body, his muscles were just front and center.

*They were so big, and when he flexed, I wanted to run my tongue along the veins.*

This morning there was a knock at my door and when I opened, there was a black box with green bow outside the door.

Trevor's gift was so sweet and thoughtful, but it made me substantially more nervous about going tonight. Attached to the box was a card that I'm doing everything in my power not to let get to my head.

> Kitten,
> You asked what you should wear to the game tonight. I vote for my jersey. I'd love to see you in the stands with my name on your back. ;)
> Hope you and Natalie enjoy it.
> -Trevor

It's the '*my name on your back*' with the damn winky face that has me spiraling down a rabbit hole in my mind as I walk up to the front of the arena looking for Natalie. She waves at me from the line. Thankfully, it didn't take us long to get inside, and once Natalie changed, we went to grab drinks.

I've been to hockey games before, but it didn't feel like this. The energy tonight is exciting. I was actually at a Cyclones game earlier this year with Tom, he said it was date night. Looking back, I realize he spent all night meeting with board members that were there, so I'm pretty sure I was only there as a prop.

Maybe it's the fact that I have better company tonight or that I'm here to see Trevor, but either way, I'm already enjoying this game more than any previous one. It definitely helps that he got us glass seats, which are a million times better than the stuffy suite I'm usually in.

Down here, it's electric. Between the action happening just a few feet in front of you to being surrounded by excited fans and the beers everyone's drinking, it's getting a little rowdy out here.

I fucking love it.

There's a guy next to me who cheers loudly while giving everyone in the row a high five anytime something happens. He's a whole vibe, and I'm here for it.

The game has been nonstop back and forth, but it's flown by. Watching the guys battle it out on the ice, flying on those tiny little blades and trusting that they aren't going to impale themselves in the process, is impressive. They give off this power and excitement that kept Natalie and me on our feet for most of the game.

It's been brutal the entire night. The other team came out swinging, but the guys fought back on the ice, both with and without gloves. Both goalies have had to make an impressive number of saves, but somehow, both teams managed to score twice.

"Okay, why have we never been to one of these before? This is so much fun!" Natalie shouts in my ear as she holds her beer in one hand and nachos in the other.

"I don't know. I went with Tom a few times, but it was never like this—it was always so stuffy and boring.

This is so much fun. Hell, I can't believe there's only two minutes left." I smile for the first time in a while. I like this feeling. The feeling of being able to do something I want and enjoy my time out with a friend without worrying about who I was pissing off at home just for having a life.

"We have to come to more. This is so much fun. Addison would love this," Natalie says, her drunk rambling beginning. "She'd have so much fun watching, but also all of the food. She loves this type of food."

"She really would love this..." I start but lose my train of thought when I watch Trevor break away with the puck, flying down the ice and leaving everyone behind.

It's just him and the goalie.

Fuck, I feel like I can't breathe. We're all holding our breath as we wait to see what happens.

In mere seconds, Trevor has gone from center ice, handling the puck like it's an extension of his body, making quick work heading straight towards the goal. In a quick move I wasn't expecting, he skates to the left of the goal, appearing to hold onto the puck. Instead, he fakes it, skating to the right of the goal as he passes the puck behind his back, sliding it right into the goal a second before the buzzer signals the end of the game.

I can't keep my eyes off Trevor as he smiles wide, skating to a stop in front of us. The whole team is practically on top of him, celebrating the win, but his eyes stay on me the entire time. I can see the pure joy on his face. As he stares at me, his smile grows even larger, then he winks, and turns to his team.

Happiness looks good on him.

"Girl, that man looks like he wants to eat you alive," Natalie tries to whisper in my ear, but her voice is far too loud.

"Oh, stop it. No he doesn't," I say, but the words feel wrong, like I know damn well what she saw because I saw it too. And in what world is a woman going to complain about being eaten alive?

"Lies and we both know it. But continue on."

"Gladly.

---

I DON'T THINK I'VE EVER BEEN HAPPIER THAN IN THIS moment that my best friend is the world's biggest extrovert. I hate meeting new people.

Tonight, after the game, we met up with Trevor to say hi and thank him. He convinced us to come out to the bar with them. Apparently, he and his friends always go out to a particular bar after their games. Thankfully, though, I've at least met one of them since he said his friend Rex will be there with his girlfriend and her friends.

And when I say that he convinced us, I mean that he mentioned it, and before I could even process his words, Natalie had already agreed to it. If his face hadn't lit up like Christmas, I probably would've said no, but he looked so excited that I didn't want to let him down, even if it did mean a lot of social interaction.

I'm not too good at peopling, especially when it's new people. When it's just Natalie and I, I'm totally fine. Put me in a random restaurant or bar and tell me I need to mingle, and I immediately want to crawl into a hole.

*Blindside Love*

My night was originally going to consist of being in my bed watching reruns of Paranormal with a pint of chocolate brownie ice cream, but instead, I'm in a crowded bar at a table full of Trevor's friends, most of whom are hockey players. His friend Rex coaches the Ice Hawks, and his other friend, Max, plays for him, but the rest of the guys all play with Trevor.

"So, how did you and Trevor meet?" Sawyer, Rex's girlfriend, says from across our table. No warning, just straight to the point.

She's made this night so much fun. She and her friend, Cassie, have been so welcoming. They made Natalie and I feel right at home. But how much of this story I should actually tell is still unknown.

"Well, he's my neighbor. I moved into the building just a couple of weeks ago," I say with a shy smile, trying not to go too far into detail—but my bestie likes to see me squirm, and she definitely likes to embarrass me.

Natalie's smile should've told me everything, and I should have just smothered her.

"I mean, I'd say your first meeting was a tad more interesting than that," Natalie says, watching as Sawyer's eyes brighten with excitement. "Let's just say that my friend Ellie hasn't had a proper orgasm in weeks."

With that, my face turns bright red as I feel all of their eyes snap to me.

*I'm going to kill her. I'm going to smother this woman in her sleep and when I get arrested, I'll just explain myself. They'll understand. They'll realize that she had it coming.*

"Well, this sounds exciting," Cassie says with a raise

of her glass. "Does this mean we get story time? I love story times. We can always get Sawyer to tell us how she met Rex. It's scandalous and fun and will probably make you feel better about whatever happened to you."

"I doubt that," I grumble, earning a laugh from Natalie that quickly turns into a grunt when I kick her under the table.

"I don't know," Sawyer says with a shrug. "Mine included a strip club and me wearing a tiny red lace set that didn't leave much to the imagination."

I glance up at the girls and can't help but smile. "Okay, then maybe you get it. It was honestly just mortifying. I was moving my stuff into the apartment and was carrying a box. Well, it fell, and uh... I was trying to catch the elevator, but everything exploded in the parking garage. And, let's just say that when it broke, I had some electronics fall out."

"Did they break? Or were they playing something? Like, did you have a spicy audiobook playing, and it blasted in the elevator?" Cassie guesses like she's on a gameshow and refuses to lose.

"Nope. I wish that's what happened, at least that I could've managed. But no, uh, it was battery operated and—"

"She dropped her vibrator into the elevator. It turned on, and it definitely wasn't a little one," Natalie says with a wink before I can finish.

"Kill me now," I groan as all three of them start laughing.

"Oh shit, that actually gives Sawyer a run for her money on the most scandalous meet cute. I would pay to have seen that," Cassie adds. "I can only imagine Trevor. I bet he got all awkward. For some reason, he doesn't seem like he'd handle that too well. A little on the vanilla side if you ask me. Like a real-life golden retriever."

Blegh, minus one point for Trevor. No offense to anyone who is into vanilla sex; it's just not for me. I've wasted far too many years of my life with a vanilla man; I don't need to continue that trend.

I'd like to come at the hands of a man at some point in this decade.

Sawyer shakes her head at Cassie. "I wouldn't assume too much. I've heard some of the conversations he and Rex have, and well, let's just say he seems like the exact opposite of *vanilla*."

"I have to agree with Sawyer," Natalie interjects, like she actually knows him well enough to have an opinion. "What? Don't give me that look. Besides, it's the way that man stares at you that makes me think he's not all vanilla. Ma'am, he looks at you like you're his prey, and he's going to catch you and devour you whole. It's hot as fuck."

"I've seen that look tonight," Sawyer says as she glances toward the guys who are over at the pool table still, but she smiles as she looks over their way. "In fact, he's giving you that look right now. Jesus, I think I just got pregnant just from watching the way he's looking at you."

"Oh, stop it, you crazy people. He's not looking at me like that. It's not like that between us. Neither one of us is really in a place to date... me especially, with my daughter and everything. Besides, Trevor and I are just friends."

"Just friends, my ass. Unless you mean friends who want to get naked together."

Before I can say anything, Trevor, Rex, and two of their friends I haven't met yet come to join us at the table with another round of drinks in hand.

"What are you ladies talking about?" the friend with the blonde hair asks with a grin as he looks between the four of us.

"Oh nothing, Harry, nothing at all," Sawyer says as she bumps him with her elbow.

"I don't believe that at all, but I'll let it slide because we have newcomers here." Turning his attention to us, he grins, showcasing a perfect white smile with bright green eyes that just scream trouble. "I haven't had a chance to meet you ladies yet. I'm Harris."

He offers his hand with a sincere smile, but the second I take it, I feel eyes on me. When I look behind me, I see Trevor. And he looks angry.

*Is he jealous? Of me? Of his friend touching me?*

Turning back to Harris, I offer him a polite smile, but he must notice my nervousness because he grips my hand a little firmer and offers a friendly wink as he glances over my shoulder toward Trevor.

"It's nice to meet you too. I'm Ellie."

"Oh, I know who you are," he says with a smile before taking a step closer, his hand still gripping mine. It almost makes me uncomfortable because I barely know the guy, but then he chuckles as he whispers in my ear. "I'm sorry if I'm making you uncomfortable. I was only helping a friend out."

"What do you mean by that?" I ask.

"Just had to give someone a little push in the right direction, help them realize what was right in front of him and how pissed off they'd be if someone else swooped in before they realized they were fucking up," Harris says with a smile right as he takes two steps back, putting some distance between us.

"It's time to go," a deep voice says behind me, immediately making my body tingle like it's filled with electricity.

I look up and see Trevor standing in front of me, blocking me from Harris, although I don't miss him winking at me as he walks towards Natalie and the other girls.

"What? Where are we going?"

"We're leaving. Grab your things," Trevor says as he impatiently waits.

Everything inside of me tells me that I don't take directions from anyone, especially men, but dammit, something in his voice is so commanding, so domineering, that the next thing I know, I'm grabbing my things, and he's practically manhandling me as he pulls me out of the bar.

Worst of all?

I *love* the way him being in control makes me feel. Him telling me what to do is so hot, and my body definitely agrees. My vagina has basically thrown caution to the wind and is kneeling at the altar of Trevor. I can only imagine what she'd make me do if he ever actually touched me.

Fuck my life.

I should stop this, but truthfully, I don't want to.

# Chapter 10

## *Trevor*

This was not part of the plan. In fact, *this* is exactly the opposite of my plan for tonight.

Tonight, I was just supposed to invite Ellie and her friend to the game to try to form a friendship with her. Not that this isn't exactly what I crave, exactly what I always think about doing anytime I see her, think of her, imagine her. Which pretty much takes up 95% of my mind each day. It always ends the same, with me grabbing her and slamming my mouth on hers right before thrusting my cock deep inside of her.

But that's not what should be happening the first time I get her to come hang out with me.

But as I pull her out of the bar and around the corner, I realize I've thrown logic out the window and am driving full force into desire. Lust. Something that feels so primal, I can feel it deep in my bones, just begging to be set free. The way I crave her should be illegal, and some of the things I want to do to her are probably illegal in at least a few states.

"What's going on, Trevor? What's wrong?" Ellie asks, her voice a little frantic as she struggles to keep up with my long strides.

How do I explain to her that nothing is wrong, yet somehow everything is wrong all at the same time? That I want her, yet I know I shouldn't. I know I'm no good for her, that I can't be everything she needs, but goddammit, what I wouldn't give to get a shot at trying.

I spin her, pressing her back against the brick wall of the building, one hand pinning her hips in place as I press my erection into her stomach. She lets out a soft moan, almost like a whimper, as I bring my mouth to her ear.

I feel like the world around us has stopped, like nothing exists anymore. All the noise has stopped, and the only thing left is her.

She's staring up at me with these big doe eyes, dark with lust, as her tongue darts out to lick her lips. Her eyes are filled with question like she's waiting to see what my next move is.

"What's wrong is that I haven't felt something like this since I first started playing hockey. It's been years since I've felt it, and I don't know what to do. Everything has felt mundane, boring, and predictable, and I loathe it. But then I met you, kitten. I'm not sure how to explain it, and I'd probably get it wrong if I even tried, but something about you feels different, reminiscent of that rush I used to get with hockey. I feel like I'm chasing a high with you."

"What do you mean?" she whispers, our lips almost

touching. I could lean forward and graze her lips, but I'm scared.

"I mean that every time I see you and the more time I spend with you, the more excited I am to continue spending time with you. To get to know you better, to earn your trust. But then tonight, watching Harris with you, smiling at you, touching you, seeing you smile at him, it made me fucking crazy, and I know I have zero right to be upset about who touches you. I have absolutely no claim. But fuck, it made me... it made me feel insane."

"Are you trying to tell me that you were jealous? Of your friend and me?"

"Yes. I wanted it to be me you were smiling at, not him," I tell her truthfully, only pulling back far enough to look her in the eyes. My hips continue to press into her, holding her right where I want her, pressed between my body and the wall.

"I'm smiling at you right now," she says, a devious smile playing on her lips, her eyes blown with lust as she slowly lifts up on her tippy toes, sliding her body along my length.

"I wanted it to be me you were touching, not him."

"It was a handshake, nothing more," she murmurs, her face turning so her lips just barely graze mine as she speaks. "Besides, it's you I'm touching now, not him."

She's right, but I still hated seeing Harris touching her. I know he was fucking with me. I saw the little glint of trouble in his eyes when he saw me watching her. But even knowing he was up to no good, I still couldn't handle watching them together. What if she started to enjoy it? I mean, hell, Harris is charismatic, that's for damn sure. He's charmed the pants off of plenty of women in New York.

"It was too much, kitten. If he was thinking about you the way I think about you..." I mumble, leaning forward to press a gentle kiss to the corner of her mouth and slide one hand up to grip the hair at the nape of her neck. Pulling gently, I hold her in place as I look down at her. "If he imagined half of the things I have, I'd lose it."

"How *do* you think about me, Mr. Adams?" she asks, and the way she says my name sends all sorts of tingles throughout me. More importantly, almost all my blood immediately rushes to my cock so fast I feel lightheaded.

Fuck, she's going to be the death of me.

"Like I'd do anything to know what you taste like. What your lips feel like. Fuck, what I'd give to know how this tiny body feels beneath me, quivering below me as I make you come over and over until you're begging me to stop. It's all I can think about any time you're around, and it's getting harder and harder to hold myself back,"

"Then why are you?"

"Because you aren't ready," I tell her, my grip tightening on her hair as I tilt her head up even further. She winces at the pressure, but her eyes sparkle, telling me she definitely likes this. Leaning in, I brush my lips against her neck; her quick intake of air makes me smile into her neck.

Fuck, she smells good.

"Says who? Are you my father?"

"I'm not your father, but I'm definitely not opposed to you calling me daddy," I growl, my lips brushing against her neck until I find the spot right behind her ear and kiss gently.

"Is that so?" she purrs, one hand sliding up from her side to start drawing circles on my chest. It feels like she's burning a hole straight through my shirt into my skin, like I'm two seconds away from being engulfed in the fire that is her. "Then kiss me, Daddy."

I use my grip on her hair to pull her lips up towards mine as my mouth slams down onto hers. My lips take over, control hers as I take exactly what I want from her mouth. She's tentative at first, but it doesn't take long until she's attacking my mouth with the same intensity as me.

As our tongues tangle, I hear her moan and feel the vibration of it in our kiss. We don't slow down. If anything, it spurs us on.

Faster.

Harder.

*Just more.*

We continue making out, slammed against the side of this building in a dark and quiet alley as we finally take this little moment to explore each other.

Her hands slide down my body, sliding into my back pockets as she grabs my ass, holding me tight against her as she grinds her body against my erection.

Fucking hell. I could come without even touching her. Without *her* even touching *me*. What am I, a fucking virgin?

I pull back, tilting her head to the side with my hand still gripping her hair as I run my tongue up the length of her neck, my teeth nipping at her jaw as she squirms in my hold.

"Fuck, what I wouldn't give to bend you over right here, fill you with my cock until you screamed so loud people in the bar would know my name," I groan, using every ounce of restraint that I have to not keep going. I was barely able to stop myself as it was.

Even though tonight proves what I'd figured, Ellie isn't as unfazed by me as she tries to let on; I know something is still holding her back. While I'd love to get naked with her, I'd like to do it more than once, so I'm trying to be patient.

"Then why aren't you?" she asks quietly, some of her confidence deteriorating. I can see the defeat in her eyes.

Shit.

"Kitten, I want to kiss you, don't twist this. But I want you to want it too. If I saw it in your eyes right now that you weren't afraid, that you weren't afraid of me, of this, of taking this further, I'd be carrying you all the way back to my bed right now. But that's not what I see. I see someone scared by what they want, and that's okay. But until you're one hundred percent sure, I won't cross that line," I tell her, leaning down to brush a kiss against her lips.

When I pull back, she's smiling, and damn, I wish I could take a picture to remember this feeling.

"Fine, pretty boy," she grumbles, but she's still smiling so I'll call it a win.

"Let's get you home before you freeze to death."

> **MOM**
> Dinner is at 6. I'm making your favorite.

> I can't make it tonight, sorry.

> **MOM**
> Unless you're bleeding, broken, or dead, I expect you here.

> I feel like my brain is bleeding, does that count?

---

"Trevor Michael, cut the shit," my mother snaps into the phone, obviously over our texting conversation already. She's not actually grumpy. Hell, she's rarely ever grumpy with anyone, well, unless you *really* deserve it. "I don't want to hear your weak ass excuses. Unless you're broken or bleeding, you'll be here for dinner tonight, if you know what's good for you."

Mama don't play when it comes to our weekly dinners, *especially* when it's a last-minute cancellation. She looks forward to weekly dinners just as much as I do, so she needs a heads up to mentally prepare to not see me.

At least that's what I tell myself—she'd probably just be annoyed she spent all day cooking for me.

"But I'm tired, Mom. We had the game last night, and the team got together after. It ended up being a late night."

"You do not get to bail on dinner just because you're tired. Besides, I heard you had an early night last night.

That you and some girl ended up bailing on the outing? Or at least that's what my spy said this morning when we bumped into each other at Mickey's."

"What? Dammit, woman. Stop making Cade tell you my secrets—you can't withhold your jam just for secrets."

"You can't stop me. I can and I will. I'm a grown-ass woman. Besides, what good is learning to make delicious jam if I can't use it to barter secrets about my son's love life?"

"You're incorrigible," I chuckle, knowing damn well that she held Cade up at the cafe until he spilled everything he knew. We'd pretty much tell her anything if she tried to withhold her jam, it's that damn good.

"See you at six, right?"

"Fine, woman. I'll be there," I grumble.

"I can't wait for you to tell me all about Emily," my mother says cheerfully.

"Her name is Ellie," I say far too quickly based on her little giggle.

"Just making sure you were listening, sweetie. See you tonight!"

With that, she hangs up.

There's something to say about the conversation with my mother. She always gets what she wants, and she's fucking effective, that's for damn sure. I guess she had to be, though, with my father working a lot, my sister playing softball and soccer in high school, and I was basically playing hockey full-time, so she was always busy.

I love her more than life, but damn, I'm not ready to be interrogated. Not because I don't want to tell her. No, if Cade hadn't told her first, I would've. She and I are close. She knows I got messed up when I broke up with my ex back in college, but that was over twelve years ago. I think ever since then, she's taken a bigger interest in my love life. Or lack of love life.

But honestly, part of it was I couldn't exactly tell her the real reason that my first girlfriend, Jessica, and I broke up. She knew that she had broken up with me and that I was heartbroken over it, but she *definitely* didn't get the full story. How could I tell my mother that she broke up with me because she thought I was disgusting, or at least that my taste in the bedroom was 'disgusting and repulsive?' I think she also may have mentioned that it was violent.

The worst part? All I had done was give her a little love tap on her ass when we were having sex. After we were done, she turned around and slapped me and told me I was repulsive. Truthfully, the way she moaned and her pussy clenched around my cock when I slapped her makes me think now that she was actually just repulsed with herself.

Sucks to be her, though, she missed out on some fun adventures and crazy fucking.

But because I wasn't about to tell my mother the truth, for obvious reasons, I've spent years with her piqued interest in my love life. Secretly, I love our talks. I love her interest in that aspect of my life because she truly just wants me to be happy.

I guess all I can hope for is that she goes easy on me tonight.

SPOILER ALERT: SHE DID *NOT* GO EASY ON ME tonight. In fact, I'm pretty sure she missed her calling as a lawyer. Or an interrogation specialist. She's ruthless.

After we had lasagna and my parents told me about their week, my dad had to take a call from someone at the university, which left me alone with my mother, who insisted we go to the living room. She was practically foaming at the mouth the second we sat down, not waiting to jump right in.

"So, are we going to start with the reason you're in a shitty mood, or go straight for juicy details and tell me why you've been checking your phone every five minutes like you're waiting for a phone call during the draft?"

"How does neither sound? Why don't you tell me about the book you read for book club this month?"

"Trevor, I am more than willing to tell you about the duke and his rather promiscuous thoughts, but my guess is that you'd rather not hear about that," she says pointedly.

"I guess we can talk about my bad mood then. But only if you promise not to tell Dad. I'm not ready for that," I say quietly, slipping my shoes off and wiggling around to get comfortable on their oversized couch.

"Trevor, that is not a phrase a mother wants to hear. Did you get someone pregnant?"

"First off, I'm thirty-five; I'm not a teenager knocking someone up. Second, it's definitely not that. No, this is about hockey," I tell her, noticing her brows furrow like she's thinking about something. She gets this look when you can tell the wheels are turning in her mind, and she just kind of stares. I used to try to talk to her, but it was always better to just let her have her little moment to think.

"But you don't want me to tell your father?"

"Not yet, look, I... I'm not sure when it started, but honestly, I'm getting tired. My body feels more worn out by the day. Hockey used to be my reason, but I'm starting to realize it's not anymore," I spill out, immediately feeling like a weight was lifted off my shoulders now that she knew.

Mama always knows how to make me feel better. She makes me work for it, but I always feel better after a talk with her.

"So, what's the issue?"

"Hockey has been our life for so long. You and Dad have sacrificed so much for me to get to where I am now. You're both at every game, and Dad calls me a couple of times a week to check in on practices, and I just feel like I'm letting you down."

"Hockey was *your* life, Trevor. *You* were our life, which is why hockey became so important to us," my mom says, her lips quirking up into a soft smile. "Look, sweetie, I can't tell you what to do. Neither your father nor I can. What I can tell you is that you need to follow your heart. Find your reason. Your father and I will be with you every step of the way."

Relief hits me that I didn't realize I needed. I've been so afraid of letting my parents down. I'd always joked that I wanted to play until I was at least forty, and now, at thirty-five, I'm already considering hanging up my skates. I know I still need to talk to my dad, but knowing I have her support makes that conversation seem a lot less scary.

"Thanks, Mom. I appreciate that more than you know. I'll talk to Dad soon."

"Good. Now, get to the juicy details. What's going on with this girl that Cade was telling me about?"

She looks like a teenage girl waiting to hear the latest gossip.

"There's not much to tell. Her name is Ellie. She's my neighbor. She's sweet and pretty and really funny."

"So you like her," she says nonchalantly.

"No, I... uh, no. I barely know her. She's just..." I drift off, not knowing exactly how to explain Ellie.

"Different?"

"Exactly. She's different in a way that's exciting. She makes me want to know more about her."

"Then why does it seem like that's not what you're planning on doing?"

I think about this, and I don't really know how to explain the complexity of the situation. The fact that Ellie is a mom and is going through a divorce makes me feel like I would be way too much for her. But I hate that. Because what if I was just enough?

"She's a mom," I say, watching my mother's face absolutely light up—definitely not the reaction I was expecting.

"How wonderful! Does she have a son or a daughter? Oh, I just love kids."

"Her name is Addison. She's five. She's a spunky thing, just like her mama." I smile, thinking about Ellie and Addison. They're a fun little duo.

"Well, I hope to meet her sometime, Trevor. Bring them to dinner sometime."

"I'll ask, but she's got a lot going on. She's in the middle of a divorce with an absolute douche."

"Shame. But, Trevor, life isn't about knowing exactly what we should be doing at all times. Sometimes, it's the messy moments, the moments where we believe we are doing exactly what we *shouldn't* be doing when we find ourselves in the perfect moment, like some beautiful mistake."

Before I can even think to respond, my dad comes out of his office, he's nothing but impeccable at timing. We spent the rest of the night watching hockey reruns before it's time to watch *Survivor* or whatever the new show is now.

I left with a full belly, more food than I know what to do with, and a smile, because for the first time in a while, I realized that maybe it's okay not to have everything figured out.

## Chapter 11

## *Ellie*

It's seven in the morning, and I have unloaded the dishwasher, cleaned my entire apartment, and folded the three loads of laundry I've been neglecting since Addy got home last Sunday. I guess this is what happens when you wake up at four in the morning on a Wednesday. Even worse is the fact that I could have slept in since there's no school today.

I'm not sure what woke me up, but as soon as my eyes opened, I was wide awake. When I looked at the clock, my first thought was that somehow I slept all day, but Addy is here, and she doesn't sleep past seven-thirty usually, so that was out of the question. Once I was awake, though, there was no going back to sleep.

I refused to get out of bed until after five, it seemed to be a more reasonable time. I stayed in bed scrolling through my phone and watching reruns of NCIS; it's my comfort show. Tony and Ziva are perfect, but something about Gibbs is just *chef's kiss.*

But now I'm watching the sunrise, drinking coffee, and feeling restless. Almost antsy. Then it hits me, clear as day, like a freight train.

I want to paint again.

It's more than that, though. It's like I can see it, imagine it, almost feel in my bones *exactly* what I want to paint.

Without another thought, I've refilled my coffee and am walking down the hall to my makeshift studio. Even though I haven't painted in this apartment, Natalie set it up exactly like I had it at the old house, so my body is moving on autopilot. I practically float around the room, turning on the music and lighting a candle before I move on to setting up the canvas and mixing the oil paints.

I enjoy painting with all different types of paint, but to this day, there's nothing quite like using oil paints. Don't get me wrong, I still paint using watercolors and acrylics, but I always go back to oil painting. I feel like I can better capture my emotions in my painting this way, like it's easier to blend the colors, replicating the image in my mind. The brush transfers the image filled with color, passion, and so much vibrancy onto the blank canvas.

The second my brush touches the canvas, I feel my body relax. I'm no longer thinking about what my next move is or what chore I need to do next. I'm not stressing about my failed marriage or the hot guy next door, who I had the hottest kiss of my life with almost a week ago and who I've been hiding from like a wimp ever since.

My body has taken over as I listen to the music and realize for the first time in ages, my mind is quiet.

I don't know how long has passed before I step

back, set my palette and brush down, and take a moment to admire my work. I must've been at it for a while, though because my apartment is already bright from the sun, and my coffee is cold. I've always enjoyed my paintings, even though I know they're nothing special, but this? This one surprised me. In the best way possible.

It's a butterfly, but somehow, it's so much more than that. It feels fresh and new, and it seems like I somehow fit the entire rainbow into it in the most serene way.

When did I start to paint with color again? When did I stop only seeing the world in shades of gray? In the last few months, I stopped finding joy in the little things like I used to. I didn't want to find happiness in the colors around me, but now, something is different.

Looking at my painting, I see life, colors, and happiness radiating from it; all I can do is smile.

"Good morning, mama," Addy's little voice says from the doorway.

"Good morning, sweet girl. How'd you sleep?" I ask as she walks over to me, her sleepy eyes barely able to stay open.

I pick her up, relishing how her head rests on my shoulder, her little arms holding onto my neck as she hugs me back. I know these moments are short-lived, she won't always want her mom to pick her up and hold her, so I try to soak it in as much as possible.

"Good. I had a dream about a unicorn! She was eating pancakes." Addy giggles. "Did you paint the pretty picture, Mommy?"

"I did. I just finished actually."

"It's pretty. I like it," she says as she stares over my shoulder at it.

"Thanks, baby. Should we go make some pancakes like your unicorn dream?"

"Yes! But can they have sprinkles just like my dream? And chocolate chips? She said they were the yummiest pancakes ever, and I just *have* to try them! Pleaseeee?"

"Yes, baby. Let's sugar ourselves up."

---

I HEAR A KNOCK ON MY DOOR AS WE SIT AT THE kitchen bar and eat our chocolate chip pancakes with *extra* sprinkles.

"Mommy, is someone here?" Addy asks, her mouth practically exploding with food, bright sprinkles, and melted chocolate chips covering her face.

"I guess so. Stay here and eat. I'll go see who it is," I say with a smile, although inside, I'm nervous it's her father.

Am I always going to feel this way? Like he controls my life, and I have to make sure he's not watching me? I hate it. I hate that I don't feel completely comfortable in my new home because there is always the thought in the back of my mind that he'll come here and mess everything up. I'm afraid of how he's going to respond when he realizes he's not getting his way. Tom never lifted a finger at me; he just used his words to tear me down. I think he knew that if he ever got physical with me, I'd chop his dick off faster than he could finish, and goddamn, that's saying something. But I am afraid of what he could do with Addy. Could he take her away from me?

Either way, no matter what temper tantrum he throws, we *are* divorcing, and I'm *not* taking the blame.

When I peek through the hole, I see it's Trevor, his usual black baseball cap on backward, paired with a gray shirt, a flannel, and ripped jeans. Seeing him makes me all tingly, and I can't help but remember the feeling of his lips on mine. Why does he have to be so hot?

"Good morning," I say, as I open the door.

Trevor looks down at his watch and quirks an eyebrow at me. "Is eleven a.m. still considered morning?"

Addy and I ended up in the living room watching *Bluey* for an hour before we finally made our way into the kitchen to make the pancakes. It was nice getting some snuggle time with my girl, plus those damn dogs are just too funny in that show.

"In this house, we kinda just go with the flow. Morning is when we eat breakfast, and it just so happens that today we're having breakfast at eleven in the morning since Addy doesn't have school today," I say with a smile. To be honest, I hadn't realized it'd gotten so late.

"I like your style," Trevor jokes before checking his watch. "So, I know this is super last minute, and I totally get if you ladies already have plans, but Rex and his girlfriend Sawyer were coming to meet me at the park. They're bringing Rory over, and wanted to walk Central Park and get ice cream. Rory has been wanting to meet Addy, so she asked me to invite you both."

It's weird seeing Trevor nervous. He has such a big

presence and is a very confident man who's never anything but charismatic and charming. But right now, it would appear that I'm making him nervous, and deep down, I kind of like it.

Addy comes running from the kitchen, a huge smile on her face when she sees Trevor. "Mr. Trevor! Hi!" she says as she swoops past me and hugs his legs. "What are you doing? Were you coming to see me?"

The way she looks up to him makes my heart hurt. It's filled with adoration and happiness. He always makes time for Addy. Even if he's on the way out and we bump into him, he'll stop and talk to Addy, and I know it means something to her. Tom barely pays attention to anyone, hell, he was probably working while Lena sucked his dick under his desk.

"I was, little one." Trevor beams as she practically leaps up into his arms.

"He actually invited us to go get ice cream with him and Rex's family," I tell her.

"Yes please, mommy. I want to go. Rory and I can be friends now," Addy says with a giggle as Trevor eyes me, waiting for my answer.

Do I want to go? I shouldn't. Not after the last time we were together and were playing tongue hockey in a dark alley where I called him daddy. And the only thing I regret is that I didn't call him daddy while his cock was buried deep inside me.

But of course, I'd do anything to see my little spawn happy, so I guess we're getting ice cream.

"Can we have ten minutes? I just need to get her ready really quick," I say, looking at Addy, who is still in her pajamas. At least I got dressed, although a pair of overalls and Converse aren't exactly fancy.

"Of course. They're meeting us out front in fifteen minutes. I still need to grab a jacket, so I'll just meet you here in ten?"

"Perfect."

*Fuck*, I think as I shut the door. I have ten minutes to make both my sleepy-looking child and myself presentable. I mean, I'd like to at least look hot, even if Trevor won't actually fuck me.

"Addy, go get dressed. I'll be there in just a minute to do your hair."

She skips off, giggling the entire way.

Now what the hell can I do in ten minutes to make myself look fuckable without looking like I'm trying too hard?

Decisions, decisions.

Grabbing my phone, I text Natalie.

> Trevor just invited me and Addy to get ice cream so she can play with Rory. What should I wear to look hot but not slutty and like I'm trying too hard?

NATALIE
> Giiiirl, get it. Wear your overalls and your white turtleneck. It's cute, you won't freeze, and your ass looks fantastic in them.

> Perfect. What would I do without you?

NATALIE
> You'd die.

> Better call me later. I want all the deets.

---

Fifteen minutes later, we're all walking into the park across the street, Addy and Rory immediately taking off to the play structure, already giggling and talking about a new toy that just came out.

Sawyer and I grab a seat on the bench closest to the structure while Trevor and Rex walk around and talk about hockey.

"Soooooo," Sawyer says with a devious look. "What is going on with the two of you?"

"What do you mean? We're friends," I tell her quietly, doing my best to keep a straight face.

"Friends that look at each other with come-fuck-me eyes. Rex and I are those kind of friends too," Sawyers says as she giggles.

"No, I mean, maybe. But that's all it is," I blab, thinking about the kiss the other night and how he didn't want it to happen again until I was ready.

The scary part? As much as it's terrifying to be interested in Trevor, it also feels so right. So safe yet so exhilarating. But admitting that out loud to Sawyer feels scarier than I can handle.

"You're telling me that nothing has happened yet, and you're already looking at each other like that?" she says, fanning her face with her hand dramatically. "Y'all are going to melt all the snow in New York when you finally hook up. If the way he's looking at you means anything, that man is ready and willing to *devour* you. "

"I mean, basically." I shrug, turning to look at Addy and Rory, who have made their way to the swings, where Trevor and Rex are pushing them.

It hits me right here that Tom has never done this with his own daughter, and here Trevor is pushing a little girl he's known for a few weeks with the biggest smile on his face, like he's actually enjoying it. This might be even hotter than his forearm veins, and I constantly daydream about tracing those with my tongue.

Sawyer swatting my arm snaps me out of my daydream. "Earth to Ellie," she giggles. "What do you mean basically?"

It's weird for me to have another girl I can talk to like this other than Natalie, but Sawyer is so down to earth that we've fallen into an easy friendship, one where I don't mind oversharing a bit.

"We may have kissed. Outside of the bar the other night."

"I knew it!" she shouts.

"Shhhhh!" I whisper, checking on the guys to see if they heard her. All I need is for that man to know we're talking about him. He's already the most confident guy I know—the world doesn't need his ego to get any bigger.

"Sorry," she says quietly. "I just saw the way he looked at you when Harris was flirting with you."

"He was not—" I start.

"No, he was. But that's just Harris. It's who he is. Besides, he was doing it on purpose to force Trevor's hand."

# Lexi James

"What do you mean?"

"We've all known for a while he was into you, but Trevor doesn't usually date."

"Why not?" I say, a weird, nervous feeling taking over my tummy. Why doesn't he date? Why do I care? Do I want to date him? Do I like him like that? I mean, duh, but it doesn't make it any less scary.

Sawyer thinks for a moment before answering, biting her lip like she's processing something.

"Look, they'd both kill me if they knew I said this, but I'm honestly just trying to protect him. If he gets hurt again for the same reason, I fear that he may never open up to anyone ever again," she says cautiously.

"Your secret's safe with me, but if you don't explain soon, my anxiety may kill us both."

"Trevor, uh... likes things a little different in the bedroom," Sawyer says nervously.

"Okay?" I ask, not sure exactly what this has to do with him not dating.

"Trevor likes it a little rough in the bedroom. I overheard him talking to Rex about handcuffs and blindfolds, and I'm pretty sure I heard him say whip."

I'm doing everything I can to steel my face, trying not to let on just how much I like what she's telling me. I knew I liked Trevor and that I was attracted to him, but now I'm ready to kneel at his altar and beg to get a taste of him in the bedroom.

"Okay," I tell her, shrugging like it's no big deal. It is a big deal, but in the most delicious way possible.

"That doesn't scare you?"

"No? Why would it?" I whisper.

"It's just that Trevor's had some bad luck with women and the way they've treated him because of his kinks. He's very open and honest about it with women, but lately, he says he's just been shoving that part of himself down."

"Nah, I'm not like that. Besides, we just might be more compatible than I realized." I smirk.

## Chapter 12

## *Trevor*

"Higher! Higher!" Addy giggles as I push her on the swing.

When she and Rory ran over to Rex and me and asked us to push them, I couldn't hide my smile. This little girl is fun and adorable, and I love that she wanted me to play with them.

"I'm pretty sure if I push you any higher, you're going to fly to the clouds," I chuckle. "Besides, I thought we were going to get ice cream."

"Yes, please," Addy giggles.

"Me too, me too!" Rory adds, both jumping off their swings with excitement as they run over to the girls.

"You look happy," Rex says, bumping his shoulder into mine. We both stand there watching Sawyer and Ellie with the girls, and I realize how much I've been wanting this.

And I don't mean just this experience with anyone. I mean this feeling of belonging. Of happiness. Ellie and

Addy have been bringing so much laughter and joy into my life, and I've felt such a strong connection with them so quickly.

"I am happy," I tell him with a smile.

"That's good, man. You seem more like yourself. More content than you've been in quite some time," Rex says, his eyes never leaving Rory, who's currently talking to Sawyer and Ellie in the animated way she gets when she's excited, especially when it's about sugar. "Have you slept with her?"

The girls practically skip their way over to the ice cream cart on the corner, Ellie and Sawyer following close behind. We head towards them but are far enough back that I can still speak openly. But how much do I want to tell him?

Everything. It's Rex, my best friend and the only one who knows everything about myself that I try to keep hidden from the world.

"No, I haven't hooked up with her," I tell him. "We've only kissed. It happened that night she came to the game."

"Was this before or after you acted like a barbarian and dragged her out of the bar when Harris was just trying to get to know her," Rex questions, a knowing smirk telling me he already knows the answer.

Those fuckers knew what they were doing that night when they had Harris talk to her, and goddammit, I hate to admit it, but it worked. It was the push I needed to make a move.

But now, the ball is in her court. If she wants something more to happen between us, she needs to make it known.

"It was after," I admit. "Like, immediately after, in the alley next to the bar."

Rex starts laughing, loud enough that the girls look back at us, almost concerned. "I knew you just needed a little push."

"Y'all are fucking dicks, but you weren't wrong."

"I never am," Rex deadpans. "So why just a kiss?"

"Because I don't want to push her. She's made it clear she doesn't trust easily, and who can blame her based on her current situation with Addy's father? I stopped it before we let it get too far. Told her I wasn't letting anything more happen until I knew she was ready. That she was sure she wanted it."

"What'd she say?"

"She pouted, and then I walked her home. It was cute, even if my dick hurt the rest of the night from how hard it was."

"Well, based on how you two are today, hopefully she's figuring it out."

"I fucking hope so."

"Uncle Trevor! Daddy! Hurry up! We want ice cream," Rory says as she runs over and grabs our hands, pulling us over to the ice cream cart.

Ellie is smiling as she watches us walk over, her eyes on me the entire time. It's the first time I can honestly say I see pure desire in her eyes, and it's setting my body on fire. There's no hesitation in her eyes, no wondering. She knows exactly how she feels, and she doesn't look the least bit scared.

Of course, she looks this way when her daughter is here, and I can't do anything about it because right now, all I want to do is strip her out of those cute little overalls that make her ass look absolutely fuckable, bend her over, and tongue fuck her until she can't remember her own name. I want to give her orgasm after orgasm, bringing her to the edge of insanity as I fuck her so thoroughly that she'll forget about everyone before me.

I want to ruin her. I want my cock to be the only thing her tight little cunt wants.

Soon... very fucking soon.

"Hey," Ellie says nervously as she stands in line with Addy, who's still talking to Ro. "Thanks for inviting us. Addy is having a lot of fun."

"Are you?" I ask.

"Am I what?"

"Having fun?"

Her cheeks redden. Her blush is barely noticeable, but I love that I have this effect on her.

"I am," she smiles.

Reaching forward, I grab the loop on her overalls, pulling her towards me until we're nearly touching. Ellie glances around for Addy, but she's in the middle of some hand-song-clap game with Rory, so she's distracted.

Leaning forward so my lips are hovering right above her ear, I whisper, "All I've been able to think about is your lips. The way they felt, the way they tasted. Fuck, you're all I think about," I murmur.

"Trevor, I—" Ellie starts, but she's cut off by the attendant telling us it's our turn to order. Perfect timing.

With a quick wink, I turn to watch Addy and Rory

*Blindside Love*

order. Rex and Sawyer are sitting on a bench watching us, both smirking. Assholes.

Addy doesn't hold back and orders chocolate ice cream with chocolate sauce and rainbow sprinkles. She and Rory are going to get along just great with their love of sugar and all things rainbow... especially sprinkles.

Once everyone orders, I pay while Ellie wrangles the two girls with their identical ice creams back over to the bench where they can sit and hopefully not make too big of a mess.

"Thank you!" Addy says with a smile, chocolate already on her face.

"You're the best, Uncle Trevor," Rory says, giving me a quick hug before grabbing her ice cream.

Rory may not be my niece by blood, but I'd do anything for that little girl. When Rex found out he had a kid, I remember how scared he was and how he didn't think there was any chance he'd make it as a father, let alone be a great one. But I knew the entire time that he would be incredible, and I was right. Rex is one of the best dads I know, and his little girl has us both wrapped around her finger.

"Anything for my favorite girls," I say as I try my ice cream. I'm one of those guys who love most chocolate and fruit combinations, especially when it's orange with chocolate, so obviously, I had to get it when I saw it was the flavor of the week—even if Rory says the flavor is, "the grossest thing in the whole entire world." Even worse was Ellie agreeing. Red flag, but I guess that just means more for me.

The rest of the afternoon is low-key. No one had

anywhere else to be, so we let Rory and Addy play while we sat and talked. Addy was super excited when Sawyer mentioned her ballet studio, so hopefully, that'll be another way the girls can play together.

It's so weird to me how easy today has been, how natural it's felt. It was refreshing. The conversation was easy, and everyone got along really well. It was nice to see Ellie and Sawyer get to know each other. Sawyer makes anyone feel at home, so I'm glad they've developed a fast friendship.

The highlight of the day was definitely spending more time with Ellie. After Friday—specifically our kiss—I thought it'd be best to give her a little space to process, to think about everything that had happened between us before I mentioned that I wanted more.

I know damn well I wanted to take it further, but I need her to want it. No, I need more than that. I need her to *crave* it. To crave *me*.

But if the looks she's been giving me today mean anything, she's definitely coming to terms with her feelings for me. Feelings? Desires? The tingly things that happen to your body when you meet someone you want to get naked with *and* have a conversation with.

It's rare and exciting, but all I want is to get to know her and maybe have some fun in the process.

And maybe, just maybe, she'd like that too.

---

EARLY MORNING PRACTICES ARE ALWAYS THE hardest to wake up for. Especially on a Saturday when, for some godforsaken reason, our coach thinks we should be laced up and on the ice by seven a.m., which actually means 6:50. This morning was no different than usual but was made infinitely better when I saw Ellie had texted me on one of our ten-minute breaks.

> **ELLIE**
> Hi. I was wondering if you were free on Monday.

> Good morning, kitten. Besides practice till 10 a.m., my schedule is wide open.

The dots start and stop a few times, and I wonder if she's changed her mind about whatever she was just about to say.

> **ELLIE**
> Would you like to come over for dinner?

I can't help it, I smile.

> I'd love to. When?

> **ELLIE**
> Six?

> I'll be there. Can I bring anything?

> **ELLIE**
> Just yourself. :)

How could I not be on top of the world after having that conversation before eight a.m.? Plus, I finally scheduled a meeting with my agent to discuss my plans. As much as I know that he could work out a killer deal for me, I still can't commit to that yet. But I also can't commit to retirement until I talk to my father.

Thankfully, we have our weekly dinner tomorrow, and my sister will be there. Hopefully, that'll help take some of the heat off of me when I talk to Dad. And now that Ellie just invited me over to dinner, I have that to look forward to the day after. It seems like this week is finally looking up.

I'd be lying if I said I wasn't nervous about dinner, though. I've hung out with Ellie before, but usually in a more public, less intimate setting. It's nearly impossible to keep my hands off of her when we're in public; how the hell am I supposed to when I'm at her place? All I can think about is the way her body felt in my hands, her tongue on my own, and the way her eyes looked up at me like I hung the moon. And in that moment, I decided it had become my life's mission to see that look in her eyes as many times as humanly possible.

"Whatever little daydream you've got going on up in your head, close it down, bud; it's time to get back out before coach reams our asses. I don't wanna bag skate the rest of the morning," Harris grumbles as he makes his way past me.

"I'm fine," I snap as I follow Harris out onto the ice.

We're doing shootout practice for the rest of this morning. Coach is still pissed we lost a game in a shootout a couple of weeks ago, so he makes us practice this constantly.

"Are too. I saw you texting. Then you got this big, dreamy smile. It was adorable. But adorable doesn't score goals."

"That's still to be determined."

Out of the ten shots I took, I made nine. Harris made six.

I guess adorable *does* score goals. Now, if only I could score her.

## Chapter 13

### *Ellie*

I wake up to the sound of footsteps as they pitter-patter into my room.

My girl is awake.

Addy climbs in bed and snuggles up, her big brown eyes staring up at me. "Mommy, I want to watch cartoons," she says with the biggest smile she possibly can.

"Okay, baby, go turn them on, and I'll meet you on the couch. Mama needs coffee first," I tell her with a smile.

She jumps up and runs out into the living room, excitement radiating off of her.

It's adorable how something so simple as watching cartoons together on a Sunday morning can make her so happy. It makes me feel special, and I love it. I follow behind her but make a beeline for the kitchen. Coffee first, everything else second. Once I get the coffee started, I find myself lost in thought, still waking up.

Normally, on Sunday mornings when she's here, I

have her get everything ready to go back to her dad's when she wakes up, and then I let her watch cartoons. But this morning, all I've been able to think about is how much I *don't* want her going back to her dad's every other week. She's been complaining that she doesn't see him much and that she's usually at the house with a nanny or Lena.

The thought of Lena being with my child makes me furious. If I had my choice, she wouldn't be able to be near my daughter, but of course, my only reasoning is that she's a backstabbing ex-best friend who broke up a family.

It's weird, lately, I haven't been as angry about their betrayal as I was in the beginning. I'm sure it's all just a part of the grieving process, but part of me wonders if the reason I'm not as angry lately might have something to do with my very friendly next-door neighbor, who I'm starting to have very friendly feelings for. The touchy-feely kind that I know will just get me in trouble. But maybe just this once, it's okay to want to be bad because these feelings only spur on my fantasies, and my fantasies do a damn good job of making me cum, especially with big pink back in my life.

But I want the real deal. I want him. I want his body.

The smell of freshly brewed coffee is enough to snap me out of my daydreams. Filling my cup, I walk into the living room, where I find a snuggly Addy curled up in the blankets, fast asleep with *Bluey* on. When I snuggle in next to her, her eyes immediately pop open, wide awake.

"Morning, sleepy head," I murmur into her hair as she snuggles into me.

"Morning, mommy," Addy says, quieter than usual.

"What's wrong?"

"Do I have to go to dad's?" her tiny voice asks.

I feel like I've just been kicked in the stomach. My heart cracks at the sadness in her voice. Squeezing her tighter, I kiss her forehead.

"Oh, baby girl, I wish you didn't have to," I tell her truthfully. The thing about Addy is she's very observant. Although it breaks my heart that she doesn't have a relationship with her father, I truthfully don't think she misses *him*. She misses the idea of a father who is present. Tom has never been that, so she really isn't all that attached to him.

It breaks my heart but I'm also proud of her for being so strong. No child should have to be.

"Okay, mommy," Addy sighs. "I love you."

"I love you too. I'll try to get everything figured out."

---

AFTER A COUPLE OF HOURS OF HER FAVORITE cartoons and some pancakes, we made the sad walk down to the lobby.

I really, *really* hate having to let her go. Look, I'm a firm believe that all children should get to spend time with both parents... if they act like an actual parent. He doesn't. He only wants her, so I can't have her, and then he sticks a nanny or his assistant with her, and that sucks for us. But now is not the time to bring that up.

Right now, I'm about to ask, no beg, if I can have Addy a day early for my birthday. It's not until next month, but I want to make sure I'm providing enough time so he can't complain that it was last minute.

As we walk out of the elevator, we see Tom standing in his usual spot directly by the door. He looks irritated as he ends a phone call and looks up to see us.

"Hi, Eleanor," Tom sneers before turning to our daughter. "Hello, Addison. It's nice to see you."

"Same to you, dad," she says, dragging her suitcase behind her as she walks over to him.

"Tom, may I speak with you?" I ask nervously, his eyes brightening just a bit.

"Of course, Eleanor. What is it?"

"So, uh, my birthday is the day before my week with Ellie," I say, feeling like I'm tripping over my words.

"I know," he says, looking bored.

"I was wondering if I did one less day the week before if I could have her on Saturday instead of Sunday that week so I can spend it with her. Then—"

"No," Tom scoffs, cutting me off.

"But—" I start, but he raises his hand, immediately cutting me off.

"I said no, Eleanor. You made the choice to leave. Deal with the consequences."

"You're really putting this on me, aren't you? Are you delusional? How have you convinced yourself that this is my fault?"

"Who filed?"

Oh, for fucks sake. What the fuck did I ever see in this man? I can't even say that I was dickmatized because he didn't know how to use it. The fact that he's being so rude and adamant that he can't even be slightly flexible on *my* birthday is ridiculous. And now, to blame the divorce on me just because I filed? I didn't fucking destroy us.

He did.

"For the millionth time, you thick-headed jackass, YOU cheated on me. You are the one who caused us to fall apart, and I will not let you convince anyone otherwise."

He just smirks like what I'm saying doesn't matter to him, and I fucking hate it.

"Well, I've already convinced my father, and he's the one selecting someone to represent me in court. He says it wouldn't look good if I did it myself, so be prepared to lose your daughter, Eleanor. Now, I've got to go. I have places to be," Tom says before turning on his heel and walking out to the car where his driver is already buckling Addy into.

It breaks my heart that she's not here with me right now. Her little hand waves as they pull away, and I can't help the tears that well in my eyes.

I don't want to do this. I don't want her to be at her dad's every other week because he doesn't give her anything she needs. He doesn't give her love or comfort, and he sure as hell doesn't give her his time.

It might just be fucking time to crack down and find a lawyer willing to go up against his father's firm. It might be tough, but I'm sure I can get someone to see my side.

At least, I hope I can.

I don't know how long I stand there staring out the window in the lobby, but a deep voice snaps me out of my trance.

"Hey, kitten," Trevor says, and when I turn to look at him, he's as handsome as ever. He looks absolutely delicious wearing black jeans, a white shirt, and Converse.

"Hi."

I feel like an idiot. He's all smiley and happy, and I'm sitting here moping around because I have a week without my girl, and somehow, all I can muster up to say is hi.

His face falls, and he looks concerned as he takes a step forward. My natural instinct is to take a step back, but for a reason, I stay put.

"Oh... he just came to pick her up, didn't he?" Trevor asks solemnly, looking around like he's going to be able to spot Addy and go get her back for me. Unfortunately, there's nothing that can be done about it. Yet.

I just nod, afraid that if I talk, I'm going to cry. I *hate* not having her with me all the time, but not enough to go back to the home where she'd never learn what a family should look like.

If I go back to that house, all I am doing is letting him control our lives, control our happiness. He doesn't care about either of us. The only thing Tom cares about is himself. His image, his reputation, his job, his money, but most of all, his status.

He doesn't care who he has to hurt or manipulate in the process of climbing the ladder; he just wants to get there, and he wants to use me and Addy in the process.

I can't let him do that.

"I'm sorry, Ellie. That really sucks," Trevor says, his thumb tipping up my chin until I look at him. "I really am sorry. You're the best mom in the world, and that little girl adores you. From what you've told me and the brief encounter I had with her 'father,'" Trevor adds air quotes for dramatic effect, "He's a piece of shit all around and isn't deserving of attention from either of you girls."

I feel my eyes welling, tears threatening to fall as his words hit me right in the gut. I've only ever wanted to be a good mom, and this man is praising me, making me feel deserving of a daughter as special as Addy. He's making me feel like I'm the mom I've always dreamed of being.

When his thumb presses against my cheek, swiping the tears away, he freezes, holding my face in his hands as we stare at each other.

"Please don't cry," he says.

"I've waited my entire life, well, my entire adult life, to hear those words, and until this day, no one has ever told me that. You say it so effortlessly like it's the truest thing in the world, and I don't know, I guess, thank you."

He smiles, and his whole face brightens with it. It stirs something in my tummy, flipping around like butterflies are taking flight. But that's not the era I'm supposed to be in! I'm supposed to be catching flights with my daughter, not feelings with the hot hockey star next door. But when he says things like this and takes the time to check on me and make sure I'm okay, all the while looking like an image straight from my spank bank, I can't help but realize that I *already* have feelings for him, I just haven't been ready to act on it.

Because truthfully, I know that I can't bring another man into my life until I've gotten Tom out of it. Especially not someone with so much to lose. Trevor is in the spotlight, famous in his own way as a killer player in the

NHL. If Tom were to realize I was interested in someone else, let alone dating someone else, there would be hell to pay, and I'm sure he'd take down Trevor, even if it was just collateral damage.

I can admit I care about Trevor enough to not let that happen to him, which is why dating him is out of the question. But that doesn't mean I'm against having some fun with him.

"You don't have to thank me, kitten. It's not a secret. Anyone around you can see just how incredible of a mom you are. You're a very special person, and I feel lucky to even know you." He smiles as he looks down at his watch before looking back up at me. "Do you have plans this evening?"

"No, I was probably just going to drink a bottle of wine and watch trashy TV while crying into a tub of ice cream," I tell him, far too truthfully to paint myself in a good light.

"Well, you can still do that, but I have a better idea, if you're interested?"

"What is it?" I ask cautiously.

"Just trust me. Meet me down here at five, you'll have fun, I promise. I just have to go run a few errands, but I'll be back to pick you up."

"Uh, alright, I'll bite."

"I hope you do." Trevor grins before he turns around and walks out.

What did I just sign up for?

"So where are you taking me?" I question as I sit in the passenger seat of his G-Wagon. I'm slightly surprised by his car. I'm not sure why I figured he'd drive a sports car like a Ferrari or something. Yeah, this is fancy, but somehow it still seems practical.

I just don't imagine a bachelor caring much about practicality.

"To dinner."

"Do I get to know where?"

"My parents' house," he says nonchalantly as his lips turn up in a boyish grin like he didn't just drop a bomb.

His parents? They don't know me, and I'm supposed to show up to their house for dinner? How the hell did I forget that it was Sunday? He always talks about his Sunday dinners at their house, usually with his sister Celeste, too.

"Breathe, kitten. Why is this a big deal?"

*Because it's your parents. I'm supposed to come face to face with your mom when I've been getting myself off every night to the thought of your cock even though I've never even seen it.*

"It's your parents?"

"And? Ellie, you said we were friends."

"I mean... yeah..."

"So, I'm not seeing a problem. I've brought Rex over before."

"This is different," I murmur.

He's right. If we were just friends, this wouldn't be an issue. At all. But deep down, I know there's a deeper connection between the two of us, which apparently is just going to become more and more apparent quicker than I anticipated.

His grin tells me he knows exactly what I'm thinking. "Is that so? Please explain." He looks like a cat that got the canary, all smug and on top of the world. He's been much more straightforward and forthcoming about his attraction to me; it's me that's been dragging my feet.

It's almost like I know it's not just a physical attraction, even though I'm going to pretend that's all it is. People who enjoy each other's company *and* want to fuck, but that's it.

"Don't be an asshole. We both know why." I glare, biting my cheek to force myself not to smile.

"Fine, fine. But really, I called them earlier and told them I was bringing you. They were both excited about me bringing a *friend* to dinner. Plus, my sister will be there. Celeste is awesome, a little bit of a wild card, but she's the best."

"Ugh. I'm not talking to you right now," I tell him, unable to help the little smirk fighting to take over my face. He's sweet for bringing me tonight after knowing I was in a bad mood, and I love that he didn't want to leave me to be alone with my feelings.

He just smiles as he drives us to his parents, letting the music keep us company.

It's peaceful, and that's not something I ever feel when Addy isn't with me.

---

## Blindside Love

This has to be the most normal family in the history of the world. They are so kind, so loving, and down to earth that I almost feel like I'm in an alternate universe.

It's easy to realize how Trevor became the man he is today. His father is so welcoming and funny as hell. They are like two peas in a pod laughing, usually at his sister's expense.

What surprised me even more than the family dynamic was watching Mr. and Mrs. Adams interact. They are obviously still so in love that I couldn't look at them without smiling. At one point, while she was cooking dinner and we were all in the living room, I peaked in to see him spin her away from the stove and slow dance with her.

That's the kind of love I want, the eternal kind. You can tell they are best friends and lovers and that just seeing the other person makes them smile bigger and their eyes brighter.

Trevor notices it too. I caught him watching them with a smile more times than I could count.

"So how do you know Trevor?" Celeste asks as we sit at the kitchen bar after finishing up dinner, a bottle of wine opened between the three of us girls.

"They're neighbors," Mrs. Adams says, a little twinkle in her eye as she watches us.

"Yeah, I moved in about a month ago. I'm right next door."

"In the apartment that's been vacant forever?" Celeste asks.

"Yeah, it's my dad's place in the city, well, one of

them. They never use it, and when we needed a place to live, he offered it to me."

"We?" she questions.

"My daughter, Addy and I. I'm kind of in the middle of a divorce with her father. He's—"

"Trash and not worth your time," Trevor cuts me off as he and his father walk in the kitchen, a glass of bourbon in hand.

Both Celeste and her mom look at him, eyebrows raised as they look back at me.

I just shrug.

"He's not wrong. I did a very bad job of picking out a father for my little girl. We tried to make it work, but I don't want my daughter to grow up in a loveless house, at least from him. He wasn't a good husband, and he's not a good father, so leaving was the best choice I could make. At least this way, she knows happiness and love in one of her homes."

I look around and see the four of them watching me, and I realize I just word vomited my life problems, at least part of them, on this family at their lovely dinner.

I'm about to apologize, but his mom beats me to the punch.

"Well, he sounds like a grade-A asshole, and I'm glad you kicked his ass to the curb. You seem like a good girl with a good head on your shoulders, even if you are choosing to be *friends* with my son."

Then, Mrs. Adams winks at me like she sees right through my mind to my secret thoughts about this evening, wondering what it would be like to be a part of a family like this.

*Blindside Love*

If they welcomed me to dinner as his friend, how would they treat me if we were more? I expect his mom to be disappointed finding out about Addy and the fact that I'm in the middle of a divorce. I guess I can't even say I'm in the middle of a divorce. I've filed, but the lawyer I filed with no longer wants to represent me once Tom threatened to destroy his career. Now, it seems like no one is interested in taking my case.

"Calling him a grade-A asshole still feels too nice for him," I say truthfully, earning a laugh from everyone.

"Well, Trev can be an asshole, but he's still okay to be around," Celeste says, earning a shoulder to her side from her brother, who's leaned against the table next to her.

"Oh, fuck off," Trevor adds, earning a glare from his mom. "My bad."

I want to laugh at his almost immediate apology from a single look from his mom, but it's cute that you can tell he's a mama's boy from just a night of seeing them together.

"What? It's not a lie. But you're usually only an asshole to people who deserve it."

"Like you," Trevor says, putting his arm around Celeste.

"You two are ridiculous," Bernard says before turning his attention to me. "Is that why she's not here tonight? Is she with her dad?"

"Yeah. He's fighting me for custody. I requested primary custody because he will be the first to tell you that he doesn't care about being a father. He spends time with Addy for photo ops and public appearances, but besides that, she's either with his parents or a nanny."

"So why is he fighting you for custody if he doesn't want her?"

"Because it's his way of trying to control me," I tell him truthfully, not interested in feeding into the belief that I did anything wrong by leaving. "He wants to control the narrative of our divorce. I left because he sucks and cheated on me with his assistant, who used to be one of my best friends. He wants me to say it was me who cheated because he wants to look good so he can make partner at his firm."

"He's a lawyer?"

"Yeah."

"You good if I make a few phone calls? I know quite a few lawyers, and I might be able to put some feelers out."

"Oh, I don't want to be any trouble. Thank you, though."

"It's no trouble at all. It sounds like he needs someone to stick it to him."

"I'll gladly do it," Trevor says, which makes me smile.

"Thank you, Mr. Adams."

"Call me Bernard, dear. Any friend of Trevor's is a friend of ours."

# Chapter 14

## *Trevor*

I didn't think this through when I invited Ellie over for dinner.

When I told her that she needed to make the next move, I meant it. But goddamn, having her in my space with my family has changed my brain chemistry.

I've never brought a girl to dinner at my parents, and they were shooting me all night when they knew she wasn't looking.

My mom pulled me to the side at one point and said if I had any brains up in my head, I would try to get the girl. She's not wrong, but it feels much more complex and challenging than they know. But at the same time, it feels so easy, so right. I watched her all night as she laughed and joked around with my sister and mom as they consumed more wine than their tiny selves should, and it's like something snapped into place, and I knew I wanted her in my life.

It feels far too soon to be having such big thoughts,

but I know the first thing I need to do is convince Ellie to give me a chance. To do that, I need to show her that I'm here to stay.

As we head up to our floor, I catch her sneaking little glances my way before she immediately snaps her eyes back to her feet, her cheeks blushing. But the little smile and the glazed look in her eyes tell me she's a little buzzed and losing her filter, so it's quite obvious she's attracted to me.

"I told you it would be harmless," I tell her as we step out of the elevator and walk to our doors.

"It was not harmless. I am tipsy now with nowhere to go, and I don't want to lose my buzz. It feels warm and happy," she slurs.

Buzzed Ellie is a very cute Ellie. She's happy and smiley and doesn't seem like the sad shell of a mom I saw earlier. Addy is her whole world, and I completely understand that, but that doesn't mean I'm okay with her being broken on her weeks off.

"Want to come have a nightcap and sit on the patio? I'm not tired yet and feel like sitting outside before it starts raining," I say as we stop at my door.

"Yes please. But only if I get to DJ."

"I'll give you a chance, but three strikes, and you're out. I don't want to listen to that pop shit people are listening to nowadays."

"Deal, grandpa. Now take me to your kitchen. I'm losing my buzz, and I'm not ready to meet the hangover that I'm sure will hit me tomorrow."

Ten minutes later, we're sitting on the patio couch, each with a blanket, as it's still cold as hell, but the bourbon is helping keep us warm. I have a patio fire pit that we've turned on to keep warm, but it feels like it's charging the air instead. You could cut the tension between us with a knife, but goddammit, I *need* her to make the move. Hell, I just need her to give me the slightest indication that she wants something to happen between us, and I'll consider her move and take it from there.

"Okay, first song," she says with a smile as she turns on Shania Twain's "That Don't Impress Me Much."

If she was expecting me to hate it, she's sadly mistaken.

As I sing the beginning word for word, Ellie bursts into a fit of giggles.

"What? Weren't expecting me to be a fan of the great Shania? My mom and sister used to crank this on the radio when we would clean the house on the weekends. My dad and I would roll our eyes but secretly loved it. He used to make her stop cleaning just to dance with her, and her eyes would light up as she jokingly scowled at him for making her stop what she was doing."

"That's cute. My parents were never like that. They didn't even show affection around me. I thought it was normal until I went to a friend's house in high school and saw their parents actually touch each other, and it was just something as simple as a hug. If my parents ever slow-danced in front of me, I probably would've passed out from shock. But seeing your parents made me realize that the love they share is the kind I should strive for. I want Addy to be able to witness something real."

"I get it. That's what I always thought about as I

watched them growing up. Hell, even now I think about it. They have something so pure, so real, that it's almost effortless. I'm not saying they've never had their problems or that they've never had to work at anything, but they've always done it together."

"It's sweet," Ellie says as she looks down at the phone she's currently picking a new song on. She starts giggling as she plays some Taylor Swift song, which I know all the words to because I, of course, have a sister.

"You're different than I expected," Ellie says as she watches me intently. She's curled up into her blanket, slightly shivering as she sips her bourbon. I don't respond, waiting for her to elaborate. "I thought you were going to be all high and mighty, the playboy who loved all the attention, but you're just like your parents, so down to earth. If you hadn't told me, I never would've expected you to be an NHL star."

"I don't know whether to be happy or offended," I joke.

"Shut it, I just mean you're humble. I like it," She smiles, still shivering. I take off my blanket and cover her in it.

"Stop it. Now you'll be cold," she whines.

"I'll be fine," I tell her, but she's not wrong, it's cold, but honestly not cold enough that I'm willing to go inside and risk this night ending.

She surprises me, though, and lifts her arm, holding the blanket up and gesturing for me to get under with her. I hesitate, not because I don't want to, but because I don't trust myself to keep my hands to myself if we're that close.

"Hurry up, it's cold," she says, and I slide in next to her, slipping my arm around her shoulder. "There. Now we'll both be warm."

I smile, afraid of what I'll say if I open my mouth. The feeling of her next to me is almost unmanageable. I feel my hands vibrating with the desire to touch her, but I'm trying to distract myself.

"What were you and your dad talking about when you went to his office? It was obvious when you two came out that you were thinking about something. You do this little thing with your eyebrows where you scrunch them together, it's cute," she says as she pokes the spot in between my eyebrows and giggles. She scoots over just enough that our thighs are pressed together.

I can't help but smile, especially when her cheeks turn rosy, and she looks away to her phone quickly where she selects a country playlist and sets her phone back down.

"Not what I went in there to talk to him about, that's for damn sure," I grumble, shaking the ice cube still in my glass. "I wanted to talk to him about the possibility of me retiring, but instead, we only talked about how this season has been going."

"Retirement?" Ellie questions, shocked by my response.

"Yeah, I've been considering it, I just haven't been able to bring it up to my dad yet. Whenever I think it's the perfect time, something gets in the way. It's usually something ridiculous like a phone call or someone showing up unexpectedly, but I just haven't found the right time. When I tried to talk to him about it tonight, he spent fifteen minutes telling me how much he loves watching me play and how he can't wait to see what my contract extension offer will be. It terrifies me because I feel like I'm letting him down if I retire," I say, staring out at the city.

It's dark now, but there are still the bright lights from all the buildings lighting up the sky, enough so that when I look back at Ellie, I can see her solemn face staring at me, her eyes filled with sadness.

"I'm sorry that you're struggling with this. If my opinion matters at all—"

"It does," I tell her matter-of-factly, earning me her usual shy smile.

"Look, your parents love you. A lot. Your dad loves watching you play because he knows you love it. That's how parents are, well, how they're supposed to be. Just talk to him. Having just met them tonight, I can already tell you that they will support you in anything you do—including retirement."

I think about what she's saying. They do love me, that much I know. I just get scared that he and I won't have anything to talk about if I retire. But I know they'll support me regardless of what I choose. We all know retirement is happening eventually; I can't exactly play hockey for the rest of my life.

I sit there thinking, letting the voice of Cody Johnson singing "The Painter" calm my mind. But when I look at Ellie, I feel this connection, this sense of calmness that hasn't been in my life, probably ever. I don't need to be terrified of making big decisions because as long as she's in my life, everything will be okay, even if we are just friends.

Standing up, I look down at Ellie, who looks confused, and offer her my hand. "Dance with me."

She looks between me and my hand, back and forth, like she can't quite decide what to do. Before I'm able to rethink what I'm doing and how crazy it is, she puts her hand in mine and stands up.

I pull her close to me, my hands resting on her hips as I hold her flush with my body. When her hands move from my shoulders up to my neck, I feel fire move through my body. A simple touch, and she's set my body on fire. I can only imagine what would happen between us if we crossed that line and gave in.

I feel her watching me as she rolls her lower lip between her teeth, but I continue moving us to the music, one hand on her lower back. All I can think about is how much I love how her body fits right in with mine, like two parts of a whole.

"You keep surprising me, Mr. Adams," she says as she looks up at me, her blue eyes staring deep into mine as desire has coated the air between us, making it almost difficult to breathe.

"What do you mean?" I ask as I grab her hand and spin her away, pulling her back and lowering her into a dip. Her hands are gripping my shoulder tightly as she licks her lips.

"You have this knack for making a girl feel special. It's like you can read my mind and know exactly what I need at that moment. It's a gift."

"It's only with you," I say, pulling her back up and continuing to sway. "You make me like this."

She pauses momentarily, but in one quick motion, she reaches up on her tippy toes and presses her lips against mine. It's slow at first, almost like she's questioning it, hesitating. But now that she's made the first move, it's go time. I won't let anything go too far, but I can't resist having a little fun with her. She's had enough alcohol to impact her decision-making when it comes to me fucking her. Kissing is fine, but I want her to be level-headed when I fuck her. I don't want her to regret a single thing we do.

I move my hand from her hips to below her ass, lifting her into my arms with ease. Her legs immediately wrap around my body as the kiss quickly turns from tame to feral.

Her mouth opens, and our tongues, teeth, and lips clash as we both fight for control. Holding her up with one arm, I slide my hand up to her neck, gripping her ever so slightly so as not to alarm her but to silently demand her complete attention. When she pulls back from the kiss, her eyes meet mine, her shy, nervous look from earlier now replaced by pure lust.

"Easy, kitten. You're not in control right now," I murmured against her lips, her quick intake of air and the gentle roll of her hips the only indication I need to know she likes to lose her control, at least with me.

My lips press against hers, returning to our kiss, only this time it's more frenzied, more frantic as her hands grip my hair, slide under my shirt, and grip me tightly like she's holding on for dear life.

I pull back, needing a moment to catch my bearings, and remind myself why I can't let this go too far. But fuck, what I wouldn't give to feel her body against mine, reach between us and feel just how wet she is for me.

"What are we doing?" she mumbles, her arms wrapped around my neck as she grinds her hips against me again. I press kisses down her neck, all the way down to her collar bone, where I run my tongue across to her pulse point. "We're supposed to be friends."

"We are friends," I groan, trailing my kisses down her cleavage, right to where her shirt meets her skin. Using my teeth, I pull it down, her breast popping free as my mouth latches on her nipple, rolling it between my teeth as she moans above me.

"This doesn't seem like something friends do," she says through a moan as I repeat the same thing to her other breast, alternating between the two, sucking and biting as she moans, her hands gripping my hair and holding me in place.

"Really? I think I'm being very friendly."

She swats me with her hand. "Trevor, I'm serious. What are we doing?"

"We are two adults who find each other very attractive. We are enjoying ourselves by enjoying each other... just a bit."

"What do you mean, just a bit?" Ellie asks, confused.

"I'm not going to fuck you tonight," I tell her, hating the hurt in her eyes. "But it's not because I don't want to. I want you sober. I want there to be no chance of you regretting a drunken decision when I sink my cock into your tight little cunt for the first time. I want you level headed, going into it completely willing so that when I take you, and I take your control and have you screaming my name, there's no way you could regret it in the morning.

"So, we're friends? But that kiss..." she says, biting her lip.

"For now." I wink, earning me a cute blush. I look down at her, her tits out, chest rosy from my bites and her desire, and goddamn, I want to drop to my knees, reach between her legs and taste her. Unable to help myself, I drop down on the couch, holding her in my arms so she's straddling me as I resume our kiss.

"How wet are you right now, kitten?" I groan, my thumb reaching down to her jeans and flicking the button open. I'm not going to fuck her, but I'm pretty sure I'll perish if I don't taste her tonight. Now. Right this minute.

"So wet," she groans, her body quivering as I slip my hand into her pants.

All thoughts have gone out the window, at least mostly as I move my fingers down to her core, sliding them through her wetness. I feel my cock harden even more, which I wouldn't have assumed possible, as I press one finger into her, coating myself in her juices. Sliding it out, I bring my fingers up to my mouth, her eyes widening as I suck every last drop of her from my fingers.

"Fucking hell, kitten, you're going to be the death of me. You taste so sweet, I could drown in your cunt and never come up for air."

Her eyes flare as she puts her hands on my shoulders, sliding back until she's standing. Before I can even think to say anything, she's dropped down to her knees, between my legs, and her hands immediately move to my belt.

"Ellie, you don't have—" I start.

"I know I don't *have* to. I *want* to. Please, let me do this," she begs, slowly undoing my belt and making quick work of undoing my pants. Watching me intently, she pauses, almost waiting for the signal that she can keep going.

There's not a fucking chance in hell I'm stopping her right now. She watches me, waiting for some sign on whether to proceed. She slides my jeans down and frees my cock.

I'm rock hard, my cock throbbing, as pre-cum slowly beads on the tip of my cock. When her tiny hand grips me, wrapping around my length, I nearly blow. Her fingers can't touch, as she uses both hands to jack me off. She's licking her lips like she wants to taste me, but her eyes are still wide as she watches herself fuck me with her hands.

"What's wrong, kitten?"

"You're... big. Like, really, really big."

I grin, unable to help it. It's hard not to smile when a pretty girl is complimenting your cock like it's a masterpiece.

"I promise you you'll be fine," I tell her, leaning forward to caress her cheek. "We'll take it slow. There's no pressure here. We'll go at your pace. I'll make sure you're ready for me."

"That's not it," she says quietly, her lip curling up in a sly grin. "I'm not afraid."

"Then what is it?"

"I don't care that you're fucking huge. It turns me on. I... I want you to fuck my mouth."

My jaw drops.

And I don't mean that in the metaphorical sense of just being shocked out of your mind. No, I mean that my jaw actually dropped, and I have to stop myself from drooling.

Her cheeks redden, and she looks down, away from my face but directly back to my cock, which is still standing at attention, practically just begging for her to take me in her mouth.

Does she want this? Does she actually know what she's asking me to do? I'm all for a blow job, letting her control the pace, control how deep she takes me, letting her take the reins. It's a whole different ball game when a woman asks you to fuck their face knowing damn well that turns a man into a savage.

"Are you sure?"

She nods, quickly responding with a very eager yes. Her hands are still gripping my cock, much tighter now with her excitement.

I'm nothing if not accommodating, though, so if this is what she wants, this is what she shall receive.

"Move your hands then, kitten. Release me. I want to watch you touch yourself while I use this pretty mouth to make me come."

She immediately lets go, moving her hands and slowly bringing her fingers down to her pussy. Her eyes never leave my cock.

"Good girl," I tell her, sliding one hand into her hair, grabbing a hold just tight enough to force her to look at

## Blindside Love

me. "You have to tell me if it gets to be too much, promise?"

She nods, lowering her mouth down to my cock, licking her lips as she opens wide to take me in. Using my hand in her hair, I guide her the rest of the way, sliding myself in deeper. She starts to gag, but the moment I start to pull back, she shakes her head, one hand holding me still. I give her a moment to adjust to my size, her eyes watering as she struggles to take me. She starts circling her clit, swallowing around me while I'm still in her mouth. She slides me in just a little further, her fingers rubbing fast circles around her clit. I feel the moment she moans around my cock, the vibrations alone nearly doing me in.

Between the feel of her mouth on my cock and watching her touch herself in front of me, I know there's no chance I'm lasting. Any extra stimulation is bound to do me in.

With my hands in her hair, I slowly start to move, sliding in and out of her mouth, thrusting my hips until I finally hit a rhythm we both seem to like.

*Be careful, dude. You don't want to scare the girl off the first time you actually get her to touch you.*

She surprises me, though, when she pulls back against my grip, my cock popping out of her mouth, covered in spit.

"Harder, Trevor. Pull my hair like you own me," Ellie says before sliding me back in her mouth.

One of her hands slides up, gripping my thigh, her nails digging in as her legs slowly start to quiver, her eyes dark with desire, as the beginning of her orgasm consumes her. I'm not far behind her, though, the tingling already beginning at the very base of my spine, threatening to explode like a firework throughout my body.

"God, you're so fucking pretty like this, kitten. Sucking my cock like such a good fucking girl," I tell her, my hand in her hair gripping tighter as I force her eyes to me. "Make yourself come. I want to watch you explode while I come down your throat."

Like the good girl I've learned she is, Ellie's movements turn frantic, her fingers rubbing against her clit as her other hand begins fingering herself as she leans forward, her mouth meeting me thrust for thrust as her body begins to vibrate, her orgasm taking over.

It's her moan that does me in, as she practically screams around my cock, her legs shaking as she rides out her orgasm before falling back on her heels. Pulling out of her mouth, I stand up, looking down at her. She looks so fucking perfect, spent from her orgasm, saliva coating her lips as she watches me stroke myself.

"Open up, kitten," I growl, one hand gripping her jaw as she opens wide. Pumping my cock, I come in her mouth, loving the way she looks, grinning up at me with pride.

"Get up here," I tell her, grabbing her hand as I sit down, pulling her into my lap. Without hesitation, I grip her jaw, pressing my lips to her, her mouth opening as I slide my tongue against hers, loving the taste of her cherry lips mixed with my release.

Our kiss turns passionate quickly, and I have to force myself to pull back before I slide her down on my cock.

Releasing her hair from my grasp, I slide a piece behind her ear before gripping her throat.

"I told you we had this 'friend' thing all figured out," I say, knowing damn well we don't have anything figured out except that I like the way it feels when she makes me come.

# Chapter 15

## *Trevor*

> Hey. Are we still on for dinner tonight?

**ELLIE**
> You better be here. I'm starving.

> Are you sure I can't bring anything?

**ELLIE**
> Just yourself. ;)

---

19... 20... 21... 22...

Dropping down from the pull-up bar, I grab my towel and wipe my forehead before sitting down to stretch on my mat. I'm sweating like nobody's business, but I'm not surprised; I've been practically killing my body today, just trying to exert as much pent-up energy as possible. I'm so antsy, but every time I try and sit down to try and relax, all I can think about is the way Ellie looked on her knees, looking up at me, as she asked me to fuck her mouth.

*Fuck, it's like she stole the words straight from my dreams. The way she took charge and asked for what she wanted.*

See! Even now, after doing three rounds of at least twenty pull-ups, I'm still getting hard just thinking about her. I'm pretty sure I can't even jerk off anymore because at this rate, I'm bound to rub my dick raw.

So instead, I've worked out, gone to hockey practice, then ran five miles afterward to try and exhaust myself so I don't become overwhelmed with thoughts of her.

She's such a contradiction, and I find it's one of the most intriguing things about her. She's happy, easy going but damn, she can be feisty as fuck if she needs to... or if she just wants to be. She's such a cool chick and fun to hang out with, but I love our conversations most.

I'm constantly in awe of how smart she is, and not just about typical everyday things. When we were at the bar after our hockey game a few weeks ago, she and Cade got in a friendly competition about music knowledge. The woman somehow stumped Mr. Music with her knowledge of different artists, albums, their sounds, and a million other things music-related that my unmusical ass couldn't understand.

But after that, she was able to talk to Sawyer about parts of her business before turning to settle a debate between Rex and Harris about who had the best fantasy football team the year before.

Throw in the fact that I fully anticipated a different sexual experience with her because I *definitely* did not

*Blindside Love*

expect her to drop to her knees, beg me to fuck her mouth, and then proceed to tell me to pull her hair harder. Twice because I still wasn't doing it hard enough. That's *never* happened to me—usually, I'm with a girl who wants a gentle slap on her ass, not the girl who wants to gag on my dick as her eyes water as I fuck her relentlessly.

It was so unexpected and completely contradictory to my first impression of her that it's now the only thing I can think about as I do anything today.

Forcing myself to stand, I look down at my watch; it's finally five, which means it's time to shower and get myself ready to go over to her house.

Heading to my bathroom, I turn the shower on to heat up before walking over to the sink; it's not just girls who want to make sure they're at their best when going on a date. Guys like to feel confident too. Tonight might not technically be a date, but after last night, I think it's rather obvious we both are attracted to each other, at the very least.

After brushing my teeth, I trimmed my beard, which was starting to get a little out of hand. It's one thing to have the whole scruff look going, but I was well on my way to full-on lumberjack.

*Now to just make it through a quick shower without thinking about Ellie.*

By 5:45, I'm dressed and ready to go, pacing around my living room, waiting until it's a little closer before going over. I picked up a bouquet of flowers and a bottle of wine I remembered she enjoyed at my parents' house for dinner. Although she told me I didn't need to bring anything, my mama taught me to never go to someone's home for dinner empty-handed.

Besides, the flowers reminded me of her, it's a light pink bundle of a couple of different flowers that I couldn't tell you the name of if I was being held at gunpoint. But they were the color of her hair and immediately made me smile, so I had to buy them.

My phone vibrates, and I immediately look down like it's going to be Ellie asking me to come over early. Nope, just the group chat doing their worst.

**HARRIS**
Did you get the flowers?

**CADE**
He's not an idiot, Harris. Of course, he did.

Yup.

**MILES**
Condoms?

**HARRIS**
Lube?

**MILES**
Handcuffs? Blindfolds?

**HARRIS**
Whips and chains?

I chuckle to myself as I type out a response. I love them for this because they're smart enough to realize that I might just actually like this girl, so I'm nervous as fuck for tonight. They may be annoying as fuck for

*Blindside Love*

giving me a hard time, but it's nice to laugh at their ridiculousness.

> Calm down, Rhianna.

REX
> Yeah, guys. Chill out. Our guy is good at making do with his surroundings. He doesn't need to bring things over and look like a serial killer.

HARRIS
> You say serial killer, I say prepared.

MILES
> Po-ta-to, po-tah-to.

CADE
> Go get em' tiger.

PUTTING MY PHONE BACK IN MY POCKET, I SAY FUCK it, five minutes early is fine by me. Before letting the nerves take over, I grab the flowers and wine and head next door.

When I get to her door, I smile when I hear her typical Taylor Swift playlist playing in the background. Knocking loudly to make sure she can hear, I wait for her to come to the door.

When the door opens, I feel like all the air has left my lungs. She's dressed differently than her usual overalls, but she still seems casual and comfortable, like I know she loves to be. She's got on an old, distressed band tee that I can tell is actually aged, not just one of the new ones they made and tried to pass off as 'vintage.' It's torn up, showcasing her toned stomach. Beneath that, she has a pair of faded, torn-up jeans with no shoes on, her toes painted a surprising shade of black that I can imagine seeing with her ankles at my ears.

"Hey, Trevor," she says with a smile, opening the door far enough to let me in. When I pass her the bouquet, I see pure joy mixed with surprise in her eyes as she closes the door. The moment stops as she leans down, smelling the flowers, her eyes closing as she smiles even wider.

*I love that I'm the one putting that smile on her face.*

"Hey," I say, breaking the moment.

"Thank you for these. They're beautiful," she says, leading the way into the kitchen, where she already has a bunch of ingredients out on the counter. If I were to guess, I'd say we're having Italian, so hopefully, the wine I bought is perfect.

"You're welcome, kitten. I was out running errands this afternoon and saw them. They immediately made me think of you—specifically your hair. I couldn't help but smile and had to buy them."

Her hand instinctively reaches up, grabbing a piece of her hair and twirling it around her finger. When she looks up at me, I can already tell she's overthinking something.

"You like my hair?" she asks, confusing the fuck out of me.

That wasn't what I was expecting at all.

"Yeah? Why wouldn't I?"

*Blindside Love*

"I mean, you don't think it's, I don't know... odd? Unprofessional?" she asks.

I don't think I ever pegged her as being insecure until this moment, and I hate it. The uncertainty deep in her eyes, the way she's trying to distract herself by playing with her hair, refusing to make eye contact with me.

The only thing I can think of is that this has to be Tom's fault.

There's no question in my mind that the motherfucker made her feel this way, and I'll be damned if she gave her all to someone who used his power to break her down and make her feel less than.

I set down the bottle of wine and take the three strides to her. Gently gripping her jaw, I tilt her face up until she's forced to look at me.

"I want you to listen to me, mmkay, kitten? You're gorgeous, absolutely, without a doubt, stunning. Your hair is just one part of who you are. You're an incredible mom, an amazing friend, and a damn good neighbor," I tell her with a wink, earning me a smile as she turns away to hide her blush. "I love it, though. It's part of you, it's badass, and somehow, it fits so well with your wild spirit."

"So, you don't think it should be my natural color? That I'll be taken more seriously if I was a blonde instead of a pixie?"

"What did he say to you?" I ask, her jaw still in my hand, and I feel her swallow nervously, her eyes quickly looking to the side until I growl, "Ellie."

"He never liked it when I strayed from what he deemed 'appropriate,' and he always made it known. Whether it was my clothes, my hair, my damn nail color, he had an opinion about fucking everything," Ellie says. "When I left him, the first thing I did was buy hair dye and had Natalie help me make the change. I also chopped it off because he loved my long hair, and honestly, I hated the fucking idea of him loving anything about me, let alone having control over anything."

"Good for you, kitten," I tell her, my thumb gently caressing her cheek as I continue gripping her jaw, my other hand leans on the counter next to her, holding her in place, trying to fight off the urge to touch her more. "The next time that motherfucker has anything to say about literally anything to do with you, tell him to come talk to me. I don't care what color your hair is, pink, purple, blonde—none of that matters to me. You're fucking amazing regardless."

She blushes, so I know I've embarrassed her, but as she looks up at me, she no longer seems uncomfortable, she seems strong.

Leaning forward, I press a kiss on her forehead before taking a step back.

"Now, wine first or are we starting with cooking first?"

"I think we should save the wine for later, you know, that way, I know you have a clear head after dinner." With a wink, she steps past me, moving over to where she's laid out everything to make our dinner, grabbing an apron and starting to put it on. "I figured we would start with something a little on the easier side. Besides, I don't trust anyone who doesn't like pasta, so if you had a problem with it, I'll have my answer about you."

"Your answer for what?" I ask.

"On whether or not I can keep you around." She grins as she ties her apron. "So tell me, what can you cook?"

"Cereal and anything involving the microwave. Well, as long as it comes with instructions that are actually correct."

She raises an eyebrow with a cute smirk as she shakes her head at me. What? It was one time! I put the ramen in the microwave for the right amount of time. Apparently, I forgot to put water in the bowl, so... rookie mistake.

"Okay, let's start with the basics. We're making spaghetti and meatballs with garlic bread because, well, duh. I'll start getting everything together for the meatballs. Would you grab a pot and put water in it to start boiling for the noodles?"

"Yes, ma'am." I smirk, grabbing the pot she pointed to and fill it with water. I sneak a quick glance in her direction and see that she's grabbing an onion. She's all bossy and in control in the kitchen, and it's sexy as fuck. She's so confident in what she's doing that somehow, I'm getting turned on watching her dice a damn onion. She catches me staring at her and blushes but immediately points to the stove. "Finish what you're doing, mister. Then you can come help me."

"So, bossy... I like it," I tell her as I bring the pot to the stove and turn it on before returning back to where she's compiling a bunch of random things into a bowl. She's put hamburger, onions, breadcrumbs, eggs, and some random cheeses and spices. I'm sure these are going to turn out to be meatballs, but I couldn't tell you what to do next.

"What can I do now?" I ask, hating the feeling of helplessness I get every time I'm in the kitchen. I like to help people out, especially when I'm over at someone's house, but I don't know jack shit about navigating a kitchen and couldn't cook an actual balanced meal from scratch if my life depended on it.

Thankfully, Ellie is patient with me and helps me roll the meatballs, fry them up, and pop them in the oven to finish up. I felt like a baby deer trying to ice skate, completely out of place, while she maneuvered around me so effortlessly.

"You salted the water, right?" she asks as she goes to open the container of spaghetti noodles.

"Salted the water? Why the fuck would I salt the water? It's... water," I tell her, completely fucking confused. You don't need to salt water, do you?

I must look like an idiot because she busts out laughing. "You're so fucking cute, Trev." She smiles. "You salt the water to season the pasta. It also helps make it not so gummy. Or at least that's what my grandpa used to tell me."

"Lesson learned. Salt the water. Now... where's the salt?"

She points at the cabinet above the stove, which she's barely tall enough to reach. "It's up there," she says, reaching up, leaning rather close to the boiling water.

Reaching forward, I grab her hips, pulling her back into me ever so slightly, getting her away from the open flame. But I don't expect her body to immediately melt into mine, a soft sigh falling from her lips. It lasts just a second before I reach past her, one hand still on her hip, and grab the salt.

"Here, kitten," I say, passing her the salt. "I don't like you reaching over the stove like that." I tell her, annoyed that she could have been hurt.

"Well, Addy sometimes likes to try and 'cook,' which usually means mixing up a bunch of spices and making a big ass mess for me to clean up, so I hid them." She shrugs it off, adding the salt into the water and the spaghetti now that it's boiling. "How come you never learned to cook?"

I think for a moment, not quite sure how to explain this. It's not that I didn't want to learn to cook. It was more that my mother loved providing that part of our lives for us; hell, she still does for me half the time. It's sacred to her. I almost felt like if I learned how to do it on my own, she would feel like I didn't need her. It sounds ridiculous, but it's the truth.

"My parents got married really young, my dad was a rookie in the NHL, and my mom was one of his teammate's sisters, and before you ask, yes, it was as dramatic as it sounds, but somehow, now they're the best of friends. My dad moved a couple different teams in his first couple of years in the league and it was hard for my mom to find a steady job with how often they were moving, then she got pregnant with me."

Ellie scoots up on the counter, watching me intently as I explain something so mundane with bright eyes like I'm Santa Claus.

"After she got pregnant, my dad decided that maybe she should be a stay-at-home mom, because that way, they didn't need to pay for childcare, and she was free to go to away games if she wanted without having to request time off of work. It was a win-win for them. My mom took the whole homemaker to the next level, from baking to crafts and everything in between. That includes taking pride in our meals. Once I started playing sports competitively, she did research on what I should be eating and basically tailored the entire family's meals around that. She loved it, so I just never learned. I didn't want to take it from her because it seemed to make her so happy. I know how dumb that sounds," I tell her truthfully.

"It's not dumb at all, honestly. In a weird way, it's really endearing that you wanted to preserve that tradition for your mom. That even though you're a grown-up, you're allowing her to still have a role in taking care of you. You're a very thoughtful man, Mr. Adams," she says, her voice deep and sultry as she says my name, and I nearly snap.

She jumps back to talking about dinner, telling me about the sauce and how it's off to the side heating up but that we'll add the meatballs to it once they're done, but I'm not comprehending anything she's saying as I have this sudden urge to kiss her.

Walking over to where she's now putting garlic bread in the oven and setting a timer, I spin her, pressing my hips against her to hold her in place against the counter.

"Wha—" she starts as I press my lips to hers, gentle at first, giving her time to make up her mind. She's slow at first, but as I press on and start to kiss her harder, my tongue begs for access against her lips. I feel something snap in her as her kiss becomes passionate, almost frantic.

Sliding her hands up around my neck, she pulls me closer. I'm about to say fuck dinner and carry her to the nearest couch, bed, chair; I don't care, just something so I can get her naked and riding my cock.

DING!

The oven timer goes off for the meatballs and bread, forcing us to pull away, both of us panting, nearly out of breath. Looking at her, I expect to see shock, maybe confusion, or that unsure look she gets when she's nervous, but I'm pleasantly surprised when the only thing I see looking back at me is pure, unadulterated lust.

## Chapter 16

### *Ellie*

Trevor Adams is turning out to be even dreamier than I could've ever imagined, and trust me, I've dreamed of his sexy ass more times than I care to admit.

Not only did he jump in and help me every step of the way with dinner tonight, but he even made me sit down while he did all the dishes. Then, when he noticed the boxes by my studio for bookshelves, he built all five for me and refused to let me help.

"So, what are all these bookshelves for?" Trevor asks as he leans the last bookshelf up against the wall in the living room. There must be something in the air tonight, or I'm hormonal because everything this man has done is sending arousal straight to my core. Between everything that transpired last night and the kiss earlier, I can't decide if I want to pounce on him or get naked and let him pounce on me. Either way, I'm tired of fucking around and not fucking him. It's time to see him naked.

But of course, Mr. Gentleman wants to help me with all these things instead.

"Two of them are for art supplies, but the other three are for my books," I tell him, passing him a glass of ice water.

When he reaches for the glass, his fingers graze mine and I feel the heat from his touch flow through my entire body. He must feel it too, because he pulls the glass back quicker than expected, nearly splashing water from it. When our eyes meet, his deep green eyes are blown, filled with lust, and I hope he's having the same thoughts I am.

"You have enough books to fill all these bookshelves?" he rasps out, swallowing some water.

"Honestly, I'll probably still need more. Want to see?" I ask, surprising myself. All of my books are in my studio, where all of my art is laid out or up against the walls, and that's a part of myself that I *don't* share with others. Especially not someone I've known for just over a month.

"I'd love to," Trevor says with a smile, gesturing for me to get up. "Lead the way, kitten. Show me this mini library you're curating. What all do you collect?"

"I mean, I'll read pretty much anything, especially a good thriller every now and then or a mystery, but my go-to is romance." I look up at him with a slight smirk, attempting to feign innocence. Let's be honest, if the book doesn't have the word cock in it at least fifteen times, I don't want it. If he knew the absolute filth I read, I'm sure he'd look at me completely different.

Not that I care. It's not my fault these authors make it

so damn enticing to have four guys all pining over you only to decide in the end that they're willing to share and do the dirty with you at the same time. I mean, a girl can dream, right?

"What are we talking about here? Like *The Notebook*? *A Walk to Remember*?" Trevor asks as we step into my studio and turn the lights on.

"Nothing against Mr. Sparks, but I like my romance to have a much higher percentage of naked time, and it pisses me off when it's just *implied*. I don't want any of that closed-door bullshit; gimme all the details. Give. Me. The. Filth," I confess, earning me a rather pleased yet surprised look from him.

"Oh really? And is that what these books are?" Trevor asks as he walks around to the side of my studio covered in books.

"Yes. Every single one of them," I tell him.

His eyes widen, but he smiles.

"And what is it about these romance books that have you collecting what looks to be hundreds of them?"

I think for a moment, I could give him some bullshit answer or tell him the truth, as slightly depressing as it is. "Um, I guess I read them because I love that there's always a happily ever after. It's a guarantee with the books I read, and given that for the past six years, I've been living in my own personal Happily Never After, I've needed consistency in my life. Plus, these books make me believe that men are actually capable of giving a woman an orgasm, unlike with my ex, where the only orgasms I had were self-inflicted and solo. I guess you could say I've been living vicariously through these women who find a man who can do it all. And by all, I mean the kind of man who can be your best friend one moment, a kick-ass partner the next, and who can still make you scream his name every. Single. Night."

His pleased look morphs into a rather naughty one as he picks up one of my books and flips through the pages. I notice he starts reading somewhere in the middle, his lips immediately curl upwards, and he glances at me. "You're a constant surprise, kitten," Trevor says as he continues reading on, completely engrossed in a paragraph of one of my rather spicy books. "This is what you like?"

I collect these books like trophies, needing to have all my book boyfriends safe on my shelf. I have everything you could think of: Kandi Steiner, T.L. Swan, Elsie Silver, I've got it all. Gimme all the forbidden, naughty vibes. And cowboys. Because, let's be real, cowboys are just hot, especially when written by Elsie. But if I'm being honest, she could publish her grocery list, and I'd pre-order that shit in a heartbeat.

The book Trevor picked up has a hot, shirtless guy on the cover and it happens to be one of my all-smut, no-plot books. With the smile on his face, I'm damn near positive he's reading something good.

I want to be embarrassed, but for some reason, I'm not. I'm actually happy he knows. It's exhausting being ashamed of who I am and the things I like. Life's too short for that shit.

Why should I be ashamed of what I like to read and what I like in the bedroom? It's only a small fraction of who I am, and I'm proud of the woman I've become, every smut-loving, spicy sex-having bit. Tom used to make me feel bad about reading smut and told me it made me a slut. I guess it never occurred to him that he was the actual slut in our relationship.

"You're a naughty, naughty little kitten," he says as he sets the book down, his eyes never leaving mine. The tension between us is so thick I feel like I'm not even breathing. In three quick strides, he's standing in front of me, his body just inches away as he looks down at my mouth before grabbing my hips and spinning me, pressing my back against his chest as he holds me in place, one hand gripping my neck as he nuzzles my ear, grazing it with his teeth.

"Is this what you like? To be manhandled. Tossed around? Moved as I please? Want me to fuck you into oblivion until I'm pulling orgasm after orgasm from your body, and you're falling apart around my cock? "

I can't breathe, and it has nothing to do with his hand gripping my throat. Everything he is saying is exactly what I want, and more, but the last time I told a man that I got slut-shamed and told I was dirty.

But this is Trevor. I'm not sure what it is about him, but I feel like I can trust him. Unable to speak, I nod, feeling his hand grip just a smidge tighter. His nose drops to my neck, pausing for a moment before sucking on the sensitive spot right beneath my ear. I feel my pussy clench. It's like I could come just from his words and his mouth.

"Use your words, kitten. Tell me all the naughty things you dream about doing. I'll give them all to you and then some," he says, his mouth pressing kisses along my neck. "I promise."

"Pinky promise?" I whisper, my breathing shallow against his palm.

"Pinky promise," he says, his eyes filled with curiosity.

I think for a moment, wanting to trust him, but part of me says I can't trust anyone. But not everyone is Trevor, and if I'm being honest, Trevor is probably the only reason I have any faith in the male population; he's just a damn good man. Not only that, though, if last night tells me anything, it's that Sawyer might've been right, and Trevor does also like it a little rough, just like me.

Inhaling deeply, I take a leap of faith.

"I don't like to be in control, well, in the bedroom. I don't like having to make decisions, it stresses me out, even if it's for fun. I overthink and can't enjoy myself," I explain. "I love having a man who's so confident in what they can do to me and knows that he can push my body to the very edge of my limits but never actually cross them."

Trevor doesn't say anything right away; he just watches me as his other hand slides up my side until he reaches the tiny sliver of skin between my shirt and jeans. Sliding his fingers against me ever so gently, he presses them along the very edge of my jeans until effortlessly popping the button.

"You want someone to own you," he growls, his voice sending tremors through my body like it has a direct connection to my pussy. "You want them to control you, use you, give you unimaginable amounts of pleasure while they take their own from you, and use you how they please. I understand, kitten," he says, his nose nuzzling deeper into my neck as he breathes me in. "I can give you that," he says, his fingers sliding down and toying with my zipper, sliding it down just enough to slip his fingers between my legs.

Sliding through my core, he dips one finger deep inside me, coating himself in my wetness before bringing his fingers back to my clit, rubbing slow, firm circles against it.

"What you haven't told me is just how far I can take it. That's what I need to know," he says, and I don't see the typical confident man I'm used to, but instead someone who's on edge. He's waiting for clarification before continuing on.

I know he's into rougher stuff, Sawyer told me. That's why I was more willing to take what I wanted last night. It didn't seem like he was likely to turn me down or, even worse, treat me the way Tom did and shame me by saying good wives don't drop to their knees.

"I... I like pain," I tell him, and his eyes light up like a boy staring at Christmas lights. "I like your hand around my neck. And I liked how your hands gripped my hair last night. I like when a man loses control with me and shows no mercy, whether it be by face fucking me or spanking me, I want it all," I say, pausing before I go into too much detail. I don't want to scare him off until I've at least learned if there's an actual reason behind all the sexual confidence that radiates from him.

"I can give you that, but I need you to let me know if I'm taking things too far. Use the color system. If you say yellow, I'll know we're close to your line. If we find your line, say red, and I'll stop"—he pauses, his face turning serious—"but, Ellie, if you ever refer to another man putting his hands on you while my fingers are inside of you, again, I'll find him and kick his ass."

Without warning, he removes his hands and lifts me into the air, my legs wrapping around his firm body for the second time in twenty-four hours.

*Remind me again how we're just friends?*

"Which one is your bedroom?" he grumbles as he carries me out of my studio.

"Second door on the left," I manage to spit out before his mouth slams against mine.

He walks through my apartment with such confidence, carrying me like I weigh nothing. He's so much bigger than me, so much stronger, and I've never felt safer than I do at this moment with his arms wrapped around me as he holds me.

When he makes it into my bedroom, he walks over to my bed, tossing me down with a smile. Grabbing my ankle, he pulls me to the edge of the bed, and his hands find the edge of my shirt, lifting it over my head before climbing on top of me. It feels like he's everywhere all at once, yet I can't get enough. His hands are touching my body wherever he can, palming my breasts as his lips find mine again, his teeth nibbling on my bottom lip.

I grab the hem of his shirt and lift it up his body, sliding it off before tossing it onto the floor. Grabbing his belt, I undo it faster than ever, the urgency I feel only building with every second that passes. Trevor must feel it too, as he pushes up, bringing us both up to stand. Undoing his jeans, he slides them down, briefs and all, stepping out of them, leaving him completely naked, his cock already hard and more than ready.

*Fuck, I want to taste him again. Feel him in my mouth. Make him lose control.*

Sliding my jeans down, I feel his hands along my back, unhooking my bra before sliding it off as I step out of my pants. The second we're naked, he's on me, kissing me as he falls onto the bed, bringing me down with him so I'm straddling his hips.

His cock slides through my core as I move up and down, grinding myself against his length. Every time I press down on him, his breath hitches, and his eyes close like the sensation is almost too intense.

*I get it. Everything with Trevor is intense.*

Gripping my hips, he slows my movements down, lifting me until I'm moving in the air, sliding up his chest as he places me directly over his face.

"Wha—what are you doing?" I stammer, holding my weight on my hands and pressing down on the bed beneath me. I may be small, but this man sure as hell doesn't need my weight suffocating him.

"I want to taste you. See if you're as sweet as you were last night. Now, stop fighting me and lower yourself. I want you sitting on my face," he says, wearing a shit-eating grin as he pulls my hips down, so close I can feel his breath on my clit, but not close enough that he can touch me.

I push back again. There's no way I can do this. I asked Tom if we could do this once and he told me I was too big to do that. I never asked him again.

"Trevor, I'm so much heavier than you realize. I am

*not* sitting on your face. Let me down," I say, panicked, nervous I'm going to hurt him.

"Ellie, first off, you're not even half of my warmup weight, so don't flatter yourself by thinking you're too heavy for me. I could lift you in my sleep. Second, even if you could smother me, I'd go out in the best way possible with your cunt riding my tongue. Show me a man who wouldn't call that a dream come true, and I'll show you a liar."

I feel my cheeks heat at his confidence and excitement for me to do this. He likes this too, I realize. It's not just for me. My body is tingling with nerves as well as excitement over what he's offering.

*If he wants me to sit on his face, who am I to deny his deepest desires?*

Lowering myself down, I feel his tongue immediately swipe through my core, pausing just a moment when he reaches my clit and does a few lazy circles. His hands grip my hips, guiding them, pulling me down as he grinds me against his face.

The pressure is intense. It's so different from having a man go down on you while lying down. When his lips cover my clit and suck, I see stars.

"Oh, fuck," I moan, an orgasm quickly building as his mouth licks, sucks, and bites my flesh. His fingers dig into my hips before he releases one. The next thing I feel is two fingers circling my entrance, dipping in just slightly before pulling back.

He repeats the movement a couple of times, going in just a tiny bit further each time. It's overwhelming, these feelings, these sensations that are building. I don't even know what to focus on first. In one quick movement, Trevor has his fingers slid all the way inside of me, his mouth latching my clit again, sucking hard as he slides his hand in and out, faster, harder.

"Trevor! Don't stop," I moan, my orgasm teetering on the edge, just a moment away from completely consuming me.

But Trevor reads my body and listens to it so well that I'm convinced my body speaks a language that only he understands because, within moments, I'm exploding, my body shaking as the orgasm completely overtakes me. I see stars, my eyes going black as I shudder, his tongue still circling my clit as he draws out every last drop of my orgasm before pulling his hand from inside me.

Grabbing my hips, he tilts me to the side, laying me back down on the bed. I can't help myself, I lean over and kiss him, tasting myself on his lips. His hard cock is between us, and I'm ready for more. I want him, I want it all.

And when we lock eyes, his gentle look from before is gone, replaced by a dark, sinister one that promises all sorts of naughty, delicious things.

I want them. I want him to own my body, to claim me, and make me his.

Even if it's just for tonight.

## Chapter 17

### *Trevor*

It's official. I'm a goner when it comes to this woman. I've never once in my life believed that people are made for each other, but I'm damn near certain that this girl was created for me and me alone.

She's shy and quiet, yet confident and strong.

She's calm, yet wild. A perfect combination of passion and adventure all rolled into a hot as fuck little submissive package.

One that I'm about two seconds from sinking into. Her hands are holding onto my hips as I grind on top of her, our tongues tangling as we do our best to become one. Breaking the kiss, I lean back, her legs straddling mine as I look at her.

"Ellie, I'm going to ask you this one more time; after that, all bets are off. Are you absolutely positive you want to do this? I don't think I could handle it if you woke up and regretted this in the morning," I tell her, watching her eyes for any hint of apprehension, but there's none.

She wants this, I'm almost positive, but I still need to hear the words from her.

"I promise you, Trevor. I won't regret this. I want this. Tonight. I want you."

That's all I need to hear before I lean over to find my pants. I could waste time trying to figure out what exactly she means by 'tonight,' but she's telling me she wants this enough that now I'm only thinking with my cock.

"What are you doing?" she asks.

"Trying to find a condom," I tell her, not sure where my pants ended up and not quite willing to get off the bed just yet.

"Oh, duh," she responds, chewing on the corner of her thumb.

"Why?" I ask, her pause making me wonder if she's second guessing this.

"We can use them... or we could not. I'll leave that up to you."

I feel like everything around me is spinning. I've been with a puck bunny a time or two who tried to get me to go without a condom, but I always refused. Hearing the offer come out of Ellie's mouth, though? I'm positive there's nothing else that would make me happier than sinking my bare cock into her tight, wet cunt just begging to be filled.

"Are you on birth control?" I ask, one hand gripping my cock, slowly stroking myself as I stare down at her. My eyes peruse her body, from her bubble gum pink hair that's surrounding her like a funky halo, her lips are pink, slight beard rash from my stubble around them, and fuck, it looks sexy.

"Yeah, ever since Addy, I've had an IUD. I... uh, I haven't been with anyone since Tom. I got tested after that since he had a dirty dick."

"What did I say about talking about another man's dick when you're with me?" I growl, leaning forward until my mouth is just above her ear. "Especially when I'm about to ruin you for every man before me. And any man that ever considers trying to own you better than I can."

She shudders beneath me, her eyes darkening as I grip my cock, slowly sliding it through her slit, coating myself in her wetness as I watch her nibble on her lip.

"We get tested in the league, and if I'm being honest, I haven't been with anyone, in any capacity, in quite a while, so I can promise you, I'm about as clean as you can get, practically a born-again virgin," I tell her, the thought of going in raw with her is enough to make me feel like a virgin, ready to blow my load before I've even felt her.

But I need her. I need to be able to feel her pussy clench around me every time I hit her clit just right. I want to feel everything with no barrier. I watch her, waiting for the final confirmation, the final approval that this is what we are doing. She's biting her lips like she's thinking or waiting for me to decide, but it's not my choice to make.

"I trust you. Besides, now that we've talked about this, fucking you bare is a new fantasy of mine."

She smiles, nodding her head again. "I trust you too, Trevor. Now, stop talking and show me just what this body of yours is capable of," she whispers, which quickly becomes a scream as I slide in deep, burying myself to the hilt in one fluid motion.

I drop my head to her forehead, pausing for a moment as her cunt clenches around me, the feeling so intense that I'm afraid if I move, my orgasm is going to explode.

When Ellie's eyes open, it's like she's possessed, driven by feeling instead of her usual cautious outlook. Her lips tilt up in a soft smile before she leans up just enough to press her lips against mine. It's slow at first, cautious almost as she catches her breath.

"Fuck, I'm not sure you're going to have any room to move," Ellie whispers, her voice deep and sultry as her nails dig into my shoulders, and she slowly starts to rotate her hips just enough to move around a little.

"Oh, kitten, you should know by now not to doubt me. I'm going to prove to you just how much your perfect cunt can handle," I tell her, sliding one hand up to grip her throat, tightening just enough that a tiny twinkle in her eyes tells me she loves it. "You're going to take my cock, and you're going to take it so fucking well. Now put your hands on my shoulders and hold on," I groan as her hands grip my shoulders, and I pull back just an inch before sliding all the way back in.

Each time I slide in, I circle my hips, making sure to build up friction against her clit, knowing that will make this more enjoyable for her in the beginning.

It doesn't take long before she's meeting me thrust for thrust, her nails digging into my shoulders as I pulse in and out of her at a quick pace, my grip on her throat tightening as her moans become more frantic.

"Oh my god!" she screams, her body shaking around me as she comes around my cock. I keep thrusting in and out, my thumb now circling her clit as I do everything I can to draw out every last sensation from her orgasm.

"Fuck. That was incredible, Trevor," she groans.

"That was just the beginning, kitten," I growled. "Now, on your hands and knees. I want this sexy little ass up in the air."

I expect a little fight from her, especially by the dickmatized look she's sporting right now, but not even a second later, Ellie has flipped over and put her hands on the headboard, her stomach nearly touching the bed as she lifts her ass up in the air giving me a perfect view.

Fuck, she has the prettiest pink pussy I've ever seen, and I could spend hours—no, days—with my tongue between her legs just getting drunk on her taste. Leaning forward, I grip one hand on each side of her ass, massaging roughly as I lean forward, unable to help myself as I swipe my tongue through her wetness. Her hips rotate just enough that I know she's still sensitive, but goddamn I love her taste.

Pushing back onto my knees, I slide one hand up her spine, moving slowly as I slide up her neck until I grip a handful of her hair. "Ass up, kitten, let's see what you can handle."

Gripping my cock, I position myself at her entrance, and instead of taking it slow like I did last time and giving herself a moment to adjust to my size, I slam in hard, immediately pulling out to do it again and again.

I hear the headboard hitting the wall every time I thrust forward, yet all I can focus on are her muffled screams as her face is buried in a pillow, my hand in her hair as I hold her in place. Shadows are bouncing around the room from the lit-up buildings outside, the city never fully sleeping, but the only thing I can pay attention to is her.

Fuck, it's so frustrating and so fulfilling at the same time that she's both the biggest unknown in my life, yet easily the more dependable, happy part of my life lately.

As I thrust in and out, I feel the tingling begin at the base of my spine, and I know that I need an act of God if I'm going to hold off much longer. Her moans keep getting louder and louder, and I feel her tightening around me, her body gripping my cock as her orgasm builds.

"Trevor, fuck. I think I'm going to come again."

"Touch yourself, kitten. I want you coming around my cock at least once more before I fill this perfect little cunt with my cum," I growl, her body trembling at my words as she moves on hand from the headboard and starts to circle her clit.

"Good girl. You listen so fucking well," I groan, reaching back with my hand and striking it across her ass with a firm slap.

I wait nervously for a negative reaction, but the way her cunt tightens immediately and the scream she lets out leads me to believe she fucking loved it.

"Don't stop, Trevor. Show me what a naughty girl I've been," she whimpers, and I snap.

"Is that what you want, Ellie? For me to tell you that you're being my perfect little whore? That you're taking my cock like a champ, and that your cunt is so needy to be filled? Or that I want to spank your ass until I can trace my handprint, one slap for every day that you've tortured me."

"Tortured you?" she whispers, her voice barely audible.

"Yes, kitten. One smack for every day you teased me with your smiles, your body, your laugh, knowing all I wanted was to feel you, taste you, yet you held strong. It's been torture."

"Do it," she says as she moans when I pull her neck back further, my grip on her hair tightening as I bite down on her neck, knowing damn well I'm leaving a mark.

Releasing her neck, I push back up on my knees, gripping her hips in my hand as I pull her ass back up in the air. Rubbing gently across her ass, I slide my cock in and out at a slow, torturous pace, slamming in roughly at the same time my hand comes down on her ass. Three times in fast succession.

Between my grip on her hair, her fingers circling her clit, and my cock buried deep inside her, the spanking sends her over the edge. Ellie's body starts to tremble, her hands moving frantically as she tries to grip onto anything she can, the moans falling from her lips are practically screams.

Her pussy clenches around me, sending me over the edge as my entire body shatters around my orgasm. I pump deep inside her, knowing I'm bare, knowing I'm filling her with my cum, but for some reason, I can't find it in me to care.

It turns me on knowing I've marked her.

## Lexi James

And I want to do it again.
And again and again.

## Chapter 18

### *Ellie*

When I finally manage to pull myself out of bed the next morning, I sneak off to the bathroom before grabbing both of us a water bottle from the kitchen. It feels like I didn't sleep at all, which is probably accurate, seeing as we were still up when the sun was coming up. My whole body feels like mush, but like the good kind where you're all tingly and happy from an abundance of orgasms.

"What was that room we were in last night? The one with all the books," Trevor asks, leaning his back against my headboard, his water bottle in hand and his chest still shining, his muscles more prominent than before as the shadows bounce off his body.

"That's my studio. It's still a mess because it's the only room I haven't fully set up," I tell him, unsure how detailed of an answer he actually wants. Sometimes, questions are just to fill time, and I'm not always the best at deciphering which one someone is looking for.

"For your paintings? Have you been painting again?" Trevor asks sincerely.

"How do you know I haven't been painting?"

"That night at the bar, Natalie mentioned your art and how you hadn't been doing it as much. I believe her exact words were, "a narcissistic douchebag stole your joy."

"Sounds like her." I shrug. "She's also not wrong. When I was with Tom, he always tore down my art, and made it seem like it was taking me away from my responsibilities. I stopped wanting to paint because everything in my mind was black, and anytime I would go to paint, I just felt sad and hopeless."

"And now?" he asks calmly, his eyes staring intently at me, hanging onto every word.

How we are sitting in my bed, him in a pair of briefs and me in just a t-shirt and nothing else, is blowing my mind.

"I've been wanting to paint more. I feel like in these last couple of weeks, I've been finding that happiness, that joy that was gone, so it's been fun to paint more. Do you... do you want to see it?"

"I would love to, but only if you feel comfortable showing it," he says, and I feel my heart swell three times its size.

I'm not used to having a choice. I'm not used to people caring about what I want. I'm used to people taking. The fact that he's asking me and honestly cares about my answer makes me feel powerful. Like my words and my feelings matter to him.

Which is why I know that last night was the only

time this can ever happen between us. There's too much at stake. I can't afford to lose a friend like him, a friend who understands me, understands my daughter, and seems to value us both. If we were to lose Trevor, it'd probably hurt worse than losing Tom, and we were married.

But Trevor is a friend. An amazing, incredible, thoughtful friend who just so happens to be skilled with his tongue. And cock.

But I can show my friends my art. I show Natalie all the time. Trevor may be different in every way possible, but tonight, I'm pretending that doesn't exist. Standing up, I smile, tilting my head towards the door as I lead the way.

I feel... excited. I figured I'd be nervous, maybe even a little anxious to show someone new my art, but it's Trevor. Trevor makes me feel so confident and safe that I know he's going to be supportive.

When we enter the studio, instead of turning on the usual overhead light, I turn on my painting light. I use it when I want to paint with emotion. It helps when I need to turn off my brain and just feel the art. Feel the paint brushes mixing with the colors and transforming the canvas into something beautiful and unique. It gives off enough light that I'm not completely blind but not enough that I can see every little mistake. It helps me find perfection in the imperfection.

Lately, everything I've been painting has been about creating something beautiful from something painful. It can be seen everywhere, in nature, our planet, and other animals. We all create incredible things from our hardships, which is what I'm trying to do for myself.

I can't take my eyes off Trevor as he walks around the room, his eyes taking in my art that's leaned on nearly every wall in my studio, minus the wall holding all my new shelves. He takes his time at each painting, soaking it all in. Nervousness builds in my tummy as he silently assesses my most prized possessions.

When he turns to me, there's no other way to describe the emotion in his eyes other than pride.

"These are fucking remarkable, Ellie," he says with a smile, walking towards me, one hand outstretched as he grabs my hand in his, his other pointing to a painting, his excitement palpable, but everywhere he's touching me feels like it's on fire. There's still so much tension between the two of us that even the smallest touches seem so powerful, but I'm not surprised at all. Trevor knows his way around my body, playing it better than even I can. After my second orgasm, I didn't think my body could handle anymore, but somehow, he proved me wrong. I still feel like I'm not really hearing his words, like I can't quite believe someone could truly like my art. "You have a real gift. These... they're incredible, Ellie."

He looks between me and the paintings, his smile widening as he locks in on a piece.

It's actually one of my favorites. I painted it the night we first kissed. I'm not sure why, but that whole day was ingrained in my brain, and I had to paint as soon as I got home.

My emotions were all over the place, and I just let them drive the piece. Even though I was confused by my feelings for Trevor and how the kiss would change everything, I was happy.

"This one is unbelievable. I can't stop staring," he says, finally forcing his eyes on me. "Thank you for bringing me in here and letting me see your work. What's that one going to be?"

He nods towards something behind me. Turning around, I see the massive blank canvas I had custom-made, with no idea of what to do with it. When I originally bought it, I had the idea of doing something with Tom. Hoping we could paint something together.

Obviously, that was the dumbest idea ever, and since I haven't come up with anything else to do with it, it's kind of just sitting there in the way.

"Honestly? I don't know. I had plans for it, but that all changed when I moved out. So now I'm just waiting for inspiration."

The way he's looking at me right now could almost be inspiration enough for an entire fucking mural. He's looking at me with admiration like he's proud of me, proud of my art. He's taking the time to ask all the right questions, and it's fucking with my head. I look down his body, no shame in my game as I check him out, remembering the way his body felt on top of me last night, the way his abs felt beneath my fingers as I rode him.

His eyes darken as he watches me like he could see right into my mind, see the things I'm remembering. As he slowly takes a step towards me, his hand grips my hip, pulling the hem of his t-shirt I'm wearing up just enough that I'm pretty sure my ass is now visible. I feel like I'm holding my breath, just waiting for his next move as his eyes stare at my mouth right before he leans in and presses his lips against mine.

One hand grips my hair, tilting my head just enough, giving him better access to my mouth as his tongue tangles with my own. His other hand starts toying with the hem of my shirt, his fingers rubbing tiny circles on the inside of my thigh. I feel my legs clench, the sensation of him touching me setting my body on fire, a fire I'm ready to pour gasoline on.

Lifting my arms up, I wrap them around his neck right as he breaks the kiss, yet his mouth never actually leaves my body as his tongue traces down my neck, finding the sensitive spot behind my ear and sucking just hard enough I feel my knees buckle. Trevor's arms immediately go around my back, holding me close to him to make sure I don't fall.

"Sorry, kitten, it's so fucking hard to keep my hands off you, especially when you're standing there in nothing but my shirt."

"The only thing you should apologize for is that you stopped," I say, my hands pressing against his chest as he pulls me close.

"Last night, you said it couldn't happen again," Trevor says, his eyes dancing with trouble. He knows damn well I want him again, even though we both know I'm not ready for a relationship, at least not right now. Yet, I want him, even though I know I shouldn't.

"Let's just call this an extension of last night. I mean, you haven't left yet, so it still counts, right?" I smile, knowing I don't actually need to convince him based on his hard cock in his briefs and the way his eyes look like he's ready to devour me whole. "I want you to ruin me, Trevor."

Lifting me in his arms, I feel his hard cock brush against my bare pussy as he presses me into him. "Kitten, you're already ruined, but I'm happy to do it if you need further convincing."

He's right. I've been ruined since the first time he touched me, but I'll take that to my grave. I need no more convincing that he completely owns me, at least my body.

*But I'll be damned if I don't take him up on his offer.*

"I mean, you were okay."

I barely get the words out before he smacks my ass. Hard.

"You're in for it now, kitten. The claws are coming out."

*Fuck, yeah.*

---

I LOVE A QUIET EVENING WITH A CUP OF TEA, EVEN IF I should probably be asleep right now. It was a long night and an even longer day. It was after five when we finally called it a night, but I'm used to being up early with Addy, so my body woke me up at eight. I tried to fall back asleep for a while, tossed and turned as I snuggled into Trevor, knowing I should stay away, but I didn't want to.

Now I'm standing in front of a blank canvas in my studio, wrapped in a blanket, while Trevor naps in my bed. The urge to paint is overwhelming, yet I can't bring myself to start. I'm not sure where to start or what exactly I'm creating. I mean, I have ideas and different thoughts about what I want to create, but nothing is just right in my mind.

Instead, I've spent my morning organizing my studio, the blank 8x8 canvas lying on the ground finally dry from prepping. It's finally ready to paint on, I'm just trying to finish this up before I take up the entire studio with that canvas.

Maybe I should go crawl back into bed with Trevor, still naked from our shower. Definitely not how I expected my night ending but you'll hear no complaints from me, there's always the hope that after another round with Trevor, I might find the inspiration I've been missing.

I'll take a naked hockey player in my bed every night.

Especially when they have a heart like his.

"Hello, kitten."

Goosebumps prickle my skin at the sound of his husky morning voice, all deep and scratchy. When I turn to look at him to see him leaning up against the doorframe wearing only a pair of black briefs, his cheeky grin on full display as he watches me, assessing me as I stand here with a tiny throw blanket covering me, my ass almost sticking out. I want to feel exposed, the urge to tighten the blanket around me to make sure I'm covered is strong.

Dropping my hand, I pull the blanket down just enough that I don't feel like he can see everything just all willy-nilly. His eyes flare with my movement, but he doesn't say anything.

"What're you doing?" he asks, pushing off the wall and walking towards me.

"Couldn't sleep, felt like painting but then I couldn't

decide what I wanted to paint, so I organized and then set up a bunch of colors, but couldn't decide which ones so I opened them all to keep my options open."

He smirks, looking at the mess I've made of the room, but I couldn't tell you what he was looking at. The only thing I could do was watch him make his way to me, my fists clenching the blanket like I'm holding on for dear life.

It's not that I'm embarrassed of him seeing my body, after the things we did last night I'm not sure there's anything I'd be embarrassed about with this man. It's that I don't trust myself naked around him, especially with the way he's watching me, it's making me want to throw caution to the wind and go for another round.

"I can see that, it looks good in here," Trevor says with a smile before looking at me and the canvas in front of me. "What were you thinking of painting?"

"I hadn't quite gotten that far, I have an idea, but nothing concrete yet."

"May I watch? I mean unless that's not something you're comfortable with. I understand how personal this is, I don't want you to think I'm trying to interfere or invade your privacy."

I think about his question, the word no on the tip of my tongue, but I don't know why and that has me biting my tongue. I mean, I could agree with him, tell him it's too personal. But it doesn't feel too personal with him in the room.

I just smile and nod, turning back to my canvas and grabbing my paintbrush. I feel the blanket slip down my shoulder, exposing more of my skin, but I ignore it, trying to be in the moment. I'm not sure what I'm doing, I have absolutely no plan in mind, I just let go and start.

I don't know how much time passes as I feel him staring at me, but I feel myself moving on autopilot, like my body is moving on instinct to create something even though I'm not entirely sure what it is.

But sometimes it's okay to live by feel, to let your emotions drive you. Logical brain be damned, sometimes it's just nice to let go.

I feel his presence before his touch, but I don't flinch as he walks behind me, his finger sliding up my arm gently as he watches me gather paint. I start to adjust the blanket with my other hand, realizing I'm very close to exposing myself, but he stops me.

"Don't, kitten. In fact, drop it."

I freeze. His tone is commanding as he brushes my hair off my shoulder to one side, his nose nuzzling in the crook of my neck as he presses his hips forward against me, his hard cock rubbing against me with no hesitation. I do my best to ignore everything that's happening and just understand his directions.

He wants me to drop my blanket.

My nipples harden at the thought, the promise in his words, knowing damn well he knows what's going to happen if I'm naked.

But what's stopping me?

Without another thought, I let go of the blanket in my hand, the soft fabric sliding down my body as it falls to the floor, leaving me completely bare in front of Trevor, his mouth sucking on my neck as I stand there holding my breath.

"Now, start painting."

My body moves as soon as I process his words, my hand rising, and without another thought, I begin painting. His mouth starts pressing kisses to my neck, slowly moving lower down my shoulder.

"Such a good girl for me," he whispers against my skin, each word vibrating against my skin.

My whole body shivers, but I keep painting.

His hands move over my body, starting at my hips and slowly moving upwards until he's cupping my breasts, his fingers twisting and pinching my nipples with just the right amount of pressure to send arousal straight to my core.

I know if I reached between my legs I'd be soaked.

I slow my movements, my brain more focused on reaching between my legs and finding out for sure just how ready for him I am.

His mouth stops.

"Did I tell you to stop?" he grumbles, and I snap out of my daydream. His hands have stopped their assault on my nipples, falling down to rest on my hips as he waits.

The moment I have more paint and have begun, he's touching me, only this time his hands travel south, slipping between my legs like he belongs there.

I'd be lying if I said I didn't think he belonged there.

He slides his fingers through my center, coating them in my wetness as he brings them back up to my clit. He does small circles, gently at first. I feel my breathing changing, my body slowly getting worked up but I don't want him to stop.

When he slips his two fingers inside me, I can't help

the moan I let out.

"Oh, kitten, you're squeezing my fingers. Just imagine if this was my cock."

My hips press back against him as he whispers in my ear, telling me everything he wants to do to me. As he does I circle my hips, rubbing against his erection that's hard as steel.

That's all it takes. In just a second he's spinning me around, one hand going to the back of my neck and gripping my hair as he yanks me into him, his mouth crashing down on mine.

I'm out of sorts, out of breath, and uncertain about most things in my life right now. But I'm certain that I want this man, that I can trust him.

I walk us backward, crashing into the table behind us, paint and supplies going everywhere yet I can't find it in me to care as his tongue finds mine. His hands grip my ass, lifting me as my legs immediately wrap around his waist, pulling him in, wanting him everywhere.

He goes to turn before setting me down on the table, but it's unsteady from me backing into it and it crashes down, bringing Trevor and I falling down with it. We land on the ground, Trevor's arm cradling my head as he cushions my fall, not letting any of his weight land on me.

*If only he knew just how badly you need his body on yours.*

He lowers himself slowly, bringing his lips to my ear.

"You good, kitten?"

I lift my hips up, nearly sliding in what I can only assume is the wet paint from earlier and although I realize it'll be a bitch to clean up, that's a tomorrow problem. I graze his cock, using one hand to grip his length as I slide him through my wetness earning me a throaty growl.

"Does that tell you my answer?"

"That just tells me you want to get fucked, but I already knew that much. I want to know if you're okay."

Even with me naked beneath him he makes sure I'm okay and that's not something I'm used to. I'm not used to having my well-being be more of a priority than sex.

"I am," I moan, gripping him tighter as I position him right at my entrance, lifting my hips just enough to slide the tip in. He grunts and I just smirk, loving the sight of driving him wild.

But in an instant, he snaps—his eyes darkening as something takes over inside of him. Something rough, edgy, demanding. Something I'm starting to need.

"Good," he says, sliding all the way in one smooth motion. "because you're about to get fucked. Hold on tight."

As I grip his shoulders, he slides all the way out slowly before slamming all the way in, knocking the air from my lungs but I cry out, the feeling of him slamming against my g spot overwhelming. But he doesn't slow down; if anything he goes quicker, faster, harder.

Thrusting into me relentlessly, Trevor goes wild, driving us both towards our release yet someone keeping us both in sync.

"Touch yourself, kitten. I want you to come with me. I want you to milk my cock as I fill you with my cum, marking you as mine."

"I'm no-," I start, but he cuts me off with his hand

over my mouth.

"Right now, with my cock inside of you, you're mine. Mine to touch, mine to kiss, mine to fuck. That is, of course, if you want me to make you come," he adds with a smirk.

A smirk that makes me want to punch him. Makes me want to kick him in the junk, but I settle for annoying him. Reaching my hand between my legs, I just smile. "I've been in charge of my own orgasms for years, I can take over from here."

I barely even get a full circle against my clit before he's grabbed both my wrists and has them against the floor above my head, his hips pinning me in place.

"Not so fast, naughty kitten. If you come, it's because I allow it. "

That's the last thing he says before he picks up again, his cock sliding in and out of my body at a pace I can barely keep up with, each time he thrusts in, he slams into my g spot pushing me further and further towards my release.

My body starts tingling as his other hand presses against my clit lightly.

"Oh fuck," I moan, my wrists twisting as my whole body starts vibrating.

The moment he presses against my clit with firm pressure, I feel it begin. But the moment he whispers in my ear, his voice deep, commanding, leaving no room for argument, I know it's over.

"Come for me, soak my cock like a good little slut."

I do, like the good little slut we both know I am, but only for him.

## Chapter 19

### *Trevor*

Liam has been my agent since I first entered the league. He's easily been the best agent I could ever ask for. Through the years, we've grown to be rather close, he even comes to my parent's Christmas party every year. After being around so long, Liam and my father became good friends, so now he just kind of feels like a helpful uncle who still gives me shit. He's always looked out for me and held my best interests at heart, and I know he fights like hell for me to see me out there on the ice.

Which is why I've been dreading this conversation *almost* as much as the one I still need to have with my father. I've been a bit of a coward about this situation; I can own it. I just hate letting people down, especially when he's been one of my biggest fans from day one.

Walking into the restaurant, I spot him in our usual booth in the back corner. He waves me over with his trademark smile.

We always come to this little Italian spot. It's like a

mom-and-pop type of place, but they make the most authentic Italian food and are always so kind. Antoinette and Matteo always make us feel at home and stop by and talk to us when they get a chance.

"Good to see you, Trevor," Liam says as he stands up, giving me a quick handshake mixed with a side hug.

"It's good to see you too. It's been far too long," I tell him truthfully, even though the reason we haven't seen each other for so long is because I've been avoiding him.

Like I said, coward.

I'll go up against a 6'4", 220lb defenseman on the ice any day of the week, but hard conversations are not my specialty.

"It has. How've you been?" he says, curiosity swirling around in his eyes as Antoinette sneaks by with a glass of bourbon for each of us before heading to the table of people who just sat down. "Besides avoiding my phone calls these last couple of weeks."

He's not mad. I know that for sure. I mean, hell, he's grinning. But I still feel like I've let him down.

"I've been... busy. I don't know. It's been good though, just a lot," I say, aware I've answered his question in the vaguest way possible, but I'm still not sure what to say as he stares at me like he knows I'm not finished.

Do I tell him that hockey has become harder and harder to bounce back from after long road trips? That when we have a couple of games in a row, I feel like I'm instantly ninety years old, living on ibuprofen.

Or do I tell him about Ellie and Addy?

The two girls came into my life in the most unexpected way, but in such a short amount of time, they've become so important to me. The two of them remind me of the joy I used to get from playing hockey.

"Spit it out, son. You're thinking far too hard for a conversation with me. I can practically hear your brain misfiring. Knock it off," Liam says, grabbing his glass and spinning it. "Now, you talk to me like you know you always can, or I can tell you exactly what you're thinking and ruin all the fun."

I look up and watch as Liam just smirks, knowing damn well he's confusing the fuck out of me. I swallow a large amount of bourbon, then take a deep breath to try and calm my nerves before locking eyes with Liam.

"I... I think I'm done playing hockey," I tell him, doing my best to keep my voice strong even though it's still hard for me to say the words out loud.

I expect him to question me, maybe even get a little defensive, and tell me that he thought I had more life left in me on the ice. But Liam Anderson always surprises me, and usually in the best way.

"I know, son. Your heart has been done a lot longer than your mind has. I've just been waiting for you to catch up. Had you started to play shitty, I would've had the talk with you already, but instead, you channeled everything into the way you've been playing and are out there looking like a guy ten years younger than you."

"You've... known?" I ask incredulously, unable to fully wrap my head around his admission.

I haven't really told anyone that I've been thinking about retiring, so how does he know? I mean, Rex knows, and I'm sure the rest of the guys have started to figure it out. Then Ellie and my mom, but she wouldn't tell Liam, no, she'd make me do it just like she is with my father. Okay, yeah, I guess I have told a couple of people, but none of them explain how Liam already had it figured out.

"Trevor, I've known you for thirteen years. I've watched you turn into the incredible man you are today—both on and off the ice. That also means I've got you pretty damn well figured out. I can tell when you're loving life, happy all the time, versus now when it seems like you're going through the motions, just going through life in cruise control."

"Why the hell didn't you say something sooner?" I grumble, annoyed with myself for how long I've been worrying over this for no good reason.

"It wasn't my place to influence your decisions. If you decided to be done, it needed to come from you. All I'm here for is to support you and help you achieve your dreams. I think we've done pretty damn good so far."

"Yeah, well it would've stopped me from stressing out."

"Trevor, you're a smart man, but you sure can be dumb sometimes," Liam says, causing me to nearly spit out the bourbon I just drank. "Don't look at me all puffy-chested, it's true. You know damn well it doesn't matter to me whether you play or not. Sure, it'll suck to lose a client like you, but you're more than that. You're like family, so regardless of if you're on the ice, you're stuck with me. Honestly, I'm more baffled by the fact that you were nervous to talk to me about this in the first place."

"You sound like my mom," I say.

"Good, so you've told them. I was worried I was going

to have to keep it from your father when I saw him next. We were planning to meet up when they got home, grab some brunch and hopefully, play some golf if the weather permits. Those eighteen holes only go quickly if we pass the time with our usual gossip."

"Well, about that. I haven't told my dad, just my mom knows. I guess I've been avoiding telling him as well."

"Trevor, don't be ridiculous. Your father lives and breathes to support you. It doesn't matter what you're doing, he'll support you. Sure, he loves that you play hockey since he did too, but that's just a small part of you. That man doesn't care if you want to be the next social media star, a plumber, or become a doctor. He'll cheer you on, but you have to talk to him."

I stare at him, knowing damn well he's right. After Liam's reaction—or lack thereof, it makes me realize that I somehow have gotten it into my head that I would be letting them down, upsetting them by wanting to do something different, even if I still don't know what that looks like yet.

"Fuck."

"Yeah, son. You've been looking at this all wrong, stressing yourself out for nothing. Didn't your momma teach you that communication is the heart of all relationships, whether that's family, business, or even a new romantic relationship. *Communicate*."

Dropping my face in my hands, I run my fingers through my hair, pulling just a bit. I feel dumb.

"I guess I am a little dumb." I shrug.

"We all are every now and then; it's a part of life. Don't wait too long, though, son. You don't want your father hearing it from someone else. He'd hate to be blindsided like that."

Blindsided. That's the best way to describe how I've been feeling these last few months. Blindsided by hockey, blindsided with life, and sure as hell blindsided by Ellie.

"My parents are on a cruise right now. My mom has been wanting a vacation; this was the only time he could take two weeks in a row off. They'll be back soon, though. I promise I'll talk to him."

"Good. Now tell me about this girl your dad's told me so much about, and don't sugarcoat anything; I want the truth. But do it quickly, you've got an early flight in the morning to Seattle, and I'll be damned if I go home to Cindy late; she'll have my ass if I miss dessert."

---

Away games have sucked all year, but even more now when all I can think about is Ellie. Fuck, I was up half the night with my cock in my hand, images of her on a nonstop loop in my mind. It took everything I had in me not to pick up my phone and call her because dammit, I don't want to freak her out.

When I left her house the other day, we left as friends. We weren't going to let anything get weird between us just because we fucked. Even if we both liked it. The worst part was that we both agreed it shouldn't happen again, even if it was fantastic for everyone involved.

I spent all night thinking about her tight little cunt, the way it stretched around my cock, fitting like a glove.

Everything was so intense between us that night. We spent all night learning each other's bodies until the sun came up.

I lost count of how many times she screamed my name because I was too lost in her orbit, too overwhelmed by everything about her that I was just leading by feel, and goddamn, it felt incredible.

But now, it's our second intermission, and we are down two goals against Seattle. They're a new team, but they've come out dominating once they fixed some of the kinks. Tonight, they've done a damn good job of keeping the puck away from me; I've only been able to make two shots the entire night.

Coach let us have it and told us that we need to figure our shit out, especially since most of us have been playing together for at least five years.

"We've gotta get Trev the puck more than just twice this next go," Miles says as we all sit, catching our breath for a minute before we head back out on the ice for the third period.

"I haven't been much help tonight," I add honestly, hating that I'm not having a great night out there.

"It's not on you man; we haven't been able to get you the puck. Those fuckers are doing a damn good job of making sure you're always double covered," Harris grumbles, the rest of them grunting in agreement.

These guys have my back, even when I feel like I don't deserve it. After my talk with Liam the other day, I've been trying to think of how to tell everyone that I'm going to retire. I know I need to let my team know soon, but first, I've gotta tell my dad and the rest of my boys.

My boys deserve to know before everyone else. We've been through some shit together, both on and off the ice; they need to hear it from me. I know damn well they'll support me in that, just like they are now. But now is not the time for that conversation, now is the time to win a fucking hockey game.

"Well, let's make it fucking happen. I'm ready to break some ankles and score some goals," I growl, suddenly ready to fuck some shit up.

Besides, when I left, Ellie said that she and Natalie were going to watch the game tonight, so it'd be nice to score at least once with her watching.

Right as I stand up, Coach comes back out letting us know it's time.

We're all zoned in as we head out towards the ice. It's now or never against this new team, and I'd hate to have the first time we go against them to be a loss.

When the puck drops, Miles is on it first, passing it over to Tyler, one of our defensemen who immediately works to get the puck down on the other side of the ice, away from our goal. Luckily, I'm the closest down towards the goal this time, so I'm first to the puck, already making my way past center ice.

Seattle got a little overconfident that they were going to win the drop, so they let their coverage on me lapse just long enough.

As I skate towards the goal, their goalie, Collins, is ready. I fake a shot to the right, and right as he goes to make the save, I shoot left, making it just above his right shoulder, just barely sliding in.

"Fuck, yeah!" I shout as the rest of the team comes to

celebrate. Right as I skate past the camera, not knowing if we're live or not, I stare directly into the camera and wink.

Hopefully, Ellie's watching and realizes that goal was for her.

One down, two more to win. Let's fucking go.

Our second line is now on the ice and it's killing me to sit back and watch, but they're doing work. After two shots on our goal, our defensemen, Davis, steals the puck and passes it to Eriksson who sends the puck directly into the goal, just barely out of reach of their goalie.

*Fuck yes.*

But now that it's fucking tied, it's time to win.

The rest of the game is rough, a fight to keep the puck away from our side, taking every single shot we can. Cade and their goalie are both kicking ass tonight, holding strong this period, letting nothing slip by them. It isn't until there's just over a minute left in the game that we finally get a solid chance. They were taking a shot on our goal, everyone at that end of the ice while I waited around center ice, just hoping for a chance at the puck. Right as Lee is about to shoot the puck, Harris steals it, passing it quickly to Miles who's already on the move towards center ice, far in front of the Seattle players.

I follow along on the outside as Miles shoots, barely missing as he hits the edge of the goal, bouncing off in my direction. In a split second, I get the rebound, fake a shot, but pass it right to Miles, who hits it with a quick slap shot, scoring the game-winning goal right between the five-hole.

After a quick celebration, we get back to playing and

hold them off for the last forty seconds, securing another win and hopefully a playoff spot as long as Dallas loses tomorrow. Now that it's towards the end of the season, we're all fighting for a playoff spot, and tonight has us up one game, holding on tight to first place.

It feels fucking incredible knowing we have a shot at a playoff run, especially knowing that this is my last season before I hang my skates up.

# Chapter 20

## *Ellie*

> Great game tonight. You guys had me nervous for a bit.

**TREVOR**
You guys watched? :)

> I pinky promised you we would.

**TREVOR**
Good to know those are important to you.

> The most important.

**TREVOR**
Noted. ;)

I look down at my phone and can't help but smile. I haven't talked to Trevor since the morning he left. We left everything on good terms, but it's still awkward the first time you talk to someone you just had the best sex of your life with, especially when you both decided it'd be for the best that it doesn't happen again.

At the time, it felt like the right decision. Between everything with Addy and Tom, I can't afford to be distracted. Just because we are extremely compatible naked doesn't mean we need to be anything more than that. It sure as hell doesn't make it any easier to bring my heart into the mix.

But now that it's been a couple days since that night, I'm finding that I don't like the decision one bit. My trusty pink vibrator hasn't even been able to do the job quite as well as Trevor, and now I'm struggling to stay away from him. Part of me wants to text him about his game tonight, tell him he kicked ass. The other part of me wants to tell him to hurry his ass back to New York so he can come fuck me again.

But that's not the type of friends we're supposed to be. That was just one night.

A night of weakness, a night of following my vagina instead of my heart, and hot damn, it paid off.

To keep myself from texting him, I'm in my studio painting at midnight. As much as I should be sleeping, it's been a long time since I've wanted to paint like this, and even longer since I really took the time to do it. It probably helps that right before we watched the game, I got a text from the law firm I've been in contact with about helping me figure out this divorce and custody situation. We were going to meet tomorrow to start the process, but they texted today saying that they weren't willing to go up against Tom, that it would be professional suicide, so they canceled our meeting and would no longer be representing me.

I hate the impact he's still having on my life. All I want is a fresh start, a clean slate, so I can create my own happiness, happiness that stems from things I love.

The longer I've been away from Tom and the toxic house we lived in, the more I've felt myself come to life again. I've been laughing more and doing more of the things I enjoy, including following my dreams of becoming an artist, even if right now that just means starting to paint again, no matter how bad they might turn out.

I can't remember the moment it happened, but color started to come back into my mind, and I just got this overwhelming urge to create, put what was inside my mind onto a canvas. It feels fresh and exciting. Everything I've been creating has been bright and full of life, excitement, and so many possibilities.

I feel like I'm finally able to spread my wings and be me.

I had to grow up quickly when I got pregnant with Addy and then married by the age of twenty-one. I don't regret it for a second, but it's nice to be able to really figure out who I am now.

I'm not oblivious to the impact that Trevor has had on my outlook on life, including my art. That being said, I'm not quite ready to admit out loud that Trevor has been changing my life for the better because that means I'm opening myself up to getting hurt again.

Even if he seems different.

I'm heading into Brooklyn today to go bring Betty some supplies for the studio that accidentally got sent to my apartment. She was showing me how to order things a couple weeks ago, and apparently, I forgot to change the address.

Her art studio is my happy place, and now with Addy gone every other week, I've been able to pick up more days here, even if it's just coming in to hang out with Betty on my days off. She has this cute little spot in the heart of Brooklyn where she holds the best art shows every month. Betty does a great job of showcasing well-established artists with huge followings and new artists that Betty thinks deserve a shot.

She's been trying to get me to show her my work for years, but I can never bring myself to do it. What if I show it to her and she doesn't like it? Even worse, what if she tells me she does, lets me do an art show, only for it to really be trash, and now I look like a fool.

"Look what the cat dragged in on her day off... again," Betty huffs as she comes over and wraps me up in a big hug. She must know I need it because she squeezes tight. "Did you send another order to your place as an excuse to come see my smiling face again?"

She winks like she's joking, but we both know there's sure as hell some truth in her statement. It was even worse when I was living with Tom. Addy and I used to find every excuse to come visit Betty. When she was in school, I would often come down to volunteer and help Betty out, even if I wasn't on the schedule, because I was happier here around art than I ever was at home.

"This one actually was an accident. I forgot I was doing the order on my computer, so everything auto-populated." I shrug, passing over the new paint brushes she ordered. "Anything I can do to help while I'm here?"

"Unless you're offering to show me your art, the answer is no," Betty says with a shrug as she starts to put away the brushes I brought her. "That opening is still available, but I can't promise it will be for long. It's yours if you want it."

"What if I promise to think about it?"

"That's good enough for now."

Betty and I spent the next two hours reorganizing the art supplies in one of the side rooms, making sure it's ready for a seminar she's hosting this weekend. Think sip and paint but with teenagers and soda.

It's been a nice way to pass the day until I have to meet up with Natalie; she should be here any minute to head out for dinner. We haven't had a chance to catch up since everything happened between me and Trevor, and I've been dying to tell her about the details in person. Our schedules didn't line up all week, so we're making tonight work before I get Addy back on Sunday.

---

NATALIE IS LATER THAN SHE THOUGHT WE WOULD be, but we are still able to make happy hour for tacos and margaritas. Tacos make even the best days even better and the worst days tolerable.

Well... that and the queso dip we're sharing.

"Can you believe your birthday is tomorrow?" she asks, smiling excitedly. We both love birthdays and even if we don't get to hang out on my birthday, we decided we're going out dancing soon, and that's celebration enough.

"I can't. It's weird. Twenty-seven used to seem so old, but lately, it's not nearly as scary as it used to be." I shrug.

"Figure out any plans?"

"Painting. I told Betty I might stop by, but it all depends on how I feel. Besides, the real celebration will be when I get Addy back, and we do our usual pancakes for dinner that she demands for birthday dinners every year."

"Have you heard from your parents?" she asks quietly. She's been around my entire life, so she's well versed in the drama surrounding my parents and our relationship.

"I couldn't tell you. I put both of them on Do Not Disturb, so I haven't seen if they've messaged me in quite some time."

I've been curious, almost tempted to look, but I've just been too nervous.

"Let's look. You know I'm curious as hell," Natalie whines, holding her hand out, waiting for my phone.

I give it to her, and she finds their messages, her eyes widening.

"Your mom is a grade-A asshole," Natalie announces, closing my phone. "I honestly can't believe she believes that you cheated and then left. She said that you should crawl back to him. Get a grip, lady."

## Blindside Love

It hurts knowing she believes that, but I learned a long time ago that my mother and I don't see eye to eye on most things in life. What hurts worse is that I know my father is too weak to stand up for me, even if he probably wants to.

"So, about that dancing, let's go the next time Addy is at Tom's. I want a night out. Drinks on me."

"Yes!" I fist pump, excited to get out and dance again. Tom hated dancing and hated the idea of people seeing me dance 'like a tramp,' so he basically forbade me from going out.

So now I want to go out in the skimpiest clothes possible and dance until my feet hurt. I *want* to feel a man's eyes on me, although I'd prefer them to be a particular shade of emerald.

"Okay, now that I've got you liquored up and fed... spill—I want all the tea," Natalie says, licking the salt from her margarita before taking a long drink. "And I want it *hot*," she purrs.

"We made dinner. It was delicious. Then he built me bookshelves. The end," I deadpan, doing my best not to laugh because she'll probably stab me with a fork if I don't elaborate.

"I asked you how your dinner went, and you sent me a string of emojis as an explanation. A winky face, an eggplant, a belt, and stars do not equal an explanation."

"I think it makes perfect sense. It explains the evening perfectly. And the next morning." I shrug, reaching out to grab a chip but Natalie slaps my hand away.

"No. No food for you until you talk."

Leaning back against her chair, she folds her arms and does her best death stare, and honestly, I'm nervous for her future children because her looks are brutal.

I wanted to make her wait a little longer and make her sweat a bit because it's fun to watch her get riled up, but I don't want to deal with grumpy Natalie. She hates not knowing things; it's both her red and green flag because she's supportive as hell but also the nosiest person I know.

"Honestly, it was a fun night. We cooked. We kissed. He helped me build bookshelves. When we were moving them into the studio, he might've seen my collection of books, so we talked about them for a bit."

Natalie's eyes are wide with shock, her mouth is opening and closing like she's trying to talk. If she had a reset button, I'd press it. Instead, I just have to wait for her mouth to catch up with her brain.

"First off, you can't just casually throw in that you guys kissed in the middle of your cooking and dinner talk, *then* tell me you let him see your studio? Ellie... you don't let anyone into your studio; you do realize that, right?"

"That's not true," I glower.

"Is too. It took me two years of convincing you to let me in when you first started painting, but he gets to see it in a matter of weeks. Either you've suddenly become way more confident—as you should because you're a fucking queen—*or* you trust this guy more than you realize."

Did I really hide my studio away from everyone? I do remember Tom was pissed when I told him I wanted to be the only one in there. I mean, if he can tell me not to go into his office, why can't I do the same? But I don't remember being that secretive with other people, at least not Natalie.

But I haven't even shown Betty, so maybe she has a point. I'm not exactly the most confident about my work; in fact, I'm usually pretty shy about it. But it felt so easy to bring Trevor into the room and let him into my world for a bit. I'd be lying if I said I didn't like him there.

"Maybe."

That's all I've got. She could be right; she could be wrong.

"Maybe what?" Natalie nags.

"Maybe you're right," I elaborate, just enough to annoy her more.

What? It's my favorite pastime. Her cheeks get all red when she's pissy; and it's adorable and funny.

"Ellie Marie," Natalie growls, bringing out the big guns. Whenever she's really mad at someone, she makes their middle name Marie, regardless of what it actually is; it's her way of scolding. "I swear to god, if you don't spill, I'm going to lose my damn mind."

"Okay, yes. He saw my studio. I actually showed him my art the next morning."

"He slept over?"

"I don't think we slept, but yes, he was over until the morning," I smirk, gladly opening Pandora's box as she squeals with excitement that I finally fucked someone besides Tom.

"Tell. Me. Everything," Natalie says, ordering another round of margaritas to celebrate.

We spent the next hour going over *every single detail*, Natalie squealing anytime I told her something exciting.

She knows how incredible that night was for me because, for the first time, I felt heard. I felt understood, and even though he obliged and pulled my hair and tossed me around, I still felt cherished.

It isn't until I'm home, climbing into my bed, that I realize Natalie was right about something else tonight.

*"You realize you like him, right? Like more than just his cock. I haven't seen you smile like this in ages. I love it."*

At the time, I shrugged her off, telling her that we agreed it was a one-time thing. But when she sent me the picture we took tonight, and I could see myself glowing, my eyes bright with happiness, nothing fake about my smile, I knew she was right.

I am happier, and it's because of *him*.

# Chapter 21

## *Trevor*

I am not a planner—never have been, never will be. It's just not my thing. But the Trevor of last week thought it would be a great idea to plan an entire day for Ellie's birthday, and of course, I wanted to make it a surprise, which only made it that much more stressful since I couldn't get her input.

But I had to do something. It's her birthday, and the only thing I wanted was to make her feel special. Make sure she knows she's important to someone. She made it very clear that Tom never did anything for her birthday, not even at the beginning of their relationship. I mean, unless you count his assistant sending her a card, although he even managed to fuck that up and always sent them on the wrong day. When she told me that last little bit, I wanted to go find him and put my fist through his face.

Growing up, my parents always made a big deal about our birthdays, so they've always been important to me. I love celebrating those I care about. Although even I can admit that today is a little above and beyond what I'd do for Rex. I mean, yeah, we go out for wings and beer to celebrate, but I'm not usually planning full days for him.

I started her day by having twenty-seven long-stemmed, bubblegum pink roses delivered this morning. That's something special just for Ellie. I've *never* been this guy, but for her, it just comes naturally. Secretly, I'm loving it, and it's all because of her and that smile she gets over the littlest things.

She's all I've been able to think about lately, and not just because I like it when she touches my cock. I mean, of course, I like the way she does that, but that's just fucking obvious. It's more than that, though. She's the first thing I think about in the morning and the last thing I think about as I close my eyes... and pretty much every waking moment in between.

I like her. I've been trying to deny it, needing her to come to peace with the fact that there's actually something between us before I made my move, but it's becoming unbearable not touching her.

But that's not what today is about. Today is about Ellie and making her feel like a birthday princess, which is why I'm standing in the lobby, waiting like an idiot for her to come meet me because walking the two steps from my apartment to knock on her door felt way too casual.

Now, I have my car parked in valet waiting for us so I can take her around the city. It seems like a date, and it feels like a date, but I can't call it a date, or I might freak her out. She's not there yet and I respect that.

She's gone through a lot with her ex—she still is, and it's not my job or my right to tell her how long it takes to heal. All I can do is hope that when she's ready to take that step, she's willing to do it with *me*.

Her freshly dyed pink hair is the first thing I notice as she steps out of the elevator. Her bare legs, which are barely covered by a short black dress and matching thigh-high boots, are a *very* close second.

*Holy shit. She looks fucking incredible.*

*Remind me again why I can't touch her. Pick her up and carry her back up to my apartment. All I can imagine are those boots wrapping around my head.*

She pauses as she steps off the elevator, looking around, her whole face lighting up when she finds me waiting. As she makes her way over, her long strides making quick work of the distance, and lord help me, she looks fucking smoking hot, a black leather jacket finishing off her look.

She's a total fucking MILF, and I love it.

"Happy birthday, kitten," I say, opening my arms once she reaches me. She leans into my hug without pause, pressing her cheek against my chest as her arms wrap around me.

"Thank you, Trev," she says, looking up at me with stars in her eyes while we hug in the middle of the lobby, ignoring everyone else around us. It's like we're in our own little world, just the two of us, where nothing else matters except what we are doing. "You know you don't have to do this, right? It's just a birthday."

I press one finger to her lips, shushing her. Her eyes widen in surprise, but she manages to hold in her giggle—barely. "I'm doing this because I want to. Because I believe you deserve to be celebrated, and I feel lucky that

I get to spend it with you. Besides, making you smile is easily one of my favorite pastimes."

"You're only saying that because you want to get into my pants," she murmurs. "Why are you so good to me?"

"Because you deserve it. You moving in next to me has been one of the best things to happen to me in a long time, and before you even say it, *no,* it's not just because you let me get in your pants. I mean—you did score some friendship points for that one." I wink, hoping I'm not crossing whatever invisible boundaries she's set up for us. It's hard to navigate her at times, as she slips between fighting the tension between us and giving in.

Based on the fact that she's still standing close to me, her arms around me as she smiles up at me, I think we're both on the same page tonight. And hopefully, there might be a tad bit more of the giving-in part of our 'friendship' tonight. "Well, it's my goal to be the *best* friend, so I'm glad I'm working on tallying up some points," she says, surprising the hell out of me. "How many points until I win?"

I shake my head, unable to stop the smirk from overtaking my face. "Oh, kitten. What the hell am I going to do with you?"

"I don't know, you planned this, not me," she deadpans, finally stepping back from me. "Lead the way before I start trying to earn some more points."

She winks as she loops her arm in mine; a devilish grin on her face tells me she's in the mood to play.

Game on, kitten.

Game. On.

"So where are you taking me?" she questions as we make our way through Central Park.

The nice thing about where our arena is that it's within walking distance of Central Park, which means it's convenient *and* free parking. I'll definitely miss that when I retire, especially when I'm on a date, and she's wearing at least three-inch heels.

"Just right over here," I tell her, shooting a text to Sawyer to tell her that it's time to disappear.

She was helping me brainstorm ideas for today, and she thought a picnic would be cute. Since she knows cooking isn't my thing, she set it all up, making sure to stay until the very end to make sure everything is perfect.

When we turn the corner to see our cute little picnic set up, Ellie stops, tears filling her eyes.

I may not have set it up, but I definitely designed this to be the most Ellie picnic I could think of. AKA, lots of desserts and only finger foods because that's what her entire food pyramid consists of.

She's basically a toddler when it comes to food. She blames it on Addy, but I know she loves it.

But I forget all about that when she turns to me, an almost sad look in her eyes, her mouth opening and closing like she's trying to think of what to say.

*Have I fucked something up?*

"Did I do something wrong?" I ask slowly, almost nervous for her response, but I'm relieved when she immediately shakes her head no.

"You definitely didn't do anything wrong. Not at all,

Trevor. I'm... overwhelmed because you've done the exact opposite. You've done everything right, and therein lies the problem," she grumbles, and I'm even more fucking confused.

"So the problem is that I did everything right? Isn't that the goal?"

"It's a problem because I'm not supposed to want this. I'm not supposed to want *you*, but then you do things like this, and I start to wonder why the hell I'm fighting this so hard! These were things my husband never did, *not once*, and you do it for me—the girl who keeps telling you she can't handle being more friends. You make me feel so special, and I love it. I just don't understand why. Why me? But I know I like it, I like you. I'm not sure what that means, but goddammit, it makes me so mad at you," Ellie says, her arms crossing, really leaning into that whole toddler thing with this adorable tantrum.

But even though she's pretending to fight it, I can't stop smiling like a fifteen-year-old boy who just got his crush's number, and I don't even care if I look like a fool right now.

She just admitted she likes me, and now I feel like it's *my* birthday.

I pull her into me, pressing a kiss to her forehead. "Nothing changes until you want it to, kitten. Let's just keep being us, whatever that looks like. Let's just relax and enjoy the day."

We sit down and eat the snacks Sawyer made for us. Ellie is teaching me what a charcuterie board is, but the only thing I paid attention to was when she said meat and cheese; everything else was noise as I watched her pretty mouth talk, dreaming of all the ways I could fill it.

But it's not time for that—I still have another surprise. Standing up, I put everything back in the picnic basket for Sawyer to come collect.

I'm going to have to babysit Rory one night soon and let her and Rex have a night out for all the help she's given me. I feel like she's been my little dating coach, teaching me all the things I've slacked on learning over the years.

After we get everything packed up, I grab her hand, turning to walk towards ice cream. It's a nice day, the weather is perfect to spend outside, which is lucky in March.

"So have you been able to talk to your parents yet?" Ellie asks, breaking the silence. Her hand fits perfectly in mine as she intertwined our fingers.

Something about the way she's touching me, the way she's looking at me, makes me feel calm about something that has been so scary. I haven't even wanted to think about having this conversation with my parents, even though it's coming up.

But hearing her ask, knowing she's actually interested in my response, in how I'm doing. It's fucking nice.

"I haven't," I tell her truthfully. "But they come home in just a couple of days, so we're going to meet for dinner. After talking with my agent, I realized I was being ridiculous by being so nervous."

"I've been telling you that, silly," Ellie says, bumping her hip into mine, a little smirk on her face.

She's cute like this, relaxed, comfortable, *happy*. My

mood immediately improves, knowing *I'm* the reason she feels like this.

"I know you did. You're a mom. You know what it feels like to want to support your kid, so I should've listened. I guess hearing it from Liam, who is one of my father's best friends and also very invested in my career, made me realize it was just as ridiculous as you were telling me it was."

"Well, I'm glad he was able to talk some sense into you," she jokes, looking around as we talk. "Ooh! I love photo booths."

She smiles as we walk by a little photo booth—the ones that shoot out little strips of pictures and girlfriends always wanted to do in high school. Truthfully, I've never taken one, but the idea of doing that right now is exciting. Pulling her with me, I slip right into the little booth, pulling her right onto my lap.

In my defense, this booth only has enough room for one of me, so it's pretty much her only option.

"What are we doing first?" I whisper into her ears as I slip my hands around her waist, loving the way she squirms on top of me as I touch her.

"What—what do you mean?" she asks, her breath hitching just a touch as my hands grip her hips, holding her in place right on my cock.

"What picture, kitten? We have six seconds."

She turns to look at me, her eyes dark, cheeks red, as she bites her lower lip and just watches me. Right then, the flash goes, taking the first of our pictures, but she doesn't move right away, she leans in and presses her lips against mine, just enough that they're touching, but not enough to push for more just yet.

*Flash.*

She pulls back, turning her face away just a bit, her shy smile in place, and I can't help but stare at her; she is so damn perfect.

*Flash.*

I pull her back against my chest, her cheek against mine, and we smile at the camera as the final flash goes off.

I can't help but feel like I just went through the wringer of emotions in the 40 seconds that it took. I went from wanting to bend her over inside the photo booth to feeling cared for and then just plain *happy*. Neither of us move as we wait for the photos to print out, her hand rubbing little circles on my arm.

"Well, I guess winging it works too," I whisper, earning a laugh as Ellie stands up to grab the pictures. Stepping out, I see her smiling down at them and realize immediately why. We look amazing.

"It definitely works," she murmurs, still looking down at the pictures.

That happy feeling *I'm* feeling is evident in both of us in that picture. I don't want her to overthink it too much right now because I'm afraid if she tries to take on too much and take things too fast, she'll scare herself, and that's the last thing I want, so I just grab her hand and keep walking on.

We spent the next two hours enjoying Central Park. We rode around on the electric scooters that people always rent until she almost ran into a building. I cut her off and let her ride with me for a while. Birthdays are meant for fun, not hospital visits.

"Do you have anything planned later this evening? I don't want to assume that you want to spend your entire birthday with me. I totally understand if you don't. But, uh, if you did, I have reservations for dinner tonight at six. I—"

"Don't be ridiculous. I would love to. Besides, there's no other *friend* I'd rather spend my birthday with."

It's the twinkle in her eye that feels like a dare to me, or at least that's how my brain takes it because, for a second, I forget all about those invisible boundaries she's created and just say what's on my mind.

"Ellie, if you call me your friend one more time, I promise I'll fuck that word right out of your vocabulary."

"What should I call you then?"

"Trevor, Trev, the guy with the nice cock, Daddy, I don't care, just not friend." I wink, grabbing her hand again as we start walking.

"But I thought we *are* friends. Just friends who fuck?"

"Yeah, that was fine until I started to enjoy you with your clothes on." I smile, earning me a glare. "Now it's not enough. I want more. But I'm patient. I won't rush you."

"Trevor—"

"Nope, we aren't talking about this tonight. Tonight is about *you*. Want to go grab a drink while we wait for dinner? I know a cute bar right around the corner," I tell her as we start walking down the street, weaving our way between the people walking in every direction.

"Sounds perfect," she says, her voice barely a whisper.

As we walk down the street, turning a couple of times to make our way to the hole-in-the-wall bar I love, I see her eyes light up right as she stops dead in her tracks, her hand pulling me back.

"You know the studio I've told you about? With Betty?"

"Yeah?"

"Want to see it? I mean, if you want to. I don't want you to be bored."

I hate that she always gives me an out. She does it for everyone, and I hate it, but I *really* hate how much she does it with me.

"Stop that. Stop thinking that what you want isn't important. I would love to go to the studio. Will Betty be there? I'd love to finally meet this infamous lady," I tell her truthfully.

"Oh boy, don't tell her that. It'll go straight to her head, and she doesn't need that." She laughs, pulling me across the street to a little studio with a bright blue sign.

As soon as we enter, I'm in awe. Inside, it's cheerful and bright and exactly how I imagine Ellie's boss to be.

The immediate change in Ellie's demeanor almost catches me off guard. She's been so happy all day, smiling and laughing as we've hung out together, but right now, she just seems so calm, so content, like this is her happy place. I can't help but think of how far she's come since moving in next to me.

From being unable to paint and losing the inspiration to do it, to creating beautiful art and having a studio become her sanctuary, it's incredible. She reminds me of that painting I saw that she had been working on. It had a beautiful butterfly and completely reminded me of her in this moment, finally finding the confidence to fly.

I don't want to slow her down. I don't want to put a leash on her. I just want to be the one next to her, helping her every step of the way as she finds out just how strong she truly is.

It's even better because she's been helping me be stronger, even unintentionally. I finally feel like I'm strong enough, brave enough, to talk to my parents and just be open about my plans. She won't be there with me at dinner, but I know she'll support me before and after, and that's enough to make me feel like I'm on solid ground again.

"What are you doing here, missy," I hear a strong female voice speak, stopping Ellie in her tracks.

"I'm not here to work! Don't worry!" She laughs. "Trevor, my *friend* and I were just heading to go grab a drink, and we were passing by. Figured I would show him my safe haven."

I watch Betty throughout their interaction, and the first thing I notice is how she watches Ellie. This is someone who's definitely on team Ellie, which means I'm already a fan of her. The second thing I notice is that she looks at me with a mixture of apprehension and approval. Needing to break the silence, I extend my hand, offering it to Betty with a friendly smile.

"It's so nice to finally meet you. Ellie has told me so much about you," I tell her, hoping she sees that I come in peace.

*Blindside Love*

"I have to grab something in the back really quick. Why don't you have a look around, Trevor?" Ellie says with a smile before scurrying off, Betty quickly following.

Girls are all the same, regardless of their age. They love the tea, and they love it hot.

# Chapter 22

## *Ellie*

**TREVOR**

> I'm going to turn your ass so red the next time we're naked. Punish you for saying the word friend.

> Okay, daddy.

---

"Ellie, I may be old, but I can still run. But I'll kick your ass if you make me prove it," Betty says as she follows me into the back.

She's in her sixties, but I sure as hell wouldn't go up against her. She's from the south—Texas, to be exact. There's something about Southern old ladies; they don't play.

"Why would I be running? I just wanted to grab the paintbrushes I had sent here. I want to work on the big canvas I've had sitting off to the side," I start rambling, hoping to throw her off, but based on her dramatic eye roll and deep sigh, she's well aware of what I'm doing and is unamused.

"You think I don't know you by now, girl? That *friend* of yours is mighty handsome. Is this the neighbor you may or may not have had relations with?"

"Can we please not say relations? Something about that coming from you gives me the ick," I grumble jokingly.

"You do know that I'm married, right? For more than forty-five years. With children of my own?"

"Betty, you and your husband are like family to me. I do not want to know what y'all do in the bedroom. But to answer your question and hopefully change the subject, yes, that is Trevor. My neighbor, who I may or may not have feelings for."

"Fine. You're no fun. But I like to see that you're admitting your feelings already. You've wasted enough time on idiots, plus he's way hotter than Tom. And have you seen the way that man looks at you? It's like you hung the moon just for him, and I can only imagine the dirty things he wants to do to you... or maybe already has done."

"Betty!" I shriek, avoiding telling her about just how dirty he can be, but my cheeks blush, giving myself away.

"Hopefully, he spanks the boringness out of you. You used to be so fun." Betty winks before heading back out to where Trevor is.

I should probably be nervous that the two of them are out there conspiring together, but all I can think about is that she's right. Trevor has helped me have more fun lately, and he's *definitely* hotter than Tom. But the way he's looked at me? Have I noticed that? I mean, his eyes are always on me when we're together, and it's usually *very* obvious what he's thinking about. Still, I was hoping I was the only one who could read into his facial expressions like that, but apparently not.

Grabbing the brushes I came for, I shut the cabinet holding all our extra supplies as quietly as possible. When I peek out to the front of the studio, I see Betty showing Trevor one of her favorite pieces, and he's completely enthralled by what she's showing him. It's one of my favorite things about Trevor; it doesn't matter who you are, he gives you his complete attention. He makes everyone he talks to feel special and important, like he has all the time in the world.

For being such a busy man, it's incredible that he's this way.

I'm immediately caught when Trevor looks behind him, smiling when he sees me spying on them.

"Whatcha got there, kitten?" he asks.

I feel my face blush even more at his use of my nickname. Betty immediately smiles brightly, like she loves what she sees.

I've gotta get us out of here before she starts talking about weddings and babies and all that stuff that will immediately scare him off... and probably me too.

"Didn't you say we had a reservation? We should probably start heading that way if we don't want to be late," I say as I walk over to the two of them.

"Yeah, you kids go have fun. Get out there and celebrate this one's birthday. She deserves it," Betty says as she pulls me in for a hug. "Love you, sweetie. Now go enjoy the rest of your evening. Don't do anything I wouldn't do."

"It was nice to meet you, Betty. Thank you for taking the time to show me around your studio. It's incredible. And thank you for the advice." Trevor winks before placing his hand on my lower back as we walk out into the night.

I can feel Betty watch us as we leave, but I'm too lost in the way his hand feels on my lower back, protective, caring, and fuck what I wouldn't do to have that hand in other places on my body.

Specifically, the part between my legs that I made sure was readily available in this dress.

But this touch is different. It feels like it's the start of something new. Somehow, it's both tentative and assertive, and I'm here for it. We've never shied away from little touches here and there; it's kind of just become who we are, even when we've been doing our best to maintain the façade that we're just friends.

As we step out onto the street, I feel the tension between us start bubbling. I taste it in the air and feel like I can't breathe. All I can think about is his hand still on me, cloaking me in his heat.

I don't know how much time passes, but we've walked three blocks, and I can see the bar at the corner of the next street. It's a nice part of town. There are usually lots of people out, but tonight it's quieter, more intimate, only adding to the vibe.

I can hear the music playing from the bars lining the streets, the beat strong, vibrating through the air, the touch on my skin only amping me up even further. It's when his hand goes from my back into my own, gripping tightly, that I finally feel like my body can't handle it anymore. Something needs to give because I can't survive this. I'm only human, and fuck, I want him. No, it's more than that. I need him, crave him, fucking desire him.

And apparently, he feels the same.

The next thing I know, I'm being slammed against the cold brick wall, hard enough that I feel my breath hitch but not hard enough to hurt. Not that I'd care anyways, as his lips slam into mine, taking immediate control of my mouth, one hand gripping my throat as he pins me in place.

His lips dance with my own, his tongue exploring, tasting me, owning me, and I follow along like he's the leader and I'm his perfect, obedient follower.

And with hands gripping my hip, tightening against my throat as his mouth is on mine, I know I'm *exactly* where I want to be.

Pulling back, his eyes are hooded as they stare at me. "I couldn't... I don't know. Fuck, I'm sorry."

"You're sorry?" I say, slightly taken aback. He just kissed me so passionately that I almost imagined we were naked, and he's sorry?

"I told you that I respected us being just friends... I shouldn't have—"

"Shut up and kiss me, Adams," I growl, pulling him back down to me. He snaps, his hand tightening against my throat and his teeth nibbling my ear.

"Say it then."

"Say what?"

"That we aren't friends. At least not *just friends*."

"Trevor, I don't think we've *ever* been *just* friends, but we're about to be if you don't stop talking and kiss me soon."

His lips press against mine as one hand slides between my legs, sliding up the inside, his fingertips rubbing light circles against my inner thigh as his tongue traces down my neck.

Right as his fingers start to slide up, exactly where I want them, a delivery truck pulls down the alley, their headlights illuminating the entire place as they are pointed directly at us.

My gut reaction is to be mortified, but as we stand up and start to walk back to the street, I can't help but start laughing.

Almost getting caught fooling around is exhilarating, and honestly, I loved the rush.

Tom would've never done something like that with me. He was way too much of a prude.

I like that Trevor seems to like the rush just as much as me. I just hope it's *only* with me.

"Did you mean it?" Trevor asks as he turns me to him right outside the restaurant. "What you said about us?"

"As much as I wish I could lie to you and tell you I didn't mean it, I can't. We've always skirted the boundaries. I mean, there are such blurred lines between us already that it shouldn't come as a surprise that we've turned into something even if we haven't wanted to admit it yet."

"So... are we finally going to start admitting it?"

"To each other? Yes. To the world? I think that'll take

a little time. I've still got Addy to think about, and with nothing figured out with Tom yet, I don't need anything impacting her."

Trevor smiles, a big, cheesy grin that lights up his entire face. Wrapping his arms around my back, he pulls me into him, kissing me. It's quick, but definitely not chaste, and when he sets me down, I realize just how turned on he is right now.

But first... we need to eat.

---

"Have you two decided on dinner?" our server asks, her smile kind as she tops off our wine. I can't help my annoyance as I watch her check out Trevor; it's only little glances, but enough that I can tell she likes what she sees.

*Oh, girl, you should see what that body can do, especially naked. He's an actual fucking work of art.*

I want to be jealous. My initial gut reaction is to feel self-conscious that another woman is looking at him, but I don't. When Tom and I first got together, I always questioned the other women around him, but towards the end, I questioned him. He would make me believe it was all in my head, and I was just insecure, but obviously, my gut was right.

But Trevor's given me no reason to be jealous. In fact, he's actually shown me the opposite. Up until tonight, we haven't been anything but friends. He could have looked at whoever he wanted, but he never did. And right now, he hasn't stopped eye-fucking me since we got to the restaurant. I don't think he's even noticed that the waitress is checking him out. His thoughts about me are so loud, so intense that I can practically hear them.

His eyes scream trouble.

The deep emerald of his eyes is dark, no longer their usual bright orbs. They're swirling with the remnants of his fantasies and desires. I should run. Get up from this table and leave, knowing I'm the victim of these fantasies. Instead, I find myself wanting to jump in and dive headfirst, unafraid of drowning or what may be waiting for me. I welcome his destruction with open arms as long as he's the one catching me.

It's hard sitting in this restaurant when we've been fighting this attraction for weeks. It's becoming too much, too hard to stay away, and I either have to accept it and give in or move.

But I know deep down that moving has never been an option. I mean, look at what he did for me, just for my birthday. How can I not feel special when he does that? How can I not recognize how special *he* is after what he's done for me? He's nothing like anyone I've ever been with, especially not Tom, so how can I judge him the same way?

The least I can do is to give him a fair chance. Plus, how can I turn a man down when there's so much promise of naughtiness in his eyes?

I mean, it is my birthday after all.

I break eye contact with him, turning to smile at our server as she patiently waits for our order. Her gaze is still on Trevor as she waits for him to acknowledge her, but he's still looking at me, his hand gripping my thigh. His thumb continues to rub slow circles on my inner thigh.

"We have," I interject, her attention snapping to me, her smile in place, but I don't miss the disappointment that she can't ogle him as much. "Can we get two daily specials? Both medium rare, a side of the veggie medley and baked potatoes—loaded, please," I say, forcing a smile as Trevor's fingers slowly drift further and further up my skirt, getting closer and closer to where I want him. Where I'm craving him. Where I've been thinking about him nonstop since we made out in the alley. His fingers continue their path, grazing my flesh, and I can feel the exact moment he notices that I'm not wearing any panties.

I feel like I can't breathe. His touch is so hot, so overwhelming, that I feel like I'm on fire, like I'm going to explode if he keeps touching me, yet I would die if he stopped.

As she types in our orders onto her tablet, Trevor grins at the waitress as he slides two fingers through my center, coating himself in my wetness. His eyes darken but he doesn't stop, his fingers now rubbing circles on the sensitive bundle of nerves he always finds so easily.

I can't breathe, can't move, can't speak. I literally can't do anything because of any extra stimulation and I'm sure I'm going to give myself away and embarrass myself by screaming for the entire restaurant to hear.

Not exactly my idea of an ideal date.

My nails dig into his thighs as he continues rubbing circles against my clit, two fingers slowly working inside of me as he smiles up at the waitress.

"I'll have that right out for you," she says with a polite nod before turning and walking to the kitchen.

I can finally breathe, yet it's more of a panting, unable to control myself as the beginning of an orgasm has started, the tingling at the base of my spine taking over. But Trevor hasn't stopped,

"Trevor. Stop. I'm going to come," I whisper, my words coming out hoarse, and throaty, as I fight to hold it together, fight to not lean into my release knowing it's exactly what I truly want right now.

He leans in, his lips hot near my ear as he kisses me lightly, his movement getting harder as he brings me closer and closer to falling apart. "Kitten, let go. Come all over my hand. I want to watch you fall apart into a million pieces. That way I can put you back together and do it again and again."

That does it.

I fall apart, leaning my face into the crook of his neck to muffle my moans as I come on Trevor's hand, in the middle of a restaurant with our waitress already returning, this time with a breadbasket.

"Here's some bread and butter, could I get you anything else before your food arrives?" she asks politely, her eyes still returning to Trevor every so often, but at this moment, I can't blame her. If only she knew what his fingers could do in a short time frame, she'd really be eye-fucking him.

I can't respond though, as I fight to catch my breath as Trevor slips his fingers out of me, the sensation even more intense as my whole body is tingling. But the moment he lifts his fingers to his mouth, sucking them clean as he smiles at me with faux innocence, I realize I don't give two shits about this meal.

I want him.

Our server turns to leave before Trevor snaps out of his horny haze, finally thinking long enough to respond. "Excuse me, could we actually take our food to go," Trevor says, his voice raspy, deep, and seductive as he says the words, yet he gives nothing away as to what's happening beneath the table. "My date is hot, and I've got to get her home so I can eat." The way her cheeks redden, I know she didn't miss the heavy innuendo in his words, but I can't find it in me to be embarrassed. I like his public claiming just as much as I liked getting caught in the alley. I'd go as far as to say it's a huge turn-on if how wet I am right now means anything.

"Alright, I'll have that right out," she says, grabbing his credit card and scurrying off.

"We're leaving?" I purr, doing nothing to hide my smirk.

"We are."

"I thought you wanted to stay and have our meal? We have all night to spend together," I say, my confidence quickly leaving, and I return to the puddle of goo I've been for the last hour as he leans in, his mouth right next to my ear, making sure I feel each of his words as he whispers them.

"I made a mistake. I thought I could wait until later, but then I touched you, kissed you, tasted you, and now you're all I can think about. You're consuming me, kitten. If we're done fighting it, I don't want to wait a second longer. I want you in my bed, naked. I want to touch you, lick you, fuck you. I want to make sure that the only cock you remember for the rest of your life is mine."

I shudder at the promise in his words as he looks down at his phone and calls us an Uber. Fuck walking back to the car, it's time to get home.

## Chapter 23

### *Ellie*

The feel of his lips on mine is the only thing I can think about as his hands tangle in my hair, moving me until I'm sitting in his lap. He smells so good, like laundry soap and whiskey—not a combination I would usually think would smell so good, but on him, it's fucking perfect.

"We're here. Now take your makeout session elsewhere and get out of my Uber."

Whoops.

*I don't regret one second of it. His lips are fucking delicious.*

Trevor hands him a hundred, and the guy immediately perks up, no longer annoyed about our backseat activities. As he smiles smugly at us, we step out onto the street. Trevor's hand immediately finds mine as he pulls me through the lobby and into an empty elevator. The second we're inside, he has me pressed against the wall, one hand lifting my leg onto his and pins me with his hips, his erection grinding against my core.

We are touching in so many places. His hands and lips are all over me, but I want more. I feel frantic, out of control, as my hands move into his hair, my leg pulling him against me as we kiss like this is our last night on earth. As the elevator stops, he pulls back, breathless, as he stares down at my mouth. I'm out of breath, barely standing as he's practically holding me upright.

His mouth hovers right near my ear, his voice ragged, "All bets are off tonight. You've got about two minutes to prepare yourself before I wreck this sweet little cunt of yours." He drags me off the elevator and down the hall.

Holy fuck, that was hot. Who is this man?

Caveman Trevor is hot, his possessiveness is hot, and I want every last bit of his promise to come true.

In mere seconds, he has his door open and is lifting me into his arms as he makes his way to his room, throwing me down onto his bed. What is it with this man and his tossing me around like it's nothing?

"Sir, you seem to really like throwing me around."

"Oh, sweet girl, this is only the beginning," Trevor growls, one hand undoing his belt, quickly sliding it from his pants before setting it down next to me. He makes quick work of his button and zipper but leaves it at that. His pants are slung low on his hips as he grips the hem of his shirt, pulling it off and throwing it down onto the floor.

Looking at him like this, standing in front of me, fifty percent naked and 100 percent sexy as fuck, I feel my core throbbing with the promise of wanting every nasty, dirty thing this man has planned for me tonight.

"Flip over. I want you on your hands and knees. Ass

up for me," he growls, watching me with an intensity that is just on the edge of nervousness but still hot as fuck. I'm not sure how long I stare at him, but his irritation is evident. "Now, kitten, I think I've been patient enough."

Without another thought, I flip up, lifting my hips in the air as I slide back to the edge of the bed. I feel his hands grip my ankles, tugging me further towards him. His hand comes down on my ass with a firm slap. "Ass up, kitten. Now."

I do as he says, immediately lifting my hips up into his waiting hands.

"You're such a good girl for me, kitten," he whispers, his raspy voice barely audible as he moves his hip forward, gripping his cock as he slides it through my wetness. I can't help the moan that falls from my lips, but who could blame me? Praise and a man who knows how to use his cock? Sign me up.

He's been edging the fuck out of me all night to the point that I'm surprised I didn't come when he touched my leg in the restaurant. Lord knows I was wet enough to be ready and willing for just about anything.

He starts to slide in, not stopping as he thrusts his hips forward until he's sheathed completely inside of me, his hips pressed against my ass.

"Fuck," I moan, my body adjusting to his size as he stretches me out in one go. "You're too big for shit like that, Trev. Gotta let me warm up a bit."

He ignores me, slowly sliding out before slamming back in, his thrusts hard and steady, and each time he hits my g-spot, I feel my breath hitch, the tingling starting down in my toes.

"Our entire fucking night was just one big warm-up, kitten. You've been teasing me all night, wearing this dress and these heels. Fuck, I've been imagining bending you over and fucking you in this dress, your heels digging into my back for hours. So first, I'm going to fuck you like I wanted to in that dark alley before we were so rudely interrupted by a bunch of fucking cock blocks. Then I'm going to take my time with you, fucking you slow and sweet."

"O-kay," I moan as he slams in again, this time even harder.

He starts thrusting faster, his cock sliding in and out at a pace that's almost difficult for me to keep up with. Each time, he hits the bundle of nerves deep inside of me that I'd once believed to have been a myth. He finds it every fucking time, making sure that I shatter around him in seconds. He grips my hair firmly in his hand, pulling up just enough to force me to arch my back, the angle changing just enough that I'm seeing stars.

As I scream out, an orgasm crashing into me, I hear Trevor chuckle behind me, but he doesn't slow down. If anything, he goes harder, faster, proving just how relentless he is.

"You like it when I fuck you rough, don't you, dirty girl?" Trevor growls as his hands grip my hips hard enough that I'm positive I'll have bruises tomorrow.

I try to nod, but I'm not sure I'm successful as the hand holding my hip starts rubbing soft circles against my clit. His thrusts have slowed, but they haven't stopped.

"Answer me, kitten. I want you to use your words."

"Yes, I like it when you fuck me rough," I whisper as

he slides out of me fast enough that I fall forward on his bed, my face in a pillow as I struggle to catch my breath. I hear his pants fall to the floor before I feel his hands on me, flipping me over so that I can see him. His hands reach for my leg, his fingers finding the zipper on my thigh-high leather boots, slowly sliding it down as he slips my first boot off, setting it down with care next to his bed.

He repeats the same thing on my other boot, his eyes watching me intently the entire time. I feel his fingers on my calf, slowly undoing the zipper. Grabbing the hem of my dress, he slides it up until he can get up and over my head.

Seeing as I wasn't wearing panties *or* a bra, we're now both completely naked, and fuck, I feel my pussy throbbing, already wanting him back inside of me, and we've already orgasmed.

Greedy bitch—oh well, he made her that way.

Before Trevor, I was happy enough to just have sex, and if there was an orgasm, that just meant I was a lucky bitch that day. But with Trevor, the first two orgasms are usually just warmups, and now I *truly* feel like the luckiest bitch in the world.

He doesn't say anything as he grins, grabs his belt, and climbs onto the bed, placing the belt next to him as he leans back against the headboard, propped up on the pillows with a cocky grin as he watches me ogle him. No shame in my game. His huge cock is hard, pointed up angrily as my arousal still coats him.

"C'mere, pretty girl. I want to watch you ride my cock," his deep voice says, barely a whisper, yet I move immediately. I crawl over to him, sliding one leg over him so I'm straddling him. His hands immediately grip my hips possessively as I hold myself up against his chest.

Lining him up with my center, I start to slide down, slowly taking him inch by inch. The angle is different than before, and I still need to stretch to take him in completely.

His nails dig into me as he throws his head back against the pillows, his hands holding me in place. "Fuck, kitten," Trevor growls as I sit all the way down in his lap. "You're suffocating my cock. Unless you want this to last less than five seconds, I need you to give me a minute."

I giggle, unable to help myself, but apparently, that was the wrong choice as Trevor's hand quickly goes to my throat, gripping me tightly as he holds me in place.

"Kitten, giggling is also something I need you not to do. If you do, and you clench down on my cock again, I promise I'm going to be pumping you full of my cum in the next ten seconds."

I feel my face flame immediately, and I wish I could say it was because what he's saying is so ridiculous. I mean, hell, we've just admitted our feelings to each other. But I'd be lying if I said seeing him with Addy didn't make me crave to see him with a baby of his own one day. But with how crazy my life is right now, the thought of him filling me with his cum should not be the turn on that it is.

I moan as his thumb finds my clit, his eyes staring intently at me.

"You liked that, didn't you?" he says, his eyes watching mine as he rubs small circles against my clit. "You liked me talking about filling you with my cum."

I feel the tingling beginning again, another orgasm already starting, but fuck, I want more. Hearing him talk like this is so hot I feel like I'm ready to fall apart.

I nod, accepting the shameful truth as I see his eyes light up. If I wasn't so turned on, I'd probably comment on the fact that he obviously likes it too, but that feels like a conversation for a different day.

"Good, now don't move until I tell you to," he says, one hand moving to play with my nipples. Tweaking them, pinching them, turning them until I'm squirming in his lap. My nipples are hard enough that they're painful, but I'm doing everything I can to not move in his lap.

I need his roughness, the pain, just more of everything. So, when he grabs his belt with one hand, looping it around my neck and pulling it snug, I pray I'm getting just that.

"You okay with this?" he asks, his eyes cautious as he holds the belt to the side, snug against my neck. It's tight, but not too tight, and fuck, I love the way he controls me.

"It's a little loose, but yes," I say, and within half a second, he's tugged it tighter, just enough to hold me perfectly in place, no room for me to move. I can't help it —I love being a brat. "So, is this when you're going to start fucking me rough?"

"No, kitten, this is when you're going to fuck me rough," he says confidently, one hand holding the belt while the other hand slides around my ass, his thumb slowly pressing against my backside, the place *no one* has ever been before. Before I can complain, though, Caveman Trevor is back.

"Now put your hands on the headboard and ride my cock. I want to feel your pussy clench around me as I fill your tight cunt full of my cum."

I lose it.

My body reacts on its own, listening to his demands as I start grinding myself against his cock, his finger still pressed against my backside, slowly pressing firm circles against me that I want to hate, but they surprisingly *don't* suck.

I'm ready to explode.

When his finger slips inside, just barely, yet just enough, my orgasm releases, completely setting me off. I scream, unable to help it as my entire body starts shaking, the orgasm so strong that I fall forward, collapsing onto his chest. Trevor doesn't stop as he thrusts from below, holding me against him as he finishes, drawing out the last bit of each of our orgasms as he pumps in and out slowly.

I couldn't tell you how long we lay there, but I can tell you it was the safest and happiest I've felt in a long, long time.

Trevor is one big treat after another, so when he carefully picked me up and carried me to the shower, I shouldn't have been surprised. And when he cleaned me up before wrapping me in the fluffiest towel ever before laying me in bed? Yeah, I shouldn't have been surprised by that, either.

But as I drifted off to sleep, unable to fight it any longer, he pulled me in closer, pressing a kiss on my forehead. His touch lingered just long enough that I felt myself fall into a deeper sleep, still aware of him but unable to react.

"Happy birthday, kitten," he whispered, his lips lingering for just a moment. "I love you."

---

WHEN ADDY WALKS INTO THE LOBBY WITHOUT TOM, I should already know that I'm going to be angry. Dave, the driver he's had for years, walks her over to me with a sympathetic smile on his face.

I've always liked Dave, even if he has horrible taste in employers.

But I guess Tom pays well, so I can't blame the guy.

"Hello, Mrs. Anderson," Dave starts.

"It's Ms. Anderson, but hello, Dave. It's good to see you," I say, not annoyed with him personally, just at being referred to as a married woman.

He smiles and sneaks a little wink. "Why, yes. Ms. Anderson has a much better ring to it. It's great to see you too, dear."

See, even Dave knows I'm better off without him.

"Where's Tom?" I ask as Addy sneaks by me to the front desk to steal her usual candy.

"Well, since you'll hear it from her anyway, I'll tell you. But please, for my sake, when he asks, just say Addy told you," Dave says, looking like he'd rather be anywhere than here having this conversation right now. "He's in Aspen."

"Fucking excuse me? Since when?" I seethe, my fist gripping my phone tighter than necessary.

"Tuesday," Dave says quietly. "Ms. Anderson, I didn't know, or honestly, I would have told you. She's actually been at his parents' this week. They brought her home today."

"I literally fucking hate that man. It was my fucking birthday, and he said I couldn't have her early because he was taking her to Disney World, and he didn't even spend time with her?"

"I know. Has he signed the papers for you yet? I made sure to deliver them."

"No. Still refusing," I say as Addy walks back over, still sad, but now she has a sucker.

"I'm sorry. If I can help with anything, please let me know."

"You've done enough, Dave. Thanks for taking care of my girl."

"Always."

Addy and I head upstairs to have a movie night. I can tell she's in a snuggle mood because she's barely let go of my leg since she's been home. There's a sadness in her eyes that kills me, especially now that I know she didn't spend the week in Disney World like she was promised.

It sucks. *He* sucks.

"You grab the candy box, and I'll go make some popcorn. How does that sound?" I smile at Addy as she walks out in her pajamas, ready for movie night.

"Okay, mommy," she says quietly.

After the popcorn is done, we meet on the couch, snuggle up in the blankets, and get ready to watch Little mermaid, our favorite.

"Daddy broke his promise," Addy says quietly, her hands twirling in my hair.

"I know, baby girl. I'm so sorry."

"I knew he would. It still just sucks."

"I'll make it up to you, baby. I promise. We don't need men in our lives to make us happy, even daddies. Okay?"

"Okay, mommy," Addy says, snuggling next to me. "What'd you do for your birthday? Did you and Aunty Natalie hang out?"

"No, I hung out with Trevor from next door."

"Oh. Did you have fun?"

"I did. I missed you, though."

"I'm glad you had fun. I like Mr. Trevor. He makes you smile, and you're so pretty. I like it."

I can't hide the smile taking over my face with the feeling I get. It's like butterflies times a million. I know I'm falling for Trevor and falling fast, but truthfully, I thought my daughter would be a harder sell.

"Me too, sweet girl. He's been an excellent friend."

I leave it at that as we both get lost in the movie, only picking up my phone to check my messages. I told Trevor about what Tom did, and obviously, he was pissed too, especially because of my birthday. He's away on a two-night road trip, coming home the day after tomorrow, and I can't wait for him to return.

The man has a soft spot for me and my little girl, and I love it.

I should just leave it at that. Close my phone out for the night. But I'm too much of a petty bitch when it comes to Tom that I open up his name.

> **Why didn't you drop Addy off today?**

**TOM**
> I had a last-minute meeting and had to stay in the office late. Dave offered to do it.

> **Why? Have you finally come to your senses and are ready to come home?**

> **I didn't know your office was in Aspen.**

The dots start and stop repeatedly, and I can tell that he's on the other end of this phone freaking out because he knows I just caught him in a huge lie. We both have an agreement in our parenting plan that if one of us has to leave for more than two days, the other parent has first right to keep the child that week.

He broke that, and the motherfucker knows he just got caught.

**TOM**
> How do you know about Aspen?

> **I know everything because I actually take the time to talk to my daughter. Next time, follow the parenting plan and bring me my daughter.**

> **Also, sign the papers. I'm never coming back to you.**

**TOM**
> Go fuck yourself, Eleanor.

> **Why would I do that when my neighbor does it so much better?**

# Chapter 24

## *Trevor*

I haven't been able to wipe the goofy grin off my face ever since Ellie's birthday a couple of weeks ago. The fact that I got to witness an entire afternoon of her smiling and laughing made my day.

Hell, it made my year.

The cherry on top was definitely her finally succumbing to what we've been fighting for months. There's something between us, and it's been so fucking obvious I almost don't understand how we've fought it for so long.

But spending all night buried inside her was exactly how I'd want to spend my birthday, so I can only hope that she enjoyed it.

Ever since her birthday, things between us have been different. On the days that she has Addy, I sneak in for a bit after she goes to bed. We usually sit out on the patio, talking and kissing, but that's about where it stops. When Addy goes back to her dad's, though? That's a different story.

As soon as I'd get home from practice, she'd be at my door. We would tear each other's clothes off on the way to my room, usually stopping in the living room for round one.

It's different, but it's us.

Spontaneity has never been my strong suit, but I think that comes from the fact that I've struggled to find a partner well suited to me.

But Ellie is so perfect for me it's not even funny, which is why I'm missing her today while she's out with the girls, having lunch and getting their nails done. As soon as Ellie and Natalie met Sawyer, Gwen, and Cassie, they've been stuck together whenever free.

It's cute, but I definitely wish I had her all to myself... all the time.

Since I couldn't steal her today, I met up with Cade and Miles for lunch after a run through the city. Which was basically just them spending the entire time ragging on me for "how many rainbows and unicorns were shooting from my asshole," as Cade so eloquently put it. I can't help that I'm actually happy for once.

It's been a while since I've been okay with things in my life being so uncertain, but for once, I don't feel depressed and lost. I may not know what my plan is after hockey or even where to start to figure that out, but I do know that I want it to include her.

Both of them.

But now I know they're home, and it's taking all my energy not to go over there just to say hi, but I don't want Addy to start asking questions about our relationship until Ellie decides she's ready to talk to her about it.

*Blindside Love*

Needing to do something, I start cleaning my apartment, grabbing the pile of recycling that's built up, and deciding it's finally time to walk it down the hall. When I open the door, though, I'm surprised when I'm greeted by Ellie and Addy, their arms up, ready to knock.

"Hi, girls." I beam, excited to see them, even if it is unexpected.

"Hi. I need a favor," Ellie says, biting her lip as her pointer finger plays with her thumb nail. It's a nervous tick I've noticed she does when she's really stressed out about something, but for the life of me, I can't figure out why she'd look like that with me.

"Of course. What is it?"

"Any chance you could hang out with Addy for a bit? Usually, Natalie would come watch her in the evenings, but she's on a date tonight. I could call her, I guess…"

"I don't mind at all. Is everything okay?" I ask.

"Betty called. Her husband isn't feeling very well; he started to get dizzy, and she wanted to get home to take him to the doctor. There's a small show at the studio tonight, so someone needs to be there. Unless I can be there, she won't be able to take him. I'm just worried and want to help her, but if you're busy or are going out or whatever it is you're doing on a night off, don't worry about it."

It isn't until I hold my hand up to stop her that I feel like she finally takes a breath. I thought she was going to pass out if she kept talking like that, all rambling and stressed out. It's still one of my least favorite things about Ellie. I hate that she feels the need to over-explain herself and always give people an out when she's asking for help.

It's bullshit that she feels like she needs to do that. It just shows that people have let her down enough that she just expects it.

"Take a breath, it'll all be fine. I was just about to order pizza and watch a movie. I'd love her to come join me," I tell her with a smile, noticing that Addy has a backpack with her, so hopefully, she'll have stuff to do and won't get too bored. "Take all the time you need. We'll be just fine."

"Yeah, mom. I brought fun stuff to do. T-Rex and I are going to have fun. I told you he wouldn't mind."

"T-Rex?" I grumble.

"Yeah, I saw your name on a piece of paper, and it looked like T-Rex. It made me giggle. So now it's your name," Addy says matter-of-factly, and she's so damn cute that I don't even care about the name change.

"The show ends at ten, but I'll make sure everyone leaves right away so I can get back."

"Don't worry about it. Here, take this spare key." I hand her a lanyard from the kitchen. "Just come in whenever you're done. Don't worry about the time. We'll be in the living room watching movies."

Addy runs into the living room and starts unpacking her backpack, leaving me and her mom at the doorway. But Ellie still looks apprehensive.

"Are you sure you don't mind?" she asks, her big eyes showing just how insecure she is about the whole situation.

Reaching forward, I tilt her chin up, making our eyes meet. "Kitten, I care about you *both*. And if this means you don't have to call Tom, I'm even happier to help."

Leaning forward, out of sight of Addy, I press my lips against Ellie in a quick, chaste kiss. "Now, I know you're not used to having people you can rely on, but you can rely on me. Now, go enjoy your night. I'll text you as many updates as you want."

With that, she turns and walks towards the elevator, her sexy ass swaying with every step in her tight black pants. Fuck, I hate that she's leaving, but damn, she looks great walking away. Turning back around, I shut the door and lock it out of habit.

"What should we order, Addy-girl?"

"Pepperoni! With extra ranch, just like my mom likes," Addy says proudly. "Can I paint your nails?"

I laugh, unable to help it. Her question surprised the hell out of me. "Uh, let me order pizza then... sure?"

"Did you just answer a question with a question, Mr. T-Rex?"

"I guess I did. Why, of course you can, just give me a minute."

After two hours, we've eaten pizza, watched *Sing*, and have now started *Sing 2*. She's painted my nails twice, finally deciding purple was more my color. It's been fun. I'm surprised as hell at how easy it's been to just hang out with Addy. There's something about this little girl. I love the hell out of her and am lucky enough that she actually enjoys hanging out with me.

I start cleaning up and putting our dishes in the sink when I realize Addy has fallen asleep on the couch. Grabbing a blanket, I cover her up. I'm gathering the rest of the dishes when I hear a knock on the door. Weird, it's nearly nine at night. Who could it be?

I look through the peephole and see a slightly older lady dressed to the nines. She's dressed nice, but her face is twisted in such a sour way that she doesn't look nice at all. Opening the door, I smile and start to say hello, but before I can talk, she cuts me off.

"I'm here to see Eleanor. Where is she?" she spits out at me.

"Well, unfortunately, ma'am. Eleanor doesn't live here. Now, is there anything else I can help you with?"

"That can't be true. This is the address my husband gave me for the apartment he loaned her. Besides, isn't that my granddaughter on the couch?"

"Let's try this again, ma'am. My name is Trevor Adams. I'm your daughter's neighbor. Addy and I were watching a movie while Ellie was away for a minute, so if you don't mind, I'm going to go back to that."

"You're him," she says like it's a fact, although I have no idea what she's talking about.

"Pardon me?" my hands grip my door, ready to slam it in her face, but I don't let the intrusive thoughts win.

"You're the reason my daughter left her marriage. You're the reason she's divorcing him," she snarls, like an angry bear, but it's all misdirected and pissing me off.

"No, ma'am. Tom managed that all on his own, but that's not my story to tell. The only *thing* I've done is try to heal two hearts I didn't break. So, if you'll excuse me, I'm going to get back to my evening."

She opens her mouth, but I don't wait for her to speak as I shut the door directly in her face and go to text Ellie.

> Not to put a damper on your evening, but your mother just stopped by.

ELLIE

Fucking excuse me? She what? At your place?

> Apparently your dad gave her this address. She's a delightful woman.

ELLIE

She's a bitch, I know it, and if you've talked to her, you definitely know it.

> You said it, not me. But no lies were detected.

> She blamed me for your divorce.

ELLIE

FML. I'm so sorry.

> Don't be. I told her off and then shut the door in her face. So... sorry about that.

ELLIE

Fuck, you're even more perfect than I could've dreamed.

See you soon.

When I head back into the living room, I see Addy is awake now, back to watching *Sing*. I'm glad she slept through her grandmother visiting; I'd feel like a huge asshole if I yelled at her grandma in front of her.

"Hey, little one, have a good nap?" I chuckle as I sit next to her on the couch.

"I did. It's comfy," Addy says, playing with her hair. "Do you know how to braid, T-Rex?"

"I don't. I'm sorry," I say, bummed at the sad look in her eyes as she plays with her ponytail.

"My mommy sometimes braids my hair. Daddy never does. He tells me to have Lena do it, but I don't like her."

*Smart girl. From what I hear, she's a snake.*

"I'll learn, okay?"

Her eyes light up as she smiles up at me. "Promise?"

"Pinky promise," I say, holding my pinky up as she links with mine.

Just like her mother, this girl is quickly stealing my heart.

By the time Ellie makes it home, Addy is asleep, and I'm well on my way to joining her as we watch *Bluey* for what feels like forever. Ellie is worn out too, so even though I suggested they just stay the night, Ellie insisted Addy should get a good night's sleep in her bed.

Now that they're both gone and on the other side of this wall, my apartment feels empty and lonely, and I hate it. Instead of going to my room, I find myself back on the couch watching *Bluey*, wishing the girls were with me.

Pulling up a group chat, I type a quick text out with an S.O.S.

> Help. I need to learn to braid. Sawyer, can you teach me?

SAWYER

> Why do you need to learn to braid?

> But, yes, I can teach you.

**REX**

She's not the one you should be asking.

> Addy asked me to braid her hair when I watched her tonight. She looked so sad when I told her no, so I wanted to learn how.

**SAWYER**

This is a lot to unpack. Come over for dinner this week and I'll teach you how.

**REX**

I'll teach you how. Sawyer's version of a braid looks like a preschooler trying to draw a straight line.

With their eyes closed.

**SAWYER**

He's not wrong. Besides, he is better with his hands.

> Thanks guys. I'll see you then... with more details.

**SAWYER**

Wise, young grasshopper.

---

I THOUGHT I WOULD BE MORE NERVOUS SITTING IN A restaurant across from my father with my mother sitting next to him, but honestly, I'm just happy.

I missed them while they were on vacation. It was weird not going over for weekly dinners, so now I'm just excited to see them. I feel like an asshole, though, because after my talk with Liam, I realized how many assumptions I had to make to get to the point that I thought I couldn't tell my father about this.

Now I just have to rip the Band-Aid off.

"Why do you look like you just saw a ghost?" my father questions, his glass of wine pausing at his lips as he eyes me curiously.

I guess it's now or never. I have no poker face, so he picked up right away that something was off.

"I... I think I'm going to retire from hockey," I say, staring down at my plate like it's my lifeline. I'm afraid to look up and see disappointment in my father's eyes. Even worse, I'm afraid to find out that we have nothing else in common, and our close relationship will only last if I play hockey.

"Why are you so upset?" my dad asks, causing me to look up at him.

The disappointment and sadness I thought I would see in his eyes aren't there. Instead, it's just my dad. No different than when we would talk about hockey, my mom, or his job, he's always looked at me the same way.

It's love.

How could I ever question him? How could I ever convince myself that he would be anything but supportive? I feel like I've betrayed my dad by holding this a secret for so long.

I shake my head, disgusted with myself. "I thought you'd be upset. Disappointed in me. I... I had myself convinced that hockey was the only thing connecting us, and you'd be mad at me if I quit."

My dad's face falls, and I feel my heart start to crack.

I hate how defeated he looks, and even worse, I hate that I caused it.

"Trevor, son. I could *never*, and I mean *never*, be disappointed in you for doing what's best for you. Regardless of the reason, you're allowed to make choices for *you*. Follow your heart, son. If your time on the ice is done, then you had a helluva run and went down like an absolute legend. But hockey doesn't define you."

Hearing him say that should make me feel better, but honestly, it makes me feel worse because everything he's saying makes sense. It's exactly what I should expect him to say because he's never shown me anything different.

I let my own insecurities of leaving the game get in the way of talking to my dad about a big life choice, and that sucks, to put it plainly.

"I know that," I say solemnly.

"Then why didn't you talk to me?" he asks. He's not mad, not at all, but I can see the underlying hurt in his eyes, and it just kills me.

"I wish I could understand it myself. I convinced myself that without hockey, I was nobody. That without hockey, no one would want to be friends with me and that our relationship would suffer because we didn't have hockey to bond over. I know it's ridiculous. Rex told me I was an idiot. Liam told me the same thing. But it was Ellie who reminded me that parents only ever want their kids happy. That's when I realized I'd been an idiot and that I just needed to tell you. Unfortunately, you were on a damn cruise."

I stop talking when I see my dad staring back at me, wide eyed, almost shocked at my long-winded response.

"You let it get that far without saying something? I raised you to be a helluva lot smarter than that, son. Next time, don't be dumb, and just come talk to me. It'd save you the headache, and hell, I just like being able to be there for you. Be the person you can talk to."

"You are, dad. I promise. I just got nervous. It's a huge change, and I just kept jumping to the worst-case scenarios."

"I get it. Your mom does the same thing, so I'm used to it, but I'm still going to call you an idiot."

"I deserve it." I laugh, feeling the weight of this conversation immediately falling off my shoulders.

Did it suck? Yeah. But I'm glad he knows.

I feel dumb that I even questioned how he'd respond, but now I know. When you're a parent, you love unconditionally, always choosing the happiness of the ones you love.

# Chapter 25

## *Ellie*

> I'm resending the divorce papers. This time, sign them.

TOM

> No, it's time for you to stop your games. Come. Home.

> No.

TOM

> Tick, tock, Eleanor. I'm losing patience with your drama.

---

NATALIE

> I'm on my way up. I'm carrying a bunch of shit, so get your ass up and help with the door.

I'm excited for a night out with Natalie, although it won't quite be the night of dancing I was originally hoping for. I know it's just dancing, but the thought of having another man's hands all over my body, close enough to feel *everything* makes me cringe. I don't want to touch anyone that isn't Trevor, and I sure as hell don't want anyone that isn't him touching me.

Opening the door, I see Natalie coming down the hall holding a pile of dresses as well as what looks like her entire makeup kit.

Jesus. I know I said we were going dancing, but I figured normal makeup would work.

"What's all this for?"

"To make us completely fuckable," Natalie says as she throws the pile on the couch. "Now come on, we've got an hour until it's time to go."

Fifty minutes later, she's done my makeup, curled my hair, and squeezed my body into the tiniest black dress known to mankind. Sparkly, knee-high silver boots make the outfit just slightly less revealing.

"Are you sure this is what I should be wearing?" I mean, don't get me wrong, I feel sexy as hell, but it also feels like I'm two seconds away from a horrible wardrobe malfunction.

"You look perfect. Now give me your phone. I'm taking a picture, and you're sending it to Trevor."

"Now why would I do that?" I ask, my eyebrows raised. That sounds dumb.

"Well, the last I heard, you guys had explosive sex

when y'all played around with the sexual tension. Think of this as text edging."

"You're ridiculous."

Yet I find myself doing exactly what she tells me to, taking the damn picture and letting her send it before getting in an Uber for a night of fun at a place I never thought I'd get to go to.

---

I'VE ALWAYS WANTED TO COME TO CLUB 100, SO when Natalie told me she got us in, I originally thought she was lying, especially for a Friday night. This is one of the hardest clubs to get into. It's one of those things where you have to know someone who knows someone types of situations, and frankly, she and I don't know too many people.

But as she walks up to the bouncer and whispers in his ear, I'm surprised when he gestures us towards the front of the line, sending us up to VIP.

*Excuse me? VIP at Club 100?*

The music is loud. I can feel the beat in my chest, but the vibe is electric. Everyone is moving, dancing, drinking, and it looks like everything I want to do tonight.

*I just wish he was here.*

But a girls' night is okay. It's fun. Especially with Natalie.

As we walk up the stairs, I see a whole area with couches, the nice suede kind, and matching chairs that are low, so low they're almost on the floor. There are men sitting in the chairs by the glass walls, watching down on the dance floor, and I can't help but wonder if they're watching their girls, making sure they're safe.

"Happy Birthday!" I hear, snapping me out of my thoughts when I turn to see Natalie standing with Sawyer, Cassie, Gwen, and all the guys—Trevor included. All of who are smiling at me.

I look at Natalie, immediately smiling because I can't believe she went through the trouble of planning this, especially knowing how much I love dancing.

"Thanks, lady," I say as I pull Natalie into a hug.

"Wasn't me, El. It was the fine-ass man of yours who hasn't stopped staring at you since you walked in. Or are we still pretending you two aren't a thing?"

I stand for just a moment, staring at Trevor as he smiles at me. My mind is reeling with the thought that *he* did this. Something else, so perfect, just for me. Is he for real?

I make my way over to Trevor, staring at him the entire way. He's sitting in one of those suede chairs, leaning back as he sips a glass of bourbon. His hair is tousled, his face scruffy, and he looks incredible.

Even more, though, he looks like *mine*.

I sit in his lap, his eyes widening just barely before he steels his expression, looking at me with a curious look. But I don't wait. I don't talk. I just plant my lips on his, kissing him with everything I have.

Right now, the only thing I have to give him is me, my body. So, if I'm going to do it, I'm going to give it to him completely. Fully. All in.

He immediately embraces the kiss, his free hand gripping the back of my head gently as he holds me against him, giving me the time and space to explore, to lead the kiss.

I feel him harden beneath my ass, and that's when I remember that we're in public, and as much as I want to fuck him right here, it's not exactly socially acceptable to get naked in public.

*But if you look as good as he does, you should be allowed to get naked everywhere.*

Pulling back, I smile, licking my lips as I stare at him. He's wild-eyed, almost on edge, as he stares down at me. It takes him a moment before he finally says something.

"I thought you said we were keeping this a secret?"

"That was before I realized there was no use in denying it anymore," I replied.

"Denying what?"

"That you're mine." I grin, wrapping my arms around his neck. I bring my mouth to his ear. "That means I'm yours if you want me to be. Your pussy to touch, lick, fuck, eat, whatever you please, whenever you please."

He growls. There's no other way around it, but he grabs my hips, holding me still as he kisses me once. It's quick but rough enough that I'm sure I'm in for it when we get home. "Mine. Understand that kitten? You. Are. Mine."

"Okay, caveman. We get it. Girl yours. No one touches the girl," Cassie says as she walks over to us with Sawyer.

"But we're gonna have to steal the birthday girl. It's

time for shots, and you're not invited," Sawyer says, sticking her tongue out at Trevor. He pretends to pout and tries to grab onto me, but they just grab my hand and pull me away while Trevor goes to stand with Rex and the guys.

The girls walk me over to where Natalie and Gwen have ordered us a round of shots, but Natalie looks excited. Too excited.

"What was that all about?" she asks, cutting to the chase.

I feel my cheeks heat as I turn to look at Trevor, who's still watching me, and I choose to tell the truth.

"I guess that was us no longer hiding it." I shrug, my lips turning up as I let myself smile. Let myself be happy that for the first time in a long time, I have a man I can be proud of, one who's proud to call me his.

The girls all practically squeal as Gwen passes out a shot to each of us. These girls have an unhealthy obsession with Tequila, but thankfully, I can stomach just about anything, especially when I have a lime.

The subject is changed from Trevor and me for all of five minutes before Sawyer looks at me, and I should expect her comment by now, but it still shocks me.

"So, was I right? Is he all rough and tumbly in the bed? Dominant and hot?" Sawyer asks, holding a perfectly straight face as she asks questions that I can tell are turning my cheeks a beautiful shade of maroon.

"Based on the color of her cheeks, I'm going to say with 100% certainty that he is, in fact rough and tumbly in bed." Natalie smirks as she grabs a tray of drinks as we walk towards the table where she sets them down.

The guys are still talking, although Trevor still keeps checking on me. Often. I only know because I'm checking on him too.

"My lips are sealed." I pretend to lock them and throw away the key. My silence lasts all of two seconds when Cassie makes a joke about my legs not being sealed, and I lose it with a laugh.

"Look, you don't have to tell us, but we both know you guys have had a tough time finding a good match for yourself. If you've found that in each other, I'm happy as hell for you guys," Sawyer says, smiling, and again, I find myself blushing, but this time because I realize I have found that in Trevor. He is my safe place, my happy place, the person I can be myself with.

"Why are you blushing, kitten?" Trevor's deep voice comes from next to me, right as his arms wrap around my waist. He leans down enough to rest his chin on my shoulder, resting cheek-to-cheek with me.

I feel my body melt into his, and at this moment, I don't want to be dancing anymore. I want to be home, in bed, naked with this man.

"I'm stealing my girl. We're dancing," Trevor says as the girls start giggling. I don't pay attention, though, as he grabs my hand and leads me out to the middle of the dance floor.

Turning until my back is against his chest, I start moving to the music, letting my body take over as his hands start touching me, starting at my hips, sliding up until he's grazing my chest, his touch charged, as I feel the heat everywhere his fingers are touching me, all the way down my side until they land on my hips, holding me firm against him as he grins into me.

Jesus fuck, he's hard—very, very hard, as he grinds against my ass, his mouth pressing open mouth kisses down my neck, over my shoulder as he presses his lips against any bare skin, he can find like he can't get enough.

I like this new freedom. Being able to show affection in public and claim each other. It's nice to be able to spend time with him and not pretend that we don't have this intense attraction to each other. Or even that we haven't started to develop feelings for each other.

Either way, life was already much happier with him by my side as my friend. I can't wait to see what happens with him as *mine*.

We dance to a couple more songs before I feel Trevor's teeth nip my ear lobe, his hips grinding against me, making damn sure I know just how massive he is. "Two choices, kitten. Either A. we go to the bathroom, and I fuck you against the wall. Or B. You grab your purse, and we go home where I can fuck you on any and every surface in your apartment."

I turn around, excitement already filling me at the promise of tonight. The look in his eyes is all I need to know that he's not in the mood for games. He wants to fuck me, and he wants to fuck me hard.

*Take me home, sir. I'm at your mercy.*

"I'll grab my stuff. You tell the guys we're leaving. I'm not sure where everyone is right now. Could you make sure one of the guys gets Natalie gets home?"

He kisses my forehead, his smile wide, although his

eyes remain dark. "Of course, kitten. Now run along. It's time to go. Meet me by the door."

That's all it takes for me to scurry off, heading back over to our section in VIP and grabbing my things. Thankfully, I find the girls easily and tell them I'm leaving, and after their five million questions, I'm finally heading to the front to find Trevor.

Only when I do, there's a girl with him. A very attractive woman who's pressing up against him, her mouth near his ears as she says something I can't make out.

I stand for a moment, waiting for the jealousy to hit, waiting for the apprehension, the second-guessing, the pit in my stomach where I just know that it's happened again, they've been unfaithful.

But that was Tom, not Trevor, and Trevor proves his loyalty when he removes her hand gently and takes a step back from her. He talks to her but refuses to let her touch him.

I smile, unable to help it, especially when he looks over at me and smiles the second he sees me, ignoring the girl as she steps closer to him. I'm definitely not jealous, but I am annoyed that she's not taking the hint. Not understanding that he doesn't want it.

Also, the main point is that he's mine, so I'm not a huge fan of her grubby little fingers touching my man.

I find myself walking over to them quicker than I realize, my arm sliding around Trevor's waist as I look up at him and smile. "Ready to go, baby?"

He looks down, his eyes twinkling with humor, knowing damn well what I'm doing. He makes a show of putting his arm around my side, gripping my ass as he pulls me in tight.

Before he can respond, the girl speaks, obviously not taking the hint.

"Are we dancing or not?" she huffs, obviously annoyed.

"Unfortunately, he can't. He has plans," I say with a smile that definitely doesn't meet my eyes.

"And what could he possibly have planned that would be more important than hanging out with me?"

She starts to step forward, her hands reaching for Trevor.

"Fucking his girlfriend within an inch of her life, so, unfortunately, he's busy for... well... forever."

I look up and see Trevor smirking, his mouth coming down against mine as he kisses me quick, rough, and passionately. I don't know how long we stand there but when we finally pull back, she's gone.

"Get me home, Mr. Adams."

---

As much as I want to walk through the door and strip each other naked, forgetting about everyone and everything else in this world, I have questions. Lots of questions.

Starting with who the fuck was that lady, and why did she seem so familiar with him.

After we get inside my apartment, I walk into the kitchen, immediately pouring a drink for Trevor and me as we head out to the patio. We always sit out here for a while every time we're together.

But I feel like I'm stewing on this, and I can't figure out why. As I feel the intensity of his gaze on me, I rack my brain for what to say.

"Stop overthinking, kitten. I can read it all over your face."

For some reason, the way he says this just pisses me the fuck off, like me not liking a woman touching him is outrageous. Like I can't be nervous about women because I've been betrayed in the past.

It may not have been Trevor that caused the pain and the broken trust, but he's the one standing in the battleground with me while I try to pick the pieces up, putting them back together the best I can.

"No. I'm allowed to think, and I'm allowed to be annoyed."

"You are, but not with me."

"Don't tell me what I can and can't do, Trevor. It won't go well for either of us," I growl, my annoyance isn't even with him, but he's a good outlet for it right now. "I'm pissed at that girl, that girl that felt like she could claim you. I don't like her possessiveness over you."

His eyes twinkle as he looks down at me. "I like when you're possessive."

"Back off, Mr. Adams. I'm still grumpy that you had another woman's hands on you."

One hand grips my throat as he takes another step forward, backing me into the glass window. "Being angry and pissed off at me over something I can't do anything about is frustrating as fuck, Eleanor."

"Do *not* call me Eleanor unless you really want me to be a bitch. Now, are you just going to stand there and complain about my attitude, or are you going to come fuck it out of me?" I growl.

I barely get the sentence out before he lifts me over his shoulders and carries me to my room.

Caveman Trevor is back.

*Fuck. Yes.*

# Chapter 26

## *Trevor*

Walking over to Ellie's with Addy's iPad in hand, I realize I'm smiling, stupidly giddy over just seeing them. Ellie and Addy have been the best part of my, well, everything lately, and honestly, I'm happier than I've been in probably ever. As I walk up to the door and go to knock, I realize the door is already halfway open.

Panic hits me that something is wrong, even more so when I hear a man's voice yelling from her living room. I head in, my stomach in knots as I listen to the conversation, and when I hear Ellie, I realize she's doing just fine on her own, putting whoever is yelling at her in their place.

But then it hits me who's doing the yelling, and I'm immediately pissed.

It's Tom.

"You're being fucking ridiculous, Eleanor. Unless you agree to help me out, I'm not signing these papers, so I guess you're just making the decision that you only want to see your child every other week. What a great mother you are."

"Fuck you, Tom. Get out of my house. I'm done keeping secrets for you. I'm telling my family all about your bullshit games. At this point, you really can't hurt me anymore," she says, more confidently than I've heard her in a while, and I can't help but feel a sense of pride that I'm watching her come into her own again and stand up for herself. It's fucking badass. *She's a badass*.

As I sit and listen to them, I realize I would do anything for this woman, absolutely anything. I would protect her, fight for her, support her, all of that. But the only thing I won't do is stunt her growth. I want her to flourish and be the happy, confident version of herself that she's showing more often.

*Am I falling in love with this girl. Fuck. When the hell did this happen?*

As soon as I realize this, I want to panic, and freak out, but instead, I feel a sense of calm. This woman has brought me a sense of peace that I haven't felt in years, and I couldn't be more grateful.

Immediately, I have the urge to find her, see her, touch her, and, more importantly, get *him* away from her. As I step in, I peer around the kitchen to see Tom staring at the painting above her couch.

"I like this painting. I'm glad to see you stopped hanging up your art and finally put something professional up. Now, this is art," Tom says, his words dripping with condescension with what he believes to be an insult.

I watch Ellie's face drop in disbelief, but only a moment later, she's steeled her face, her eyes shooting daggers, but no other emotion shows as Tom turns towards her, a vicious look in his eyes as he gestures towards the art. "I've been telling you what you were doing wasn't art for years, Eleanor," he sneers, his nose curling in disgust as he stares for a moment. "This is what I wanted in our home. *This* is art. *This* is talent. This isn't some painting you hang on your fridge or your wall because your toddler did it. You're a stay-at-home mom who watches Pinterest to learn, for crying out loud, but you refused to listen. Can you reach out to the artist for me? I'd love to see their collection."

She glares at him, her mouth opening to speak, but I walk in further, cutting her off. I'm way beyond listening to this piece of shit disrespecting her in her own home.

"With that beautiful sentiment, I think it's time you left," I all but growl at him, my fists clenched at my sides as I do everything in my power not to throw him through the goddamn wall. Thank fuck I know Addy is here because it's the reminder I need to make sure she doesn't experience this fight. I refuse to let it get that far.

"And who the fuck are you? This is my wife I'm speaking with," Tom snaps, his face turning scarlet with embarrassment or anger, I'm not sure, nor do I give a fuck. It's time for him to go.

"Are you deaf or dumb? I said it's time for you to leave."

His face reddens and his jaw clenched as he just glares back and forth between Ellie and me. She's standing next to me, watching me with a look of wonder. She's looking at me like I hung the moon for her.

*Little does she know, I'd hang every star in the galaxy just to light up her smile.*

"Do you know who I am? Do you realize how big of a mistake you're making right now, disrespecting me like this? I am her husband."

"Soon to be ex," she snaps.

"Shut up, Eleanor. This doesn't involve you," Tom sneers.

And I feel something snap in my brain.

I take a step closer to Ellie, loving the way she leans into my side, letting me pull her in close as I plant a quick kiss on the top of her head, grounding myself for a moment before turning to deal with this waste of a human still standing in her home.

"First things first, if Addy wasn't in this house, I'd throw you through that fucking wall for talking to my girl like that. Speak to her like that again, and I promise it'll be the biggest regret of your life," I growl, doing my best to keep my voice down to not let Addy hear. "But Tom, of course, I know who you are. And I'm not the one who should be worried. I've made no threats. I've just informed you what the consequences of your actions will be in the future. If you decide to ignore my warnings, that sounds like a personal problem. See. You came into *my* girl's home, disrespected *my* girl, and expect it to just be okay? That's where you're wrong, you can go on and fuck yourself, sir. Now, get the fuck out."

He glares at me before turning his stare towards Ellie, but she doesn't back down. She doesn't even flinch as she leans in closer to me.

"So, this is the guy you're fucking? The reason you're

too good for me now? You just wait. I'm going to make your life a living hell. I promise you that."

"No, Tom. You aren't," Ellie says, standing taller than she has in days. "Trevor isn't the reason that you're not good enough for me, you're the reason you're not good enough for me. You fucked up or Lena did, I'm not sure. Either way, Addy has admitted she spends more time with Lena than you. That's a strike on you. Between all the text I have saved with you saying you don't want Addy, that you never have, it should be enough to get the court to see you have no desire to be a father."

Tom's eyes widen in fear, his forehead glistening with sweat that I'm sure is caused by a mixture of nerves and anger, and it's nice that, for the first time, he looks almost defeated.

"Ele—"

"No, Tom. You don't get to speak right now. I'm not finished talking. I've sent them all to my lawyers, and if you still fuck with me, I'll send them to our parents. My lawyer will not release anything unless you push me on this. All I want is to move on with my life. I want a divorce, and I want my kid. I don't want anything from you. No money, no child support. Just my kid and my life back. One without you."

"Fi-fine. This isn't fucking over, Eleanor."

"Oh, but it is, Tom. I'm not scared of what you can do to me anymore. I don't care. Do your worst. Now, go out that door, take a left, and fuck *all* the way off."

Tom stares at us for a moment like he can't quite decide what he wants to do but quickly turns to head to the door, his fists clenched. *Unfortunately,* though, I'm a petty motherfucker and can't help but kick him when he's down. You don't fucking disrespect my girl without paying the price—in this case, it's just emotional warfare.

"Hey, Tom, you know that painting you wanted to buy?" I say, earning me a very confused look as he nods. "I fucked your wife on that painting, so, no, it's not for fucking sale," I deadpan, doing my best not to smirk while I watch the anger take over his face. "Now get the fuck out of her apartment. I'd like to fuck *your* wife again before she becomes mine."

I can't help the slight smile that falls on my face as his reddens, his anger so thick the air feels heavy. I'm concerned he's going to yell, get pissed or throw a tantrum, but instead of saying anything, he just spins and walks out the door, slamming it on his way out.

The second the door clicks shut, Ellie starts laughing. Full-on belly laughs that are absolute music to my ears.

"Fuck, I wish I'd recorded that. His face was absolutely priceless when you mentioned fucking me," she says, her eyes bright with laughter.

"We might have to check your cameras. Maybe one of them caught it," I say with a smile before turning serious. "More importantly, though, are you okay? Tom's a fucking asshole. I'm sorry about everything he said."

"Thank you for asking." She smiles, one that actually reaches her eyes. "I'm actually fine, though, surprisingly. I decided that I was done letting him impact my life, positively or negatively. He lost that right. So, I figured I'd just ignore his insults because giving him any sort of reaction would only encourage his behavior and make him feel powerful. But now I feel powerful. Thank you for standing up for me."

"Always, kitten. You may be feisty, but you'll never fight alone ever again. You've got me."

"Thank you. I-I'm not always the easiest. I have a lot of shortcomings, but I fight for the people I care about. You're one of those people. I'll do everything I can to fight for you, make sure you're happy, and I just hope that's with me."

I stop her before she finishes by kissing her roughly.

"I love you, kitten," I whisper against her lips, which immediately turn up as she smiles, her arms squeezing me tightly.

"I love you too, Trevor. I probably should've told you that a while ago, but I'm a little bit stubborn if you weren't aware."

I just roll my eyes, smiling as I hold my girl, knowing I'm exactly where I'm supposed to be in this world.

*She loves me.*

———

DAYS WITHOUT ELLIE HAVE BECOME FEW AND FAR between, especially the weeks when Addy is with Tom, which made planning a surprise evening for the girls a bit challenging, especially when I relied *heavily* on Sawyer and Stella to help plan the best surprise Disney-themed day.

After Ellie told me about Tom lying to Addy about Disney World, and then leaving her with her grandparents while he went to Aspen with his girlfriend, I knew I wanted to try to help her make a new, fun memory instead.

Stella is a baker, so I had her help me recreate food you'd find at Disney World. Thankfully, she was willing and whipped up a bunch of food, mostly desserts, for us to eat. She's taking care of all of that right now while the girls are on their way to the arena to watch us play against Vegas, before our surprise begins.

Stella was willing to make sure everything was set up, so I don't have to stress, and she even made sure Addy's new princess dresses were ready so she could play dress up for our movie night.

I haven't told Ellie about any of this, because honestly, she sucks at keeping secrets, and I want to watch it unfold.

But first, I want to win this game, especially with tonight being Addy's first game.

I'm gonna fuck some shit up tonight on the ice, obviously not too much knowing Addy will be in the stands. It's nice having my girls in the stands because it helps return the excitement I used to feel just from being out on the ice. Knowing that, I'm even more convinced that next week I need to tell the team and let them know I'm officially retiring.

We have played through two periods, and thankfully, we're heading into the third period up by one. It's been such a physical game, though, and everyone is worn out. Even with a break between periods, we're still fucking tired.

At least I am, which is more proof that I'm making

the right call. So I'm going to leave it all on the ice. I refuse to lose this game.

Cade has had one helluva game tonight, making more impressive saves than he should need to, so now we just gotta help him out a bit.

Scoring would be nice too.

Luckily, the third period is different. Miles scores right off the bat, winning the face-off and making a shot right away. It was a relief knowing we had a bigger lead, but we were still hungry.

With five minutes left, Vegas is on a power play and Harris gets called for a bullshit tripping call. But our power play kills are incredible, and we're able to hold them off.

As exciting as this win feels, I'm more excited for the rest of my night with my girls and the surprise I have planned.

Now to get through showers, media, and then to my girls.

---

BY THE TIME WE MADE IT TO CENTRAL PARK, I think Addy had asked me no less than thirty-seven times what her surprise was and what was in the bag I was carrying, but I kept my lips zipped. Ellie even tried to get me to spill, but I wouldn't cave.

I stop at a bench really quickly, handing each of them their own small bag, only adding to their confusion.

"What's this?" Ellie asks, holding the bag like she's afraid of it, like I'm giving her a bomb or something.

"I just thought we could do a couple fun things. I wanted to let Addy do some of the things we got to do on your birthday. There's more, but that's all at my apartment."

Addy squeals as she opens her bag, revealing a shiny tiara fit for a princess. "This is for me? I love it! Thank you, Trevor! I love you."

She runs over to me, wrapping her arms around my leg, and I feel like this hug just healed something inside of me that I didn't even realize was broken. I look over at Ellie and see her wiping away a tear, quickly looking away from us, and this hug just became that much more important to me.

"Love you too, sweet girl. Now let's go get some ice cream and then go ride the carousel," I say, still holding her, but the second she hears ice cream, she's smiling and ready to go. She walks ahead of us, and surprisingly, she remembers exactly where it is.

"You really went through the trouble of taking us out and getting her a tiara? You planned an evening for her just to make her smile?" Ellie asks, almost cautiously.

"That's exactly why. I hated that she had this shitty memory when she wanted a fun one. A meaningful one. The least I could do was give her something to make her smile when that's what she does for me all the time.

I must have said something right because she looks up at me and shakes her head, her smile as wide as it'll go, her hand holding mine just long enough for a couple of squeezes, but it's fine by me. It'll take time to let Addy know that we're more than just friends.

For now, we are just enjoying spending time together.

After we get our cones, chocolate with extra fudge for the girls and chocolate peanut butter for me, we make our way over to the carousel, riding it at least four times before Ellie finally cuts Addy off.

Apparently, she loves the carousel, and it's always been a struggle to get her to want to come off. So, I told her a little secret when she started to throw a fit.

"So, Addy girl, there's another surprise for you at my place. For you and your mom. Which means the sooner we get there, the sooner you get to see your second surprise."

Addy smiled brightly, her happiness evident as she grabbed Ellie's hand and started skipping away.

I'm going to get whiplash from my own emotions, but I smile the entire way home, loving every second.

---

I HOLD MY BREATH AS I OPEN THE DOOR TO MY place. All the main lights are off, only the twinkling lights Stella insisted on buying illuminate the living room. As I walk in, I set my things down on the entry table as the girls follow me in. Ellie's eyebrows are scrunched together as she notices the Disney piano music playing through the speakers. I follow them as they make their way through the kitchen into the living room.

I can't tell if I'm more nervous because I have no idea what the girls did to my apartment or to see their reaction. Luckily, I don't have to wait long as Addy runs in, her immediate squeal of excitement warming my heart.

"This is so cool! Did you do this?!?" Addy asks, spinning around with a smile on her face as she looks at my living room.

She's not wrong, though, what they were able to pull off is pretty incredible. My entire apartment is Frozen-themed, with lights everywhere and music playing in the background. They already have the movie queued up, so it's looping through some of the movie.

"You did all this for her?" Ellie asks, her voice a little shaky.

I smile even wider, knowing exactly why she's nervous, but I wish she realized she didn't have to be. Even if Ellie decided that she didn't want to be with me, these two are stuck with me for as long as they'll allow.

"I did," I smirk, rocking on my heels a bit as I watch her.

"But... why?"

"Because I care, and I hate that she got hurt, that Tom hurt her. I may not be able to bring her to Disney right now, but at least I can make her smile."

"This has my name on it," Addy says excitedly, noticing the bags next to the TV. "Is this for me?"

"Yes, it is, sweet girl. Go on and open it."

I love the way her eyes light up, her whole body filling with excitement as she digs into the bag. It's even more exciting watching Ellie watch her, seeing the single tear slip down her face when Addy opens the Elsa costume excitedly.

"I thought you could put that on, and we could watch the movie and eat all the Disney snacks that Stella made for us today."

"Mommy! Look at this. Can I put it on?"

"Yes, sweetie, you can."

"Thank you, Trevor! This is the best surprise ever!"

Addy squeals as she runs to the bathroom to change into her new dress. Ellie turns to look at me, an adorable, happy smile now on her face. "You're really something else, Trevor. You're too good to us."

"No, Ellie, that's where you're wrong. You have this image in your mind of what a man is supposed to do for you and for your daughter, and it's the bare minimum, at best. That's not your fault, though, that's just what you've been shown. I want to help you reach your dreams and see your potential, but I also want to spoil the hell out of you two because you deserve it. It's still only a fraction of the happiness you give me."

She steps forward, her arms wrapping around me as she hugs me, her whole body stepping into me, as she looks up at me with a smile that makes me believe that maybe, just maybe, she cares about me as much as I care about her. I step to the side and grab the other bag for her, loving the way her eyes continue to light up. When she sees the dress inside, she starts laughing; it's an adult version of the Elsa dress.

"Be right back, get comfortable," I tell her, sneaking off to my room to change. I'm definitely not wearing a costume, but I'll throw on an Olaf onesie any day of the week.

By the time I make it back out into the living room, the girls are snuggled on the couch, practically salivating at all the food laid out on the coffee table. There's pineapple dole whip, beignets shaped like Mickey and Minnie, funnel cake, corn dogs, and what seems like a million other things, all Disney-themed to choose from. I can't help but laugh at the excitement in their eyes, happy they're enjoying themselves tonight.

"You can dig in whenever, but Addy, if you want, I can give you the Elsa braid you asked for last time. I learned how."

If I thought she was happy before, it's nothing compared to right now. At this moment, I feel like I've peaked, like everything else I do after this will be inconsequential because this is *everything*.

A night of braiding and eating treats with my girls, there's absolutely nothing better.

## Chapter 27

## *Ellie*

I feel like I've been floating these last few weeks, happy about everything and just high on life. Don't get me wrong, splitting time with Addy has still been hard, but I've filled my weeks without her with things that bring me joy, mainly painting and spending time with Trevor.

After Betty continued to pester me about the opening she had in her schedule, I finally caved and agreed to do a show. She was ecstatic while I stayed up all night looking at every piece I'd ever done, convinced everything was trash. Trevor sat and talked me through until the early morning, yet by the end, I felt stronger, more capable like I somehow believed in myself more just by having him believe in me so wholeheartedly.

It also inspired me to create new art, pieces that have excited me and made me feel things I haven't felt in so long. I finally feel ready to take everything on.

Trevor finally announced his retirement last week, and he's been the most relaxed I've seen him. He seems so light, so carefree, and it's a good look on him. We went to Sunday dinner this last week with his parents, and seeing their interactions and the way they laugh makes me so happy to know that he has that kind of relationship with his family. His mom thanked me for being a positive impact in her son's life, even if I think it's the other way around.

She said that Trevor had always been an honest man; that's the only thing he'd ever cared about, so finding a woman who truly cares about him is all she'd ever wanted for her son.

But now he and I are on our way to meet up with my parents. Apparently, they talked to Tom's parents after Trevor had a few words with my mother. They finally started to put all the pieces together, realizing they had it all wrong, and they wanted to meet Trevor and me for dinner. They want to know the whole story, and my newly found confidence is definitely coming in handy, giving me the courage to tell them *why* I'm divorcing him and *why* I want sole custody of Addy, at least for now.

It definitely helps that they already have a bad taste in their mouth about Tom. I guess my father needed to get some paperwork from Tom last week and spent over an hour trying to call Lena and got no response. So, when he headed back to the office and went into Tom's office and found them both naked, let's just say he was less than pleased.

"Are you sure you want to do this?" I ask, squeezing Trevor's hand in my own. He's refused to let go of my hand since we got in the cab, and honestly, I'm more thankful than he realizes.

"Of course, kitten. I'll go anywhere with you. Remember, they love you. They're your parents. Hear them out before you make any decisions."

"Fine, Mr. Smarty-pants. But if I'm following your rules, I better get spankings tonight. I'm feeling wound up and feisty," I grumble, earning me a swat on the butt as we walk into the restaurant.

It's easy to find my parents, and as we approach them, they both stand up nervously.

"Hi," my father says, looking between Trevor and me. "It's nice to meet you, Trevor. Thank you for treating my Ellie so well."

My heart stops as Trevor squeezes my hand, the sadness in my father's voice immediately getting to me.

They shake hands, and we all sit down. Surprisingly, it's my mother who starts.

"I told my husband about when I saw you, and you were taking care of Ms. Addy. It was... different, the way you stood up for her, but I respected you for it. Tom was never that way. He went with the flow of conversations and never stood for anything. My Ellie deserves someone to stand by her proudly."

With that bomb being dropped by my mother, the rest of our meal goes rather smoothly. I told them about my marriage with Tom and his lack of respect for our vows and our daughter, and they apologized for not supporting me.

It was cathartic and hard, but I feel relief at no longer keeping secrets from them. Although it sucked that they didn't support me, I realize I could've fixed that by showing them what I had on Tom, but I couldn't bring myself to start that battle before.

They asked Trevor a million questions, and by the time the night ended, I had to pull Trevor out of the restaurant because he found out my father loves hockey.

I feel like things have been going well lately, almost too well, so I'm constantly waiting for the other shoe to drop. So, when Trevor and I are walking off the elevator after dinner, and I see an envelope taped to my door, with handwriting I'd recognize anywhere, I get the sinking feeling that my nightmare is coming true. Grabbing the envelope, I tear it open, the feel of Trevor's eyes on mine the entire time.

"Come with me. We'll go to my place. I'm not sure I trust yours right now," Trevor says, his voice solemn like he has the same feeling as me. He's no longer the bright and cheery Trevor I know and that hurts.

Knowing Tom is causing his solemnness and that in some ways, I am too, is heartbreaking. I hate it.

Tom is officially raining on my fucking parade.

He's pissed about Trevor and me, especially after Addy told Tom's parents about everything Trevor did for her with the Disney night. My sweet five-year-old even did the damn doe eyes and told them her daddy had promised to take her to Disney World but changed his mind last minute.

Apparently, it's my fault that his father is starting to question his character and asking questions about how he was as a father and husband. Tom's dad has always said that how he is as a partner in life shows how he will be as a partner for the firm. This does not bode well for him.

*Blindside Love*

So now, instead of facing it head-on and accepting responsibility for his actions, he's trying to take further control of my life and get custody of Addy by ruining Trevor's reputation, as well as further ruining mine. It's more upsetting that he wants to hurt Trevor, someone who hasn't done anything to him, a man who has kept his reputation clear his entire life, working hard to be honest and positive, and now Tom wants to ruin that.

The envelope is filled with printed text messages between Tom and me, but they completely warp the situation. Instead of him looking like the lying cheater he is, he looks like the scorned one. *He* looks like the one brokenhearted from my cheating with Trevor. *He* looks like the one who was fighting for our marriage, fighting to get me to pay attention to our daughter.

It's all lies, it's obvious, but it's just enough to hurt Trevor's reputation. Taint something that's never been tarnished before, right when he's letting go of hockey and trying to find a new place in this world. Tom knows exactly what he's doing, spinning everything on me to make it look like he was the one that got hurt, that Trevor came in and stole me from him. Even worse, though, it makes it look like Trevor has been pushing me to spend less and less time with my daughter, which couldn't be further from the truth, but it will *definitely* impact custody.

I'm not sure if I'm more upset that Tom is trying to make me look like a bad mom or pissed that he's actually this much of a piece of shit to try to ruin our lives just because he doesn't want to face the consequences of his actions. He's threatening the reputation, livelihood, and integrity of the one man who came into my life and *hasn't* hurt me. I can't let Tom ruin Trevor's reputation or his career; it's not fair, but I know Tom, and I know he's serious about releasing this.

The only thing I know is that I'm going to fix this, but won't let this hurt Trevor. So, when I look up at him, see him looking through everything on the counter, and see the sadness in his eyes, I know what I have to do.

I should've cleaned up my mess before I got involved with him, and that's on me.

He's far too sweet, too loyal to leave to protect himself. I'll break my own heart if it means I'm protecting him. I have to play the bad guy, the villain in my own story, because I let this situation go on with Tom for far too long. It's time to end it, because I won't let anyone else get hurt.

"Ellie—" he starts, but I can't listen. I can't hear him try to make me feel better about this when I can see the fear in his eyes. He knows what bad PR like this can do to someone.

"I'm sorry," I start, his face falling like he can read my mind. "You should've never gotten involved in this mess. I should've waited until the smoke had cleared before involving you in my life. I'm so sorry."

"You have nothing to be sorry for, Ellie. You're not the one doing this."

"You're right, I'm not. But it's my fault he's including you in this. It's my fault he's trying to spin everything to make us look bad. It's one thing if he fucks with my reputation, he's already tried that. I mean, at least now I have my father on my side. But I won't let him use you."

"What are you saying?"

"I'm saying that if you're not in the picture, he has no leverage. No ammo. He can't destroy our reputation if we're not together. He can't destroy yours. I won't let that happen."

If I thought he looked hurt before, I was wrong. His eyes fall, immediately watering as he bites his cheek. I hate the hurt and the despair I see in his eyes. Even worse though, is the emptiness. It's the look he had the first day I met him in the elevator. I stared at him, unable to move because that emptiness called to me. It resembled the emptiness inside of me.

But knowing I'm the reason that look has returned is almost enough to make me take it back... almost. But I refuse to be selfish when it comes to his heart because he's the one who stitched mine back together.

"You realize you're letting him win, right? That you're letting him control your life again. You're stronger than that, Ellie. *We're* stronger than that."

I feel my tears immediately start to fall at his words. I know he's right, but I *can't* let him get hurt. Tom is ruthless. He only cares about himself, and I know he won't stop until he gets what he wants.

"I'm sorry you think that. For months, I've had someone telling me to believe in myself and that I'm capable of hard things. Now, I'm trying to prove it to myself. Prove that I can go up against Tom and win, and not let the man I love get hurt in the process. You knew I was damaged goods when you met me; you just put me back together in a pretty way."

I grab all the papers, shoving them into the manilla

folder, tears streaming down my face as I know I have to walk away, walk away from this man who wants to fight with me, fight for me, next to me.

But I can't. Not until I can fight for myself.

I need to show myself I'm strong. That I can protect those around me, and that means doing it on my own.

"Goodbye, Trevor. Thank you for loving me, showing me my worth, and teaching me how to fight for myself." I walk over to him, pressing a kiss on his face as he stares at me in disbelief. "I'll never know how to thank you for that."

As I walk away, I feel his stare on me. I hold my breath, doing everything I can to not turn around. It isn't until I'm opening the door and stepping out that he says, "Don't go."

I feel my heart crumble, my legs feel weak, but I run to my apartment, the one that doesn't feel like home anymore. Slamming the door, I fall to the ground, letting the tears fall as the reality of what I did slams into me, knowing damn well I just walked out on the only good thing to ever happen to me.

# Chapter 28

## *Trevor*

I thought I knew what pain was.

I thought breaking my leg in high school snowboarding was painful, but it wasn't.

I thought taking a stick to the face and needing more stitches than I could count was painful, but it wasn't.

Yeah, those injuries hurt, and in the moment, they sucked, but it's always been skin-deep, a type of pain that you could manage. This is a soul-deep, all-consuming pain that makes me feel like I can't breathe. It feels like my heart is going a million miles an hour, yet so weak it could stop at any moment, and the only person that can give me relief is the same person who caused the pain in the first place.

It's been four days. Four days of unimaginable pain and I'm not sure how much longer I can hold myself together.

The first day was hard. I laid in bed all night waiting for her to text me and tell me she was wrong. Every noise I heard in my place made me wonder if she was knocking on my door, coming to tell me she couldn't live without me either, but she never came.

We had a game that next day, and I was able to put on a front long enough that no one on the team questioned anything, but I definitely racked up some time in the sin bin from my short temper on the ice.

My team may not have said anything, but my friends definitely did afterward. They've been texting and calling since that game, but I haven't had the energy to answer. I haven't had the energy to answer anyone's calls.

My parents have both tried calling and texting. They immediately knew something was off after the second fight that I initiated that night, but I didn't want to talk. My agent, Liam, has called me every day too, but I've sent them all to voicemail.

We have to be back on the ice tomorrow night, and I know I need to put in some work to not look like a total train wreck in my second to last game, but I'm struggling to find it in me to care.

It was different getting on the ice, knowing I had someone watching me besides just my family and friends. Ellie and Addy weren't watching because they loved the sport, they were watching for *me*. Because they cared about *me*, and that made me look forward to my time on the ice.

But now it just feels empty, like me as I lay on my couch for the fourth day in a row watching the Disney channel because these songs are catchy, and it makes me feel like my girls are with me, even if I know they're less than two hundred feet from me in an apartment they shouldn't be at.

They should be here. With me.

*Knock, knock.*

I get up begrudgingly, not truly caring who's on the other side of the door but knowing anyone who has taken the time to come here won't stop until I answer.

When I look through the hole, though, I see the only face I kind of want to see right now. Rex.

Opening the door, I let him in, watching as he surveys the place before turning to assess me.

"You look like shit, dude," Rex says as he makes his way to my fridge, grabbing two waters and passing me one. "I'm guessing you look just about as great as you feel, am I right?"

I just nod, taking a swig of my water as he waits.

"I think that much is obvious, but if you need me to spell it out for you, just tell me," I grumble, annoyed that I'm even standing, that I'm talking to anyone because all I want is to talk to her.

"I think I do," Rex says, a smug look on his face as he looks around. "You're obviously unhappy. My guess is it's because of your lady, based on the state of you *and* your apartment."

"Yep. We're through," I tell him with a shrug.

"Care to tell me why, or are we just going to pretend this is a conversation when, in actuality, you're just going to be grunting and nodding for 95% of my questions."

I roll my eyes, but decide it'll be easier if I just explain.

"You've been spending way too much time with Sawyer and the girls, you're turning into gossip girls just like them," I say, hopping up on my counter.

"Oh well, it keeps me young," he grumbles. "Plus, I just know it's going to come again when Rory gets older, so I guess I might as well get used to it now."

It hits me that Addy was going to bring that to my life. That I was going to get to watch her get older, watch her grow into a teenager, but Ellie stopped that.

And I want to hate her for that. I want to be mad that I won't get to experience that now, but I can't. I saw the look in her eyes, I saw the pain she felt when she made the choice.

I hate the choice. It's not the choice I would've ever made, but it wasn't mine to make. I love her enough to support her, even if that means letting her handle something like this on her own.

I tell Rex about it all. I tell him about Ellie and me, how we talked about our feelings for each other, our love. I told him about Tom and how he hurt her and everything he's done or hasn't done for Addy. Then I told him about Tom and his threats, how she ended things before returning to her apartment.

I knocked on her door. I knocked for fifteen minutes when I heard her crying, but she never answered, so I finally went home.

When I finish, he's watching me, flipping his phone in his hand as he thinks.

"So, I just have one question for you," he says casually. "Are you going to continue being the dumbest smart person in the world or are you going to pull your head out of your ass and go get the girl."

"But she told me not to. No one ever listens to her or respects her choices. I'm no better than them if I make

*Blindside Love*

decisions for her, even worse if I don't respect the decisions she's making," I growl out, annoyed that he's making me question myself. I wanted to fight for her, but I convinced myself that to respect her, I needed to respect her decisions, even if that meant losing her.

But should I have fought?

"I get that. And I also get why you're respecting that. I think you're both being stupid and that *both* of you need to pull your heads out of your asses. She's fighting for you while trying to fight for herself. Don't lose a girl over her trying to play hero. *Fight with* her. She doesn't need a hero; she needs a partner, but so do you."

I think about what he's saying, knowing he's trying to be a rational voice, but my irrational brain is fighting him right now.

But I get it. I see what he's saying, and my instinct is telling me that he's right. That I need to fight for her. That I need to show her that she's worth fighting for, that they both are. That I'd rather have an imperfect reputation in the public eye than a perfect one without them.

The weight that was on my shoulders feels lighter, yet my heart feels heavier knowing I need to get my shit together if I want any chance of convincing her that I'm worth fighting for too.

"So, what do I do?" I ask, needing direction from my best friend who's faced his fair share of troubles in life but who's always come out on the other side looking better.

"Truthfully? Change your clothes, go for a run, then take a shower; you stink, that alone would have her send you packing."

"Fuck you," I grumble as I make my way to my room to change.

By the time I come out, ready to hit the pavement, Rex is picking up my apartment, headphones in one hand and a garbage bag in the other as he walks around, trying to make my apartment less of a disaster.

I don't wave, knowing he'll probably still be here when I get back. This is what we do; we're family, and family always picks the other one up when they've been blindsided, whether on the ice or by love.

---

AN HOUR LATER, I'D RUN ALL AROUND THE CITY. I did throw up in the bushes once because I believed in my abilities a little too much, but after six miles, I'd still call it a win. As I head into the lobby, my shirt sticking to me from sweat, I go towards the elevator, hoping just this once to *not* see Ellie. Not yet at least.

I need time to shower and put myself together before I go find her and tell her I'm *not* letting her face this alone, that I'm with her every step of the way.

When the elevator opens, it's not empty, but instead of being Ellie, it's her father. He smiles kindly when he sees me, immediately taking in my state. I've exchanged my normal scruff for more of an unkempt beard, which I'm sure is a dead giveaway for the state I'm in.

Seeing as he's coming down from her apartment, he probably already knows.

"Hello, sir. It's nice to see you." I smile, letting him step out before walking onto the elevator.

When I turn, though, he's standing outside of the elevator, his arm holding it open.

"I'm telling you this as a father, as someone who's fucked up a lot with his little girl but who will do anything to see her smile. Don't listen to my daughter; she loves to be the villain of her own story, she always has, and that's why she walked away from you. It's why she let us believe Tom for as long as she did, even though she could prove everything she hid from us. She tries to be strong, to be enough, but I've seen the way she looks at you. See the way her face lights up when you're around. That night at dinner, when I first met you, I knew immediately that you two were different, and it's because you're a team."

"With all due respect, sir, she left me. She broke up with me. I didn't want this."

"Like I said, son. She's thinking with her brain, not her heart. The thing is, you are her heart, which is why she's protecting you. Ignore it. Clean yourself up and meet me at this restaurant," John says, handing me a business card for an Italian place down the street. "I might just be meeting Carl, Tom's father, there for dinner. Be there by 6:45. The main event happens at seven."

With a wink, he walks away, letting the elevator doors shut.

What the fuck was that?

The only thing I am certain of is that I'm taking his advice. First shower, then restaurant, then hopefully, I can get my girls back.

# Chapter 29

## *Ellie*

Everyone talks about how hard breakups are, and it's so true, but I've never experienced a greater heartbreak than walking away from someone I'm confident is my other half.

I don't believe in soul mates, but honestly, I'm positive that man is the other half of me; as delusional as that sounds, I know it. Walking away from him was easily the hardest thing I've ever done, but I'd do it again in a heartbeat if I knew it would protect him from Tom.

That's what I keep telling myself as I sit in the back of the cab, heading down the street to meet Tom. I feel sick to my stomach knowing I have to play nice, even if just for a while. After I got the envelope of "evidence" left on my door, I called my dad immediately. Once I told him what Tom was doing, I asked for his help.

To get Tom's dad on board, I needed him to hear it firsthand, so I messaged Tom and asked him to meet me at this Italian restaurant down the street. It has booths with curtains so you can have total privacy. My plan is to have our fathers in a booth next to mine and Tom's, and hopefully make him comfortable enough that he decides to spill a little for them to hear.

The plan sounded smart when I thought of it, but right now, it just seems like a recipe for disaster. I'm not calm enough to pull this off.

But then I remember what Trevor told me. How he believed in me, how he knew how strong I was.

If he can believe in me, so can I.

As the cab pulls up to the curb, I take a deep breath, pay my fare, and step out onto the street. It's time to get my fucking life back.

---

I WALK INTO THE RESTAURANT, SMILING AT THE hostess as I walk back, heading back to the booth I reserved. Tom's already waiting, his annoyed look firmly in place as he stares down at his phone, a glass of scotch in his other hand. When I sit across from him, he looks up.

"Well, hello, Eleanor. Don't you look... nice," he sneers. I know he's lying because I specifically picked out this outfit to irritate him. Why my clothes have such an impact on his life, I'll never know. But being the petty bitch I know I am, I wore the overalls he despises and space buns because he always said I looked ridiculous with them. I'm also wearing my Converse just to twist the knife a bit more.

"No need for fake pleasantries, Tom. We both know

you hate the way I look," I say, pouring myself a glass of wine. A very full glass of wine.

"Then I guess we should just cut to the chase. I need something from you, and you need me to not ruin your life. I see you took me seriously, though, breaking things off with your little boyfriend."

"This doesn't involve him, it never has, and it never will. Leave him out of it." I clench my teeth, wanting nothing more than to throw something at him, but I can't do anything until he talks. "Unless you want to finally talk about Lena."

"What about her? We've been over this. It was nothing. Just stress relief during the day with a very willing participant."

"So, fooling around with Lena daily, while married to me, wasn't cheating because it was stress relief?" I mutter, doing my best not to scream just yet.

"See, you're starting to get it," Tom says, leaning forward, his arms on the table. "It never needed to be the big deal you made it out to be.

"So, what do you need from me?" I ask, hoping I've let him talk enough that he's let his guard down a bit and will shoot himself in the foot.

"I need you to take the blame. I need you to say that you cheated, that you left me heartbroken," Tom says, taking a sip of his scotch as he looks down at his phone, barely paying attention to me.

"Remind me again why I would do this for you."

"Because I have control over the one thing you care about. Addison. I'll sign over my rights. We both know I never wanted to be a father anyway. I'll just blame it on her, that she only wanted to be with her mother and that I wanted to make her happy and all that bullshit. But you have to give me what I need first."

I grab my wine again, taking a very, very large swallow, watching as Tom looks back at his phone, probably texting some woman, thinking this conversation will be over soon. It will be, but not in the way he's thinking.

"No," I say, sitting up tall, remembering to breathe, and reminding myself over and over to believe in myself as much as Trevor did.

Tom looks up, confusion and shock written across his face like he can't quite believe what he just heard.

"Eleanor, think about this."

"I already have. The answer is no. If you want our daughter, take me to court. Either way, sign the divorce papers, and let's get on with this. I'm done with your games. I've already turned everything over to my lawyers; they have all of the true evidence and they confirmed their authenticity. They'll be passing it along to our parents, helping them get the full picture of what actually happened in our marriage and your lack of parenting."

"Why can't you just do this one thing for me, Eleanor? After everything I've done for you—"

I snap. "Everything you've done for *me*? Buddy, let's get one thing straight here: the only thing you've done for me is give me a migraine. You forced me to be this picture-perfect trophy wife who couldn't work, couldn't follow her own dreams, all because you deemed yours more important than mine."

"That isn't true," Tom sneers.

*Blindside Love*

"Oh, but isn't it? I quit my job because you said no wife of yours would work since it would make people think you weren't providing well enough for our family on your own. You wouldn't let me pursue my dreams because it would take time away from me being at your beck and call when I wasn't solely raising our daughter because you chose not to give two shits about her while you worked your life away and stuck your dick in anything with a pulse that *wasn't* your wife. I wonder if they all had to fake their orgasms like I had to for six years."

"Fuck you, you vindictive little bit—"

He doesn't get to finish his sentence as Trevor comes around the corner, his fist slamming directly into Tom's nose.

"What the fuck!" Tom shouts as blood pours out of his nose, but Trevor grabs him by his shirt collar and slams him against the wall, splattering blood on the nice white walls.

"If you fucking ever, and I mean *ever*, speak about either of my girls like that again, you'll be waking up in a hospital in a body cast wishing I'd have killed you instead," Trevor growls, nearly face to face with Tom who looks like he's about to poop his pants from fear.

"That sounds like a threat," Tom sneers, but our fathers take that moment to step out of their booth. His eyes widen in shock, but he covers it quickly, working hard on playing the pity card. "Did you hear what he said to me?"

"No, actually, son, I didn't," Carl says, his teeth clenched as he stands there, his feet spread and his hands in his pockets. You can't deny that Carl is a big man, and right now, he's a very pissed-off man. "I was too concerned with everything I heard *prior* to what Mr. Adams here said to you. In fact, if we're being honest, I was wondering if I should fire you first or punch you for disrespecting a woman like that. Either way, I'm glad he did it so I didn't have to."

"Fired? Excuse me? For what?" Tom says, panic crossing his face, but I'm staring at Trevor, who's looking down at his fist and standing to the side of the booth, almost like he's nervous.

I want to go over there and check on him, but first, I need to finish this.

"Let's just say that you lack integrity and basic human decency, and at our firm, those are requirements. The way you treated Ellie *and* Addy is disgraceful, and until you man up, you not only do not have a job at my firm, but you also don't have a place in my home. I love you, son, but I did not raise you this way."

Tom turns red in the face, almost like he wants to argue, but instead, he looks down and grabs the pen, signing both the divorce papers and the papers that start the process of giving me sole custody of my daughter.

Would I like him to no longer have rights just so I have peace of mind that he can't come in and disrupt her happiness at the drop of a hat? Of course, but I'm also not stupid enough to want her father to give her up completely. I hope he grows up and decides to be the father she deserves, but I'm not holding my breath.

Without another word, he turns and walks out of the restaurant, leaving me wondering what the fuck just happened. I immediately look back towards Trevor, noticing my dad and Carl are talking quietly, probably discussing the firm, so I probably have a few minutes.

"What are you doing here?" I ask bluntly, still shocked he's here. I want to reach out and touch him just to make sure he's not fake. How the hell did he even know this was happening? Even better question is why the hell he cared after I broke his heart. "I-I ended things. I told you I wanted to do this alone."

"Kitten, when you ended things, I respected it. I thought that was me making the right choice, respecting you by respecting your choices. You wanted to protect me, to face him alone, and I let you do that. But you made the mistake of letting me fall in love with you, kitten, and unfortunately, I don't go away that easily. Once I'm on your team, you're never alone."

"But..."

"You didn't say I couldn't be here. A very kind gentleman invited me to come enjoy a glass of bourbon so I could be here with you. See, we all know you're excellent at self-sabotaging, and well, your father decided what we had was special enough to risk pissing you off by talking to me."

I look at my father, who has the decency to look embarrassed, but his smile tells me it's true. I love my father so much, he will always do what's best for me, even if it means protecting me from me. The only reason he didn't these last couple of years was because I didn't communicate that there was an actual problem.

Trevor takes a step towards me, his eyes locked on me as his hand reaches to grab mine. I want to step forward, to trust him, but what have I done to deserve him?

"But why? Why are you fighting for me? For us? What have I done to deserve this?"

"I love you. It's plain and simple. That means I fight for you, I fight for us, even when you can't. Because I believe in you. I believe in us."

"I love you too. Does this mean you forgive me for all of that? I'm sorry. I got scared. I was just trying to protect you from him."

"I get it. But you don't get to do that again. Next time, we fight it together. You have to promise to work on letting people help you. You're awful at it," Trevor says.

"Oh god," I groan, not wanting this lecture right now. My father's already given it to me once.

"Don't talk to him right now. He's mad at you about this too," Trevor says, pulling me up against him.

"You're ridiculous," I murmur, my words dying on his lips as he kisses me gently.

"You're stubborn," he growls, the vibrations firm against my lips, his tone dangerous, but then I remember we're being watched. By my father, no less. Pulling back, I smile as he glares. "Why the hell is it so damn hard for you to accept help?"

"It just is!" I whine. "I guess I've been conditioned that way these last few years. It might take a little while to break old habits. But I'm willing to try if you are."

"Always, kitten. You're not getting rid of me that easily."

## Blindside Love

It's crazy how life can change in twenty-four hours, how you can go from being in the darkest days of your life and feeling sadness and desperation like never before to remembering what it feels like to laugh and smile and just feel loved.

Trevor came home with me after the restaurant last night. Once we talked to my father and Carl, they told me they would help me proceed with the divorce, ensuring that they would get it done, cut and dry and that I had more than enough to take care of Addy and me.

Carl also mentioned that he was going to personally handle the custody agreement. He wanted to ensure that if Tom ever showed interest in taking a role in Addy's life, it had to be consistent and frequent before any legal changes were made.

I respected him more than I ever expected to for putting his granddaughter before his own son. It's not easy to do, but I'm thankful he's on our team.

I've felt more support in the last twenty-four hours than I've felt in years. Between my father and Carl helping me with all the legal hoops and Carl putting his son in his place, Tom's tune has completely changed, and he's been *much* more accommodating already. My mom has also been calling and checking in with me, but I haven't gotten back to her much lately. I will, but I'm just doing it on my time.

She always wants things when she wants them, but this time, she has to wait. I've spent the last eighteen hours tangled in the sheets with Trevor, making up for lost time.

He peppered kisses and promises on my skin all

through the night, reminding me how safe I was with him. Both my heart and my body are safe with this man.

It's in these moments I remember what it feels like to be *exactly* where you're supposed to be. Unfortunately for me, in forty-five minutes, I'm supposed to be at the studio for my very first art show, and I'm nervous enough that I'm positive I'm going to pass out. Or sweat through my dress.

I feel his body press against me as I try to put my shoes on, but I'm too shaky to stand upright. His hands find my hips, holding me still as he presses my back into him. He holds me while I step into each heel, his nose nuzzling in my neck, pressing soft kisses along my throat and collarbone, making me wish we could skip tonight and go back to the bedroom.

"No, kitten. We can celebrate tonight. Right now, it's about you. Show yourself off to the world," Trevor murmurs into my neck, reading my mind and knowing my thoughts before I can even voice them. "Tonight's going to go by so quickly. We'll be back here naked before you know it."

I groan, knowing he's right. He steps back to grab my jacket and holds it up for me to slip into.

Knowing Trevor is going to be with me tonight has me feeling much safer, more confident, yet I'm still very nervous about the event. Ever since I broke things off with Trevor, my anxiety has been through the roof. I go to sleep nauseous; I wake up nauseous, it hasn't mattered what I've done, nothing has helped my nerves or my stomach.

I figured now that we're back together that my

anxiety would chill out a bit, but unfortunately, it seems to be the opposite. My stomach is still turning as we walk down the street to Betty's studio.

When we stop out front, I notice Betty standing right inside, but Trevor turns me to him, a look of pride on his face as he stares down at me.

"I'm so proud of you, kitten. So proud of how strong you are, for everything that you've accomplished, and everything you've yet to accomplish. No more worries. Walk through those doors knowing that everyone inside that studio is here to see your art, your creations. That's something to be proud of."

I smile, turning to look at the studio where I see that people have already gone in, groups of people mingling as others are walking around looking at everything on the walls. It's surreal. Turning back to Trevor, I lean up and press a quick kiss against his lips before placing my hand in his and heading into the studio.

As we mingle, people stop me and ask me questions, congratulating me. I realize that this is the first time in my life that I feel accomplished, like I did something on my own. Something I could be proud of outside of motherhood. This is for me, and these people inside, they're smiling, talking about my art, *buying* my art, and I realize that none of this would've been possible without Trevor.

Trevor helped me believe in myself when I didn't want to. He helped me find the art that I'd buried deep inside of me. He returned the color that I'd lost and made everything vibrant. I stop suddenly as we're walking around, looking up at Trevor, I squeeze his hand in mine.

"Thank you. For believing in me."

# Chapter 30

## *Trevor*

Tonight's the night.

Tonight is my last night as a New York Cyclone, and instead of feeling sad, I feel excited. Hopeful. Invigorated.

I always thought that the day I put on my skates for the last time would be awful and that I would be scared. But I feel ready. I feel like as this one door closes, a million more are opening for me to choose from, and the possibilities are exciting.

I can't help but think it's the cute pink-haired girl I met earlier this year who's having this effect on me. That her being in my life isn't the reason that I'm excited about retiring, not sad and depressed.

She's my reason. She's the rush, the excitement that had been missing from my life. I'd been sailing through life clueless of what I needed, but everything clicked into place the second I met her. She's my reason to push on and be my best. She's why I wake up every morning with a smile on my face and go to sleep every night excited for our next adventure.

When I used to think about retirement, I had this fear that everything I've worked my entire life for would all be for nothing, and that scared the fuck out of me. I thought my life was going to be over.

I realize now it's only just beginning.

As we head down towards the ice, Cade, Miles, and Harris all come over to me. It's been the four of us playing together—plus Rex before he got injured—for years. Some of us started the team together, Cade and Miles coming later, but damn it's been a wild ride.

"Thanks, you guys, for everything."

"We just want you to know that we got your back, on and off the ice. Hockey is our thing, but it's not our friendship," Miles says, hitting my skate with his stick.

"Always, brother. We may not play hockey together after tonight, but we're much more than teammates," Cade says, his usual tight-lipped response traded for a more heartfelt response.

"Thanks. I thought it'd be much harder, but I realize I'm just giving up the game, not the relationships. Plus, I'm gaining more time with my girls, so to me, it's all a win."

They nod and agree, smiling as we stand there.

"Are we going to kiss and celebrate or head out onto the ice? We have a game to win, and I'm itching to celebrate tonight," Harris says as he starts to walk back down to the ice.

We laugh as we follow, knowing this may be the end

of our time together on the ice, but our friendship is far from over.

Cade makes his way to the goal, ready to go, while the rest of us skate into position. Being out here on the ice tonight feels different. I have my entire family here tonight, my sister, Sophie, included. She was able to fly in this morning, as well as Ellie and Addy plus Rex, Max, and their whole gang, all sitting in a suite watching the game. It's exciting. I feel complete knowing all the people I care about are supporting me, regardless of whether I play hockey or not.

Looking up, I see Addy and Ellie in the suite. Ellie is pointing me out for Addy. I love the smile they both get on their face as she sees me. I wave, smiling before turning back to the game. The first two periods are over in what feels like seconds. Cade is able to keep everything out of the net, but unfortunately, so is Sanchez. Going into the third period zero to zero isn't ideal, but it's an easy fix—theoretically, of course.

We just need to score.

We try everything we can think of when it's our turn on the ice, Miles and I skating out there together while Harris and Cade work to keep their shots *out* of our net, but fifteen minutes into the third, we're still scoreless. At this point, we're all getting frustrated. We're getting cheap shots, dropped gloves, and more penalties than usual, and we're just all fighting to get the puck into the net.

Sitting on the bench waiting for our next ice time, I look up to the suite, unable to keep my eyes away for too long. There's something about watching my parents, sister, and Ellie talk, smile, and laugh together. It further solidifies my thought that she was made to be a part of my life, to be my other half.

She's the one I want to spend the rest of my life with and grow a family with.

"We're up," Miles says, snapping me back to the bright lights and fast skates.

Hopping over the boards, we hit the ice, changing quickly, the other team wasn't able to switch in time, so they're all gassed. In a lucky break for them, though, Miles slips up, losing the puck, and Thompson from Nashville steals the puck.

He breaks away, making it one on one with Cade, but like the brick wall he is, he stops it without hesitation, passing the puck back out to Miles. I skate towards the goal, hoping Miles notices as it's a clear shot to me and maybe, just maybe, we could do it intimate to break away.

He must notice me out of the corner of his eye as he skates to the left, passing right, directly to me. I get the puck, turning to head towards the goal, just Sanchez and me going head-to-head.

I skate towards him, knowing his defenders are right on my heels, but I'm faster, I have more energy, and I'm not stopping unless I get this damn puck in that net. I skate right, shooting wide, but fortunately Harris gets it, shooting it again, but it bounces off the goal.

This time though, it comes directly to me. I hit it without stopping, shooting right to the corner of the goal. As it flies through the air, I feel myself holding my breath. When the buzzer goes off and the light shines, I drop to my knees, feeling the weight of tonight fall from my shoulders.

We spend the last bit of time trying to hold them off, and thankfully we do.

As I skate off the ice, I realize that this is the last time I'm getting to do this, yet as I look around the arena at the flashing lights, the crowd still cheering, I realize the only thing I'm looking for right now are my girls, and I realize I'm not missing out on anything by giving up hockey. I'm gaining time with my family, and that's invaluable.

The team and all our friends and family are heading into the city. We rented a rooftop bar to celebrate. I shower quickly, more excited to celebrate the end of an incredible season than we are to start cleaning everything out today.

By the time I make it down to the tunnel, my girls are ready and waiting for me, and I can't help feeling like even though I thought everything was over, it's only just beginning.

When I walk out of the locker room, I see my parents smiling and waiting for me. After hugging them and listening to them tell me how proud they are, I can't help but feel like I'm back in grade school, loving the way my parents support me and tell me how proud they are. I can't believe that I was questioning everything, questioning their support when I made this decision, but now I realize just how silly I was being.

After my parents, I see Ellie and Addy standing with Rex and the rest of the gang, and the excitement in Addy's face makes my whole year. She comes running down the hall, leaping up into my arms, and I love the way my jersey looks on her, almost as much as I love the way it looks on her mom.

But as I look at Ellie, Addy jumps down, running back to her mom, and I realize she's not wearing the jersey I had delivered. No, this one doesn't have my last name on it, although it still has my number. I see Ellie looking at me, nervously standing there in the middle of all of our friends and family, and that's when I see it.

*Big Sister* is on her back.

I freeze, my heart stops, and I feel like my palms are sweating. *Am I reading that right? Does this mean what I think it does?*

It's at this moment that I realize *everyone* is watching us.

I make my way towards them, still too shocked to speak, but as I get closer, I see Ellie is crying happy tears. Her tears mirror the emotions I'm feeling, making me believe that everything I've done in my life, every choice I've made, every little thing that has gone wrong, has all been leading me to this exact moment.

*This is the moment my life begins.*

*My family, my girls, and soon, our family of four.*

Without a second thought, I step closer, wrapping my arms around Ellie as I lift her in a hug. Unable to contain my excitement I spin her around, kissing her without a second thought of anyone else around us. It's quick but filled with promise and so much damn love.

When I finally stop and set her down, Addy's giggle warms my heart immediately as she runs over to hug my leg

Ellie turns to me, nervousness on her face as she

wipes her tears away. "Is this okay?" she asks cautiously, almost like she expects me to be mad, but there isn't anything she could do right now that would upset me. Do I have questions? Hell yeah, but not because I'm upset, because it's unexpected.

But sometimes, even in the moments you get completely blindsided, you can't help but love the outcome.

"Yes, it's okay, kitten. It's more than okay. I'm on top of the world right now, and it's all because of you,"

With that, we turn and look at all of our family and friends and walk out hand in hand with Addy, ready to spend the rest of the night celebrating an incredible season, a long career now over, and the new life that I've been dreaming of.

# Epilogue

## Trevor

Bacon. That's the first thing I smell when I walk into the diner to meet Rex for brunch and I feel instantly lighter. Somehow that smell is comforting and makes me feel more relaxed, probably because how can anyone be grumpy when eating bacon? Although my conversation with Rex earlier still has me on edge.

He told me he had something he wanted to talk to me about, but said Sawyer and Ro were still home and he couldn't talk about it. It was annoying because I hate not knowing, but he said that Sawyer and Ro had dance class this afternoon and Ellie and Addy were going shopping today so now we're out to brunch.

At least here I can have bacon. At six months pregnant, Ellie hasn't been a huge fan of the smell of bacon lately which means my usual weekly french toast with extra bacon has had to be put on hold. Heading past the host desk I look around for Rex, spotting him in a booth towards the back, waving me over, his usual half-assed smile nowhere to be seen.

*Interesting.*

As I slide into the booth a waitress walks by and sets down water and menus for the two of us with a quick promise to be right back to take our order. *No rush here, I want the gossip first.*

"Hi," Rex grumbles as he pulls the menu towards him, feigning interest in what he's getting when we both know he's getting a traditional breakfast with extra bacon.

I just stare at him though, not playing into his game. We both know I'm here for a reason and I'm too damn nosy to be patient. His eyes slowly look up from his menu and he doesn't look angry, or sad. He looks nervous. Excited? Fuck I don't know.

"What's going on?" I question, unable to read this situation well. "Spit it out."

"I'm…I'm going to ask Sawyer to marry me," Rex says, his voice filled with trepidation although I see his little smirk and his eyes brightening with excitement as he talks.

"Cutting straight to the point, but that's awesome," I say, smiling wide knowing that two of my favorite people in the world found each other and I couldn't be happier for them. "But why do you look like you're terrified?"

"Because I'm supposed to be meeting with Max in a couple of hours, you know, to ask his permission since their father sucks," Rex grumbles. "The little fucker is going to give me shit even if he knows damn well he's going to end up saying yes. I think it's in his blood to make my life difficult, especially regarding Sawyer."

"Well, that's your damn fault for dating your player's sister in the first place," I smirk, loving the way his eye twitches when he gets stressed.

He's fun to fuck with because his bark is far worse than his bite.

"Fuck off, Adams. I don't know why I'm stressed. What if he says no? What if *she* says no? This whole thing is fucked. I don't like not being in control," Rex says as his face falls in his hands, tugging on his hair.

I can't help it. I laugh.

Which only pisses him off more.

"Oh stop it, I'm just kidding. Anyone with two eyes can see how perfect you two are for each other, and Sawyer damn well knows it. She's going to say yes in a heartbeat dude. And Max? If he says no he knows you'll whoop his ass, besides, he loves you too, especially for his sister," I tell him with a shrug watching as he just stares at me.

All of a sudden he takes a deep breath and leans back, his eyes flaring brighter as a little smirk starts to play on his lips. Cocky fucker.

"We are pretty perfect, aren't we?" he smirks, his eyes gleaming like he's realizing just how silly he's being. "I know it's stupid. I really do, I just think until I hear her say the words and see the ring on her finger, it won't feel real."

"I get that. But I'm excited for you guys, taking that next step," I say with a smile. "Although I wish I could see Max when he gives you a hard time."

"Not a chance. Speaking of the next steps, I know you and Ellie have a lot going on seeing as you're just a few months away from baby girl, but have you thought about taking that step?" Rex says, poking a bit.

If it was anyone else I would probably push back, but I know he's just genuinely curious.

Truth is? We haven't.

She just now has a finalized divorce from Tom, and with everything with the baby and moving in together, I wanted to give her time. Give her time to get used to being her, not jumping straight into marriage just because we love each other and are having a baby together.

"I do not doubt that it will come for us, down the road. But now we're just enjoying this first step we're taking together, and watching Addy become a big sister." I tell him, smiling while thinking about it.

"Who'd have thought we'd be sitting around a table about to order brunch talking about this shit?" Rex says with a smile.

"Not me, but I'm fifty times happier than I ever imagined," I smile, right as our waitress comes over.

It's true though. I never imagined my life turning out like this, but I also never imagined being as happy and excited for life as I am right now. I wouldn't change a damn thing in my life knowing it brought me to my two, soon-to-be three girls.

## Ellie

The sounds coming from the living room are all I can focus on as I pull the cookies out of the oven, setting them on top to cool. Between the smell of the warm cookies and Addy's laughter, I can't help but feel like my heart is bursting with joy. Grabbing a cookie that's *way* too hot, I pop it into my mouth, the melted chocolatey goodness exactly what the doctor recommended.

Well, maybe not the doctor, but this little diva I'm currently growing is a fan.

At six months pregnant and still throwing up daily, you eat what you can stomach. Addy and I were out all day and I could barely stomach anything. The only thing I could think about was baked goods, and since today the little peanut has decided she wants chocolate chip cookies, I made three dozen.

She's already a demanding little thing and I just can't wait to watch her wrap her daddy around her tiny little finger.

He's going to be mush for her.

As I head into the living room I smile when I see Trevor and Addy snuggled up on the couch as they try to make each other laugh making funny animal noises.

*This* is exactly what I've always dreamed my life would be like, but I thought it was just a dream.

Until Trevor.

Before we met Trevor, Addy, and I had never experienced a home like this, never experienced what it was like to have someone on our team, someone trying to make us happy. We'd never experienced a home that's happy, warm, full of love, laughter, and smiles. But now? Now Trevor has set up a full movie night for Addy and me, Taylor Swift themed since we are watching her new era's tour movie that just released.

Once Trevor realized just how much my girl loved Taylor Swift, he jumped right on board and became the biggest Swiftie ever. The number of times they've screamed the bridge of Cruel Summer together is unknown, but I'll never forget her smile when they do it.

His either.

He does so many little things to make sure she's happy, to make sure she feels loved. He'd protect her from anything, and he's proven that time and time again. She feels safe with him, and he makes sure she always knows that she's the most important girl in the world, and damnit I can't wait to watch him be a dad to *two* little girls.

To think I only have three more months until I get to watch this man with an actual tiny baby of his own. If I wasn't pregnant right now, I would be getting pregnant, *immediately* at that thought.

"Whatcha thinking about over there with that little smirk, kitten?" Trevor says with a wink, snapping me out of my little daydream.

*But reality is even better.*

"Oh, nothing," I smile, before taking the last few strides over to them, crawling into the blanket Trevor has opened for me and snuggling in. I can't help get butterflies at the way his hand immediately goes to my belly, like he's trying to include her in our snuggle puddle.

"I changed my mind," Addy announces out of

nowhere, an adorable grin on her face. "I want to watch Avengers."

Trevor eyes me questioning but I just nod and he quickly changes the movie.

What kind of mom would I be if I said no when my girl was *finally* taking interest in one of the greatest movies ever.

How did I get so lucky? I have a cool kid, a wonderful, caring, naughty-as-hell man that I get to share my life with, and finally a finalized divorce.

Curling into Trevor on one side, I snuggle up, Addy curled in on the other side as we lay back to watch the movie. It doesn't take long before Addy is asleep.

It doesn't matter what time of the day it is, if she lays down with a movie on it's lights out. Before I can stand up to move her, Trevor glares and does it for me.

"You shouldn't be lifting her, kitten. You're six months pregnant," he grumbles as he carries her to her room. I can't help but smirk, loving his grumpiness, but also how he takes care of me.

Laying down on the couch I close my eyes, thinking about everything that's happened these last couple of years and how all of that brought me here. It might have been hell getting married to someone I didn't love, then to get cheated on.

But if all that hadn't happened, I would've never moved in next to this man.

As he walks back in he walks over to the couch, lifting my feet to sit before placing them back in his lap where he starts to massage them. Holy hell his hands are magic.

"I think we should go to Disney World this weekend since we will have Addy," Trevor says with a smile.

We're both over the moon that Tom chose to agree to part-time custody. He requested to have her every other weekend, but I know damn well one of those weekends is for his parents.

But honestly, that makes it even better.

But now to be able to celebrate our extra time with her by going to Disney World?

"That sounds perfect," I whisper, sitting up to kiss him. "I'll go anywhere with you."

# Dirty Play Sneak Peak

## Cade and Gwen's Story (Subject to Change)

Prologue

Cade

*Ten Years Ago*

*Beep. Beep. Beep.*

*That's all I can hear among all the chaos. That and the screams, but I couldn't tell you where they are coming from. The smell of antiseptic mixed with hand soap and desperation hangs thick in the air, clinging to my nose. An unwelcome reminder of why I hate this place.*

*Nurses and doctors are moving around the room at a speed I can't follow, as I stand they're staring at her, like somehow my presence could make this all go away.*

*I vaguely notice someone's hand gripping me, trying to move me.*

*I don't move, though. I don't do anything except stare, the feeling of desperation and heartbreak hitting me like a freight train; slamming into me like a blindside collision on ice. They warned me that I should be bracing for this, preparing myself for the worst.*

*I refused to accept it though, and refused to believe that I couldn't fix this.*

*I promised her that I would always take care of her, that she'd be okay. I told her I would keep her safe, protect her always, she even made me pinky promise her, saying that was the most important part.*

*Obviously not though, when I don't hold my end of the deal.*

*Everything around me starts moving at lightning speed, people moving in every direction, other staff rushing in and suddenly I'm being pulled back, my dad's voice whispering in my ear. But I can't concentrate on anything around me, overwhelmed by the realization that my entire world is crumbling around me.*

*Standing outside the hospital room knowing that in just the next room, I'm losing my best friend has to be the worst feeling in the world.*

*I'm wrong.*

*The moment the noises got louder just before the beeping flatlines, everything stops. I know what's happening even before the doctor walks out of the room, a look of grief on his face as he approaches us.*

*I feel myself slide to the floor as my dad moves to stand by my mom who's currently consoling my little sister, Kylie. His eyes keep bouncing back to me, almost urging me to come to them as he wraps his arms around them like he can protect them from this, protect them from what we are about to hear.*

*Which is why I don't move.*

*It's why I can't.*

*They deserve better, they deserve each other without*

*Dirty Play Sneak Peak*

*my poison. I don't deserve their hugs, their words of affirmation, or their comfort.*

*She's dead.*

*My sister is dead, and it's all my fault.*

———

*Want more of the Empire State Boys?*
*Dirty Play, Cade and Gwen's Story is coming Spring 2024.*

*Pre-Order Dirty Play Here*

# Acknowledgments

First off, I want to thank you, my readers. I wouldn't be anywhere without you, so from the bottom of my heart, thank you, thank you, thank YOU.

Thank you for loving these characters and their stories, it helps inspire me more than you know and I can't wait to keep bringing new swoony stories your way. Thank you for every share, post, review, and any other feedback I've received. This community has been so supportive to me as a new indie author and I'll never be able to express my gratitude fully. I love connecting and interacting with you all so feel free to say hi or let me know what you think!

To Candice. You're the best, like seriously. Thank you for being my person, someone I can bounce ideas off of, helping me with all the behind-the-scenes things, and loving these stories as I do. Let's keep writing a fun new world to escape to, one hot guy at a time.

To my Alpha readers, thank you. Candice, Shannon, Megan, and Jamie. You helped me mold this story from the beginning. You saw it when it was living on Trash Island and helped me turn it into the story I'm most proud of. All of your feedback, your support, your help with sharing, thank you.

To my Beta Readers. Again, you all are incredible.

LB, Torie, Mudge, Andi, Emily, and Jenn. Thank you for all your feedback and help catching little things that had been missed. You helped me fine-tune this story and make Trevor and Ellie's story shine. Thank you. :)

To my editor, Matti. You're incredible at what you do and this book wouldn't have happened without you. Thank you for dealing with my stressed-out self and always pushing me, you're a rockstar editor and friend.

To my family, thank you for supporting me even though you've been forbidden ever to read my books. You're always so excited about the details I share and I love that. If you've read this, that means you failed. ;)

Last but certainly not least, my husband. You pick up the slack for me when I'm off in a make-believe world and I can never thank you enough. You're my rockstar, my book boyfriend come to life, and I couldn't have done any of this without you. You believe in me enough for both of us. <3

# Want More?

*Want to go back to the beginning?*

*Read below for a snippet of Rex and Sawyer's book in Power Play.*

## Prologue

## Rex- Five Years Ago

"Your career is over."

Those words have played in my head on a constant loop since my injury six months ago, when my doctors and coaches told me I would never get on the ice again. At least not playing hockey for the NHL. I tried to ignore them, pretend none of it was real. I went through with the surgery, the physical therapy, and even tried a new trial therapy that's supposed to be promising for injuries like mine.

But if I'm being honest, I've known it was over for a while, and it fucking sucks. Hockey has always been the one thing I had that no one could take from me. It's been something I've worked for since I was a little kid and have poured my heart and soul into. I'm not even sure where to go from here or what I'm supposed to be doing. It's not like I have a backup plan. Hockey was it. It's always been it. Hell, in college, I majored in fucking communications for fucks sake. If that doesn't scream "Athlete that doesn't know what he's fucking doing," I don't know what does.

But in the blink of an eye, it's gone, all because of a stupid accident.

Now, I'm injured with no idea where to go from here. It's just me and a bottle of pain pills that will hopefully numb more than just my knee.

## One year later

Laying in my bed, I stare at the ceiling, like I do every day. It's where I think the most, which is a double-edged sword. I should definitely be thinking about my next steps, or how to pull myself out of this black hole. More importantly I should probably think about cleaning my apartment, at some point. Looking around, the stench of vodka from the random empty bottles and leftover takeout containers isn't exactly a good look for anyone.

But anytime it's quiet, I end up thinking about the accident and how I lost the one thing that means the most to me.

I'm a mess. Between the prescription pills, the alcohol, and fucking a different woman as often as I can, I'm

## Want More?

not sure where I'm supposed to go from here. Something's gotta give.

My parents have tried to help me. They even moved down here a couple of months ago to try and support me, but there's nothing they can do when I'm so unwilling to see anything positive. I'm stuck wasting away in my apartment.

In my mind everything is already over, so what's the point in trying to fight my way back? Even if I get more use out of my knee, I'm thirty-three years old. It's not like I'm exactly in my prime, just waiting for the opportunity to join another team or to get back with my old one. I'm old news. Washed up. That's a hard fucking pill to swallow, and trust me, I've had plenty of practice.

When the doorbell rings at seven a.m., I assume it's my parents doing their usual check-in, or at least my mom. Ever since I got injured, my dad and I have had an interesting relationship. He's not mad about the injury, but he's ready for me to man up, pull my head out of my ass, and start making better choices.

Throwing on a pair of sweats, I walk to the door, passing more take-out containers and liquor bottles in my living room that I've yet to clean up. My mom's going to have a field day with this mess.

But when I open the door, it's not my mom waiting there.

I recognize the woman standing in front of me but can't seem to recall her name or where I know her from. But that's not even the worst part.

The worst part is that she's standing here on my

## Want More?

doorstep, tears streaming down her face, holding a bundle of blankets in the shape of a baby.

What. The. Fuck.

"Uh, hi. Can I help you," I muster out, unease slowly creeping in as I battle the fogginess of my brain. Why does she look so familiar?

Maybe I've seen her around before. It's not unlikely, our apartment complex is weird.

"Rex?" she whispers tentatively.

*Fuck me. Who the fuck is this?*

"Uh, yeah, that's me. Who are you?"

"Miranda. We met at The Last Stop, the bar in old town. It was, uh, awhile back."

She's obviously nervous. Why is she here if she's so nervous?

"You obviously don't remember me, which isn't exactly surprising. It was a weird night, for both of us. But I remember your name, and what you looked like, and you seemed like a nice enough guy," she says, mumbling to herself and confusing me further.

It's way too damn early for this.

"Miranda, right? It's fucking early and you're speaking too fast for my brain to process anything. What did you say you needed?"

She looks upset, but confident when she says her next words.

"I need you to take your baby."

I know I'm hungover, possibly still drunk, plus it is only seven a.m., but there's no way in fuck I just heard her correctly ... right?

My baby?

## Want More?

"Uh, excuse me? I don't have a baby."

She has a strange look on her face, a mixture of sadness, embarrassment, and what seems like panic.

"So, uh, we met about nine months ago. You probably don't remember much. I mean, I was bartending, and you easily put down enough shots to forget the night, if not the week. But we ended up in the bathroom at closing time, and apparently, we didn't use protection because she's here."

*She.*

*I have a daughter.*

"Maureen . . . I . . ."

"It's Miranda."

"Sorry, I, uh, I think you have the wrong person. There's no way I'm a father, plus I *always* use protection."

It's true. I always use protection, no matter what. I mean, even when I was on the team and would hook up with puck bunnies at our games, I never forgot protection. But . . . what if I did? If my math is right, this would have been shortly after I realized my career with hockey was over.

"Okay, Rex. Well, she's here, and she's yours. This is her bag, it has everything you'll need. You're much more capable than I am, even if it does seem like you're struggling right now," she says, glancing around my apartment, tears filling her eyes. "Look, I just want her to have a shot at a good life, and that's not with me. I don't want to be a mom; I never have." I try to stop her by putting my hand up, but she easily ignores me, continuing on as if she's afraid to stop talking. "Along with all her things, in the bag is her birth certificate and the paternity test I had done. Don't ask, but I promise you it's true. You can repeat the test, and you'll get the same results. I, uh, I also signed over my rights. After this, she's yours and only yours."

The reality of the situation starts to hit me, and I realize that there's no way my apartment is a good place for a baby right now.

"Uh, can you give me a minute? Come on in, I just need to gather my thoughts."

"I can't stay long; I have a train to catch in an hour."

"Wait. You're leaving already?"

"Yeah. I . . . I can't stay. I thought I could do this, but I can't, and honestly, this is going to make me sound like the worst person ever, but I don't want to do it. I don't want to be a mom. But I'm not evil. I don't want her to have a bad life. You're her father, her only shot."

Is she serious right now? I can't even take care of myself, and yet this woman thinks I'm able to take care of a baby that I didn't even know existed.

"Can I make a phone call before you leave?"

"Yeah, no problem."

Walking past the mess of my living room, I go back into my room to find my phone. There's only one person for me to call, and I just pray she can get here quickly.

"Mom? I need you. Now. Please come over."

# Books by Lexi James

*The Empire State Hockey Series*

Power Play (Rex and Sawyer's Book)
Puck Princess (Max and Cassie's Book)
Blindside Love (Trevor and Ellie's Book)
Dirty Play (Cade and Gwen's Book, Spring 2024 )

# About the Author

Lexi James lives in Washington with her husband and their two kids. If she's not at work, you can find her out adventuring with her family, exploring trails, or curled up on the couch with a steamy book. She began reading after the birth of her kids when she needed something 'just for her' and since then she's read every day.

She's a daydreamer who always has characters and their has stories running through her mind. With encouragement from her husband and family, she sat down to write a book, giving a voice to her imaginary friends and a place to escape to when life gets crazy.

Made in the USA
Monee, IL
18 February 2025